Agent Svetlana Simonov of the government's top-secret Omega Force is sent to South America to assassinate a renegade general. She accomplishes her mission spectacularly . . . only to discover that the colonel who takes Svetlana's victim's place is planning on selling Russian-made chemical weapons to any terrorist who can come up with the money. Svetlana's young protege, Tatiana, goes on her first mission for Omega Force as the world's sexiest secret agents battle the world's most dangerous master criminals.

This book is a work of fiction. Names, characters, places, and incidents either are products of the author's imagination or are used fictitiously. Any resemblance to actual events or locales or persons, living or dead, is entirely coincidental.

To Kill Again
Copyright © 2020 Robin Gideon
ISBN: 978-1-4874-2893-8
Cover art by Martine Jardin

Published by eXtasy Books Inc or
Devine Destinies, an imprint of eXtasy Books Inc

Look for us online at:
www.eXtasybooks.com or www.devinedestinies.com

To Kill Again
Agent (Rom)antics 1

By

Robin Gideon

DEDICATION

For Uncle Ken, who gave me a cardboard box full of books, and changed my life forever.

CHAPTER ONE

Bogota, Columbia

General Martino Palmero looked at the buxom blonde beauty sitting beside him in the nightclub's booth and wondered just how far she would go. All the way? It was a tempting thought. He might even be satisfied just finding out if those tits of hers were real, or if a doctor had worked his professional magic on her. Either way, Palmero didn't much care. The woman was a turn-on from head to toe. Her magnificent breasts were only part of what excited him.

She was no naive teenager, this one. General Palmero wondered how close to thirty she was. Two or three years under the big three-oh, at most. The years hadn't been cruel to her. In fact, the years had been more than kind — they'd been generous, nearly to a fault. General Palmero had known the pleasures of enough beautiful women in his day to realize that this one — Svetlana, she called herself — was more beautiful now, in her middle to late twenties, than she had been a decade earlier. The time had given sophistication to her looks, her moves, her gestures, that hadn't been there earlier. She touched his erotic sensibilities in ways that no mere girl ever could. And that difference made his cock hard as stone — solid like it hadn't been since he was a kid in school.

The trouble was that Svetlana had not come to the nightclub with him. Colonel Alonzo Mendoza had brought her. The colonel had met her that afternoon at the outdoor market, and apparently they'd hit it off immediately. At least that was what the colonel said.

"What's wrong, General?" Svetlana asked, turning her sultry, ocean blue gaze upon Palmero as she leaned toward him in the booth.

She had a Russian accent when she spoke English, and it was slurred slightly with alcohol. The general didn't mind the fact that she'd been drinking. Over the years, slightly inebriated women had been a source of great pleasure to him. He found vulnerable women a serious turn-on. It was always erection-inducing for him to him to know that the women really couldn't defend themselves. Nothing made his cock so hard as power over a defenseless woman. It was then that he could really show a woman the kind of virile man he truly was.

"Something seems to be bothering you."

"It's nothing."

Svetlana placed her hand upon the general's knee beneath the table. She leaned toward him, pressing her extravagant breasts against his biceps. She whispered, "Have I done something to upset you? If I have, I swear to God that I hadn't meant to."

Palmero shook his head. "I was thinking of something else entirely."

"You were wishing it had been you who brought me here," she said as her hand slid higher on his leg and the blue light in her eyes became just a little more intense, "and not Colonel Mendoza, weren't you?"

Not even the years of military life he'd spent in the Venezuelan army could prevent the shock from showing in Palmero's expression. Svetlana had shocked him by accurately reading his thoughts, and though he was pleased with her awareness of the situation, a small part of his brain warned that he had let his defenses down. It wouldn't kill him to have a half-inebriated, big-bosomed tourist reading his thoughts, but it could be fatal to have a vengeance-driven counterpart from, say, England or the United States know what he was thinking.

This was not an awareness that rested easily with his consciousness.

"Now I've made you angry again." Svetlana leaned even closer and whispered into his ear. Her breasts pressed tightly against his arm. "Tell me what I'm doing wrong, and I'll stop doing it. Just tell me."

"You're doing nothing wrong," Palmero replied, patting the back of Svetlana's hand on his leg. "In fact, you seem to be doing everything right." He looked into her eyes that, he noted with a connoisseur's sense of detail, were the color of priceless jewels. "Perhaps more right than you could ever imagine."

Out of the corner of his eye, Palmero saw Colonel Mendoza returning from the restroom. Palmero had learned to respect and trust Mendoza's ability, and because of this, had never pulled rank on him. But he thought now of bullying his aide for the first time. This woman was someone worth annoying a junior officer over. Rank did, after all, have its privileges. This awareness made Palmero smile. He had power . . . and it was the greatest aphrodisiac that he had ever known.

There was something special about Svetlana, something almost magical, that he hadn't seen in a very, very long time. She was someone unique . . . and he wanted to know what it felt like to bury his hard cock deep inside her soft, welcoming body. He couldn't remember the last time he'd lusted for a woman this intensely.

"And how is my lady?" Colonel Mendoza asked as he slid into the booth to sandwich Svetlana between himself and Palmero.

"What took you so long?" Svetlana demanded, her brow

furrowed, her full-lipped mouth turned downward slightly at the edges in annoyance. "I started to worry that you'd never come back."

"Not come back to you?" Mendoza exclaimed, leaning away from her in mock horror, a hand lifting theatrically to his chest. "How could you even think such a thing?"

Palmero noticed that Svetlana placed her right hand upon Mendoza's thigh, midway between his knee and groin. Now that Mendoza had returned, she no longer had her hand on his leg. As a man who played power politics every day of his life, he understood her actions and didn't begrudge them. He didn't necessarily like what she had done, but he certainly understood it. He was a player who knew how to play the game . . . and he played it exceptionally well.

She said petulantly, just loud enough for both men to hear, "It's happened before. I'm always afraid that it'll happen again." She sniffled. "You can't blame me for that."

Svetlana crossed her legs delicately at the knee. She was wearing a dark green knee-length silk dress, the bodice of which only partially hid the sweet fullness of her bosom. Completely hiding the woman's extraordinary breasts was an impossibility, but it was clear from the tailoring of the garment that she was doing what she could to de-emphasize her more than ample charms.

The smile was gone now from her lips, and when she picked up her cocktail — a gin and tonic — in unladylike fashion, she finished it in three quick swallows.

"You need another," Mendoza said. It was a statement, not a question, and he was already raising his arm to get the waitress' attention.

"Yes, I need another," Svetlana replied. "But darling, won't you please go get it yourself? The waitress here is so overworked it takes her forever to serve the drinks."

Palmero looked at Mendoza. It was obvious he didn't like

4

the idea of leaving her again. Better to hurry off and return with more liquor than let her sober up. He didn't want her to reach the conclusion that maybe the smart move to make was to go back to *her* hotel *alone* instead of to *his hotel.*

The general could read his right-hand man as though his emotions were printed words in ink on a page. He could read all the men who worked for him like a book, and it was a skill that had served him well for many years.

The colonel slipped out of the booth and pushed himself forcefully through the mass of bodies, heading toward the bar.

As soon as she was alone again with the general, Svetlana twisted in the padded bench seat toward Palmero. Her smile was electric, and the glow in her shimmering blue eyes was intoxicating.

"You're staying at the First Imperial Hotel?" she asked.

Palmero nodded. "We've got most of the ninth floor."

"How far away is your room from Colonel Mendoza's?"

"Right next door."

Svetlana looked away from Palmero toward the crowd, as though frightened that Mendoza might return and somehow hear the conversation she was having, even though the recorded electronic dance music blaring from the innumerable speakers made such an event impossible.

"He's . . . a strong man," Svetlana explained in an almost apologetic tone. "But he's only the beta male. You're the alpha male, aren't you?"

Palmero frowned. He had a solid grasp of the English language, but he didn't have a clue as to what Svetlana was speaking of now. The fact that she spoke English with a Russian accent didn't help. When he let his confusion show in his expression, she quickly explained what she meant by alpha and beta. Only then did he let awareness show in his expression. When he looked down into Svetlana's cleavage, he didn't make any effort to hide the direction of his gaze. Her words were making his cock even harder.

"I don't want to leave Mendoza for you," Svetlana said. "Not . . . not just yet. Not like this. It wouldn't be fair to him."

Palmero wasn't inclined to gaze too deeply into his good fortune. He knew that many of his sexual conquests had wanted something from him. Quite often they were young female soldiers looking for an easy assignment in the military. Other times they were hoping to get a promotion, or a transfer to a better military outfit. But whatever it was, whenever a beautiful woman threw herself at him, it was because they wanted something. They were just using their bodies and his lust to get his good graces—and he didn't have a problem with that. For Palmero, sex was a commodity that was either bartered for, or simply bought and paid for. But whatever it was, it wasn't something that a woman gave away for free. Not ever.

"What do you suggest?" Palmero asked after several seconds of silence. For one of the few times in his adult life, he felt out of his element, confused and disoriented. It wasn't a feeling that sat well with him. He liked being in control.

"Go back to your hotel. I'll meet you there."

Svetlana put her hand over Palmero's crotch. When she squeezed him, he felt her fingers against his cock through the fabric of his trousers. He began to respond instantly. His cock had been on high alert from the first moment he'd set eyes on her. But at first he hadn't thought it would be possible that she would toss the colonel overboard for him. Now he understood that such a possibility was *very* real. The awareness added fuel to the fire in his libido.

He had close-cropped, gray hair, and though he was clearly a man of advancing years, he felt terribly young and virile.

"I don't know how I'll do it," Svetlana said, her Russian-laced speech apparently slurred by alcohol, "but I'll meet you there. And Colonel Mendoza won't know anything about it."

Palmero's eyes widened as he felt Svetlana's slender fingers caressing him intimately. How long had it been since he'd had a beautiful woman touching his cock like that? He couldn't remember the last time any woman—ugly or gorgeous, it didn't matter—had put a hand between his legs without being coerced into doing it. Whoever the fuck this Svetlana was, she was turning him on like no woman had in years.

"You're teasing me now," Palmero said quietly. The words shocked him, because he hadn't thought of actually speaking them. Svetlana seemed so sophisticated, so unobtainable, that he couldn't entirely believe that she wasn't just toying with his emotions for some bizarre, sadistic reason that he did not yet understand. "You're not actually going to come to my room."

"Promise me you'll wait for me in your room?"

"Come with me now. I'm a general and he's just a colonel," Palmero explained. "I don't know how much you know about the military, but a general far outranks a colonel." He inhaled deeply, squared his shoulders, and said, "I can make the little son of a bitch do whatever the fuck I tell him to do."

Svetlana shook her head, then combed her fingers through her blonde hair. To Palmero, it seemed an incredibly erotic gesture to make, though there wasn't anything outwardly erotic about it. Everything Svetlana did seemed to arouse him sexually.

"I know enough to realize that I want you to fuck me, and that the power you have over everyone around you turns me on. How's that? But I don't want to make the colonel angry, don't you see? Mendoza brought me here. Please"—she squeezed his cock again, then reached deeper between his legs to give his testicles some tender attention—"go back to your hotel and wait there for me. I'll be there soon. I promise I will."

Palmero felt the firm, enticing fingers toying with him, and he just knew that no woman fondling him like that could be a liar. He cast a quick glance in the direction of the bar, worried that Mendoza would return too quickly. He said, "Give me something . . . just a little something to know that you'll be by later. Do that for me, and I'll wait for you until eternity freezes over."

Mendoza was pushing his way through the crowd, moving toward the booth in the back of the nightclub. He had a vodka martini in one hand and a gin and tonic in the other. Much of the vodka martini had been spilled, apparently as he was pushing his way through the crowd of men. He was protecting the gin and tonic—Svetlana's drink—like his life depended upon it. There could be no doubt that he was more interested in getting alcohol into Svetlana's blood steam than into his own.

Mendoza set the gin and tonic down in front of Svetlana, then slid into the booth. He gave Svetlana and Palmero a careful look. He didn't trust Palmero with women, and it was obvious. At least not with women that Mendoza was hoping to keep for himself. Palmero smiled, feeling quite superior.

"My good colonel!" Palmero said, smiling broadly. There was a theatrical quality to his expression. "This has been a fine evening, but I think it is time I leave you alone with this young lady. I've stayed in this noisy nightclub too long as it is." He pushed himself out of the booth, and raised a hand when Mendoza began to put up what was at best a half-hearted protest at his departure. "I've overstayed my welcome as it is. You two stay here." He leaned over the table so that his face was close to Mendoza's. "I'll leave the car and driver here for you and take a taxi back to the hotel."

Mendoza replied, in a hushed voice that Svetlana was not

to hear, "I owe you one, sir. And I won't forget it."

Palmero nodded to Mendoza, then straightened, looked at Svetlana, and smiled appreciatively. "Perhaps we will meet again."

Svetlana replied, "Perhaps we shall." She smiled. Her gaze never left Palmero's. "I hope we do."

Palmero turned and walked through the crowd. Unlike with Mendoza, when Palmero walked, other men got out of the way.

"At last, I've got you all to myself," Mendoza said.

He put his hand on Svetlana's thigh, midway between her knee and the juncture of her legs. When she made no move to push his hand off her leg, he slipped his hand beneath the hem of her dress, touching her leg through her silk stocking.

"Yes, all to yourself." Her voice was a sultry purr. She leaned forward and for the first time kissed the colonel on the lips. When he tried to slip his tongue into her mouth, she pulled back quickly. "Wait," she whispered, "there's something important I must do first."

"There's nothing more important than this," Mendoza declared. She could tell that his own pleasure was always uppermost in his concerns. That was the way it was with most men, she understood. It wasn't a pleasant awareness. Cold facts were often exactly that . . . cold.

"You don't understand." She slid her hand up his thigh, almost to his groin, caressing him through his trousers. "General Palmero was kind and understanding enough to know that we wanted to be alone together. He even let you and me have the car and driver. The least I can do is wait with him while he gets a cab."

"I'll go with you."

"No, please. Let me thank him myself, talk to him without

you being there. I'm sure he's feeling a little old right now. He's not a young man. He's not virile like you are."

Mendoza reacted to the last comment with a smile that pulled at the corners of his mouth. Svetlana's words were caressing his ego. She knew she'd said the right thing. Her confidence surged. She had much to do, and the odds of success were against her.

"Just let me wait with him until he gets a taxi back to the hotel. That way he won't feel so alone . . . and old. Do you see what I mean?"

"Yes. You're a very kind-hearted woman, Svetlana. One of the kindest I've ever known."

"Wait here for me. I'll be back as soon as possible." She reached between his legs and gave his cock a squeeze. "Please, wait for me."

Svetlana leaned over to kiss Mendoza, and this time, when she did, it was she who initiated the French kissing, boldly thrusting her tongue between the colonel's lips to explore his mouth. And then, just as quickly as she had started, she ended the kiss and slipped out of the booth, appearing a bit breathless and thoroughly turned on. She gave the appearance of a woman literally aching to be back in the booth with the colonel, hungry for his caresses.

General Palmero had hardly made his way through the front doors of the nightclub before Svetlana grabbed his arm from behind. He turned gruffly to see who had shown the temerity to touch him, but when he saw Svetlana, his face lit up.

"You've left him behind after all!" Palmero said, clearly proud that he had won the battle for Svetlana's attention.

"No." She cast a quick glance over her shoulder, as though afraid that Mendoza had followed her. When she turned back to Palmero, there was a quality of quiet desperation in her blue eyes that bordered on idolatry.

"What?" Palmero was confused. The desperation in Svetlana's voice, in her mannerisms, was extraordinary. Almost too much to believe. Almost . . . but for a man like Palmero, not quite. He was a man who believed in himself.

A taxicab pulled up and Svetlana rushed toward it, pulling General Palmero along behind her. There was a young couple in line to receive the taxi in front of her, but Svetlana pulled several bills from her purse and shoved them into the young man's palm. It was an enormous sum for the couple — a month's income or more — and they smiled broadly.

"I've got to have this taxi," she said to the surprised young man.

She opened the door and practically leaped into the back seat of the taxi, apparently unmindful of her dress, which rode high enough up her legs to show the tops of her stocking and a thin strip of pale thigh above the embroidered and elasticized upper edge of the silk. Palmero got into the taxi behind her, though not nearly as nimbly.

Svetlana once again dug into her purse, extracting a fistful of bills. She tossed them into the front seat and said, "Drive around the block. Keep driving around the block, and don't look in your rearview mirror until I say you can."

The driver protested in Spanish, then switched to badly spoken English. "Hey, lady, I don't — "

"Just do it!" Svetlana shouted.

General Palmero was stunned. Never in his life had he felt so thoroughly and completely wanted by a woman. No, it wasn't simply *wanted.* That was too casual a word. The way that Svetlana made him feel, the phrase *ravenous for* seemed more appropriate. And because she made him feel that way, he also felt more dynamic and virile than he had in fifteen years. He felt himself to be in the presence of a goddess.

Turning to Palmero, Svetlana said, "We don't have much

time. Mendoza isn't going to be patient for long. I don't want to make him angry."

Palmero didn't know what to say or how to respond. The words *Who the fuck cares if he gets angry* nearly slipped out of his mouth. But when the blue-eyed blonde with the luscious tits grabbed his zipper and jerked it down, his mouth went desert dry so quickly he wasn't even certain he could speak, and he most definitely couldn't think logically.

Svetlana looked toward the front seat and said, "I'm sure you're going to watch, but at least don't be obvious about it."

Then, as she thrust her hand inside Palmero's trousers, she leaned over in the seat and kissed the general on the lips, pushing her tongue deeply into his mouth. She tugged his rapidly growing erection out through the fly of his trousers and began stroking him. As she did this, she continued kissing him. He began responding immediately to her caresses and kisses, his cock growing and hardening in her fist, stretching out, filling her hand even though he was only of average dimensions.

"This is just sampler of something better that'll happen later on," Svetlana said a bit breathlessly.

Before Palmero could reply, Svetlana slipped down off the seat until she was kneeling on the floor of the rather spacious though decades-old Chevrolet sedan taxicab.

"What the—"

Palmero's words died in his mouth when Svetlana's lips encircled the head of his cock. Years earlier he had thought he was done being surprised in life, but he was surprised now. Thoroughly and completely. The warmth and wetness of the beautiful woman's mouth surrounding the head of his cock was almost too much to believe. And he was responding with extraordinary swiftness.

"That's it," Palmero groaned. "Suck me."

He said other things, in Spanish mostly. Svetlana was

sucking lustily, her butter-soft lips sliding up and down over his hard cock, which literally throbbed with lusty tension. That was as much as the general could expect of anyone . . . especially while getting a blow job.

The general leaned back in the taxi, kicking his feet out to get more comfortable. He looked into the rearview mirror and wasn't surprised to see the driver watching everything that was happening. He could tell, though, that the driver, from his vantage point, couldn't actually see Svetlana's bobbing face in the neon-lit shadows.

Palmero gave the driver a condescending smile as though to say *Take a real good look and watch your betters living large. It's the closest you'll ever get to having a woman this beautiful wanting you like this, you stupid, taxi-driving, limp-dicked buffoon!*

Palmero watched Svetlana as she bobbed, taking his cock in and out of her mouth. Her lips were moist and soft upon his shaft. He smoothed her silken blonde hair away from her cheek so that he could see her face in profile. She was gorgeous with his cock in her mouth. Several seconds passed as Palmero, almost in a trance, studied the beautiful woman's features while she nodded slowly up and down, her lips nibbling softly on his hard flesh.

Palmero swore in his native language. He was certain that never before had anyone performed a blow job with the skill that was now being bestowed upon him.

Svetlana released Palmero's cock from her oral embrace. She sat upright in the back seat of the Colombian taxicab and put her forefinger to Palmero's lips. She didn't say a word. She simply looked into his eyes and smiled, then bent over at the waist once again, opened her mouth wide, and took his cock into her mouth.

Palmero swore again, spewing words that would have shocked his portly wife back at home. He saw, out of the corner of his eye, the nightclub he had been in earlier. Only then did he realize that the taxi had managed to make just a single circuit of the block surrounding the nightclub where he had, only an hour earlier, met this beautiful nymphomaniac who had sexual skills sufficient to make his spine melt. Had any woman ever sucked his cock with such expertise?

A sudden thought entered Palmero's brain, and when it did, he was angry with himself for even thinking it. But once the thought was there, he couldn't simply banish it, as though it had never existed.

Palmero asked, "Why are you doing this?"

Svetlana raised her head, letting his cock slip out of her mouth with a slurping sound. When she looked into Palmero's dark eyes, she appeared completely serious as she answered, "Because I want you to go back to your hotel room and wait for me. If you leave here unsatisfied, you'll just find another woman to give you pleasure, and then you won't be waiting for me. I want you hot to see me again." Svetlana grinned then. "Even if I suck you off now, I know you'll be excited again later on tonight. Don't think that you're too old to go twice in one night. I know better. You're the stallion I've been waiting to find, so don't try to convince me otherwise."

Before Palmero could say a single word in reply, Svetlana again ducked down in the back of the taxi and resumed giving the blow job that was steadily driving him thoroughly and completely out of his mind.

He reached beneath her arm, groping for her breasts. The feminine mound filled his hand. He squeezed firmly. Even though the caress was through her dress and bra, it turned him on enormously to be feeling Svetlana's lavish bosom.

"Do it," Palmero groaned, feeling the tingling anticipation of release beginning to build. "Keep doing it! Don't stop! Just don't stop!"

Svetlana bobbed up and down over the cock faster, noisily dragging her lips over him. As she pleasured him with her lips and tongue, she stroked her fist up and down on his shaft.

Svetlana obviously wanted to get the general to completion as quickly as possible, and to that end she used all her skills. The general was certain his cum would be squirting against her tongue in seconds.

The general's thighs begin to quiver. He knew he couldn't withstand much more of the pleasure she was giving him. She bobbed even faster, sucking hard on his cock, her hair flying around her cheeks as she salivated freely.

The harsh words the general spoke were indecipherable as he straightened out, his body angled sideways in the back seat of the American-made taxicab. A moment later, his jaws clenched with strain, he erupted, cum jetting from his balls with greater fury than in years.

Svetlana continued bobbing over the cock even as the general released his sperm. She nursed on his cock until she had drained the general's balls completely. Only then did she release him from her oral embrace. When she sat up in the back seat of the taxicab, there was a smile of confident carnality upon her lips. She swallowed theatrically, letting him know she liked drinking his salty seed.

"Your room is next to Mendoza's, right?" she asked.

Palmero nodded. He was breathing so deeply it would have been extremely difficult for him to talk.

"Good. I'll be seeing you later on tonight." Svetlana ran the tip of her tongue around her lips, as though savoring the pungent taste of the general's cum. "Like I said, this blow job was just a sampler. You're in for an amazing evening later on. I'm going to blow your mind."

Svetlana ordered the taxicab to pull over to the curb in front of the nightclub again. She slipped out into the street and hurried inside, ignoring the looks she received from other patrons. The bouncer, who was the final vote on whether someone was allowed to enter or was kept outside waiting, clearly remembered Svetlana from the first time she had entered. Perhaps he also remembered the powerful men she had been with. He opened the door wide, a faintly knowing smile on his lips as she slipped past him and entered the carnival chaos of the nightclub's interior.

Svetlana found Colonel Mendoza in the booth where she had left him. He smiled initially when he saw her, then immediately frowned.

"What took you so long?" he demanded when Svetlana slipped into the booth beside him. "You were gone for ten whole minutes."

"It was difficult finding a taxi." She smiled apologetically. "Don't be angry with me now. I want us to have a good time."

Mendoza put his arm around Svetlana's shoulders and pulled her in close to his side. He looked into Svetlana's eyes for several seconds, then dipped his face down and tasted her lips. When he touched her lips with the tip of his tongue, Svetlana increased the intimacy by opening her mouth, leaning into him, inviting his deeper exploration.

Swirling her tongue against Mendoza's, Svetlana boldly reached for his crotch beneath the table. She found him, and when she gave his cock a firm squeeze, she heard his sharp inhalation.

"Enough of this," Mendoza said when the deep, probing kiss finally ended. "I've waited long enough to have you. Why should I have to wait any longer?"

"But where can we . . ." Svetlana asked. She felt a pink hue darken her cheeks.

"In the car."

He grabbed Svetlana's hand and nearly yanked her out of the booth. As she protested, he pulled her through the crowd. She sensed that feeling her hand on his cock had set ablaze emotions within Mendoza that wouldn't be quenched easily—not until he'd buried his cock to the hilt inside her cunt and she was begging for more.

"Not in the car," Svetlana said feebly when they had made it outside and Mendoza raised his hand to hail his driver.

Very quickly a dark sedan pulled up to the curb. Inside was the soldier Svetlana had seen earlier. The young, neatly groomed man wasn't wearing a uniform, but one look at him told Svetlana that he was a soldier through and through. He opened the door for his superior officer. Mendoza pushed Svetlana into the sedan's back seat. He followed her into the sedan, immediately reaching for her, groping her voluptuous curves.

"Back to the hotel," Mendoza growled to the young driver, reverting to his native language. "And be quick about it!"

Svetlana made a point of appearing at least a little afraid of Mendoza, and he obviously liked that reaction from her. He was one of those men who enjoyed inspiring fear in women, she could tell . . . and she hated him just a little more because of it.

He grabbed Svetlana's wrist and once again brought her hand to his crotch. She didn't fondle his cock quite so boldly this time and continued casting frightened glances into the front seat at the young driver.

"Forget about him," Mendoza said. "He knows enough to keep his mouth shut."

Svetlana leaned closer to Mendoza, though she still was not smiling. She whispered, "I'm not worried about him talking, I'm worried about him watching. Can't we just wait until we get back to your hotel?"

"What's wrong? You suddenly getting shy?"

Svetlana shook her head and caught her lower lip between her teeth. She gave the colonel an impish look before turning away. She shook her head as though a thought had just entered her brain which mustn't ever be put to words.

"What is it?" Mendoza demanded.

"I can't tell you." Svetlana voice was small. When she looked at Mendoza again, there was a thoroughly naughty twinkle in her blue eyes. "You might not like the same things I do."

"Like what?"

"I have a fantasy." She glanced toward the driver, and then leaned against Mendoza again, this time pressing her breasts against his arm. She put her lips close to his ear. "I've had this fantasy, but I've never dared to act it out. What I dream about is being tied up in bed and ravished by a strong man. A commanding man. Someone who will take charge and make every decision."

"A man like me," Mendoza said. It was a statement, not a question.

"A man *exactly* like you."

Mendoza looked Svetlana up and down in the uneven light that came from the Colombian businesses outside the taxi. The grin on his face was a mixture of fascination and marginally controlled sadism. After several long seconds, he turned away from Svetlana and said to his young aide, "Can't you drive any faster?"

CHAPTER TWO

Svetlana noticed the sly, knowing smiles on the faces of the young men. They all figured she would be Mendoza's latest sexual conquest, and she knew they were right. But the young men were also envious and hoped that they might be able to slide between her shapely thighs as soon as the colonel tired of her. To that extent, they were completely wrong. Svetlana would never share her body with the young handsome enlisted men. They didn't have enough clout, enough power, to make it worth her time and effort.

Mendoza opened the door to his hotel suite, and Svetlana stepped in. It was a two-room affair, with a bedroom off to the right and a spacious sitting area to the left. Along the back was the balcony. Svetlana walked straight to it, stepping outside.

"You say that the general's room is right next to yours?"

"Forget about him." Mendoza stepped up behind Svetlana and slipped his arms around her. He cupped her breasts in his hands and squeezed too firmly, causing her discomfort. "Big!" he growled.

Svetlana moaned a bit theatrically as Mendoza crudely fondled her breasts. She rested her head back against his shoulder and whispered, "You're sure we won't be disturbed?"

"Security checks at midnight, three, and six," Mendoza answered. "They come and go without making a sound. They're silent as ghosts. You'll never know they were here."

Mendoza's voice sounded tight, hoarse with the lust racing in his veins. Svetlana suspected he wanted to throw her to the floor, rip off her clothes, then kick her around some before he pierced her body with his own. She had no illusions about the kind of man she was with.

"Bed-bedroom," Svetlana stammered. "Let's go to the bedroom."

Once again, Mendoza grabbed Svetlana's wrist and pulled her along behind him as he hurried. Once in the bedroom, he pushed Svetlana toward the bed, but she resisted.

"Wait a second," she said, sounding breathless. "Let me tell you how I want it."

"You'll get it the way I give it to you!"

"Please, let me act out my fantasy with you. Please?"

"What is it?"

"I want you to stay here in the bedroom. Get it all set up properly." Svetlana walked to the closet. As she had expected, she found an assortment of neckties, all of them silk. They'd be perfect for what she had in mind. "Use these. I'll come walking in here, not suspecting a thing. You attack me from behind. I'll struggle, but you'll tie me up and ravish me."

"I get it," Mendoza said, his eyes glittering demonically. "I see what you've got in mind."

"I want to be tied up, but I don't want to be hurt. Right? You understand the difference?" She looked into his eyes, her heart suddenly racing. She didn't trust him for a second, but she had no choice but to follow through with the plan. "No hitting. No punching." It appalled her that she felt the need to tell him such things.

"Sure. I understand." Mendoza appeared thoroughly amazed that such a sophisticated woman got her sexual juices flowing with the notion of bondage.

"I'll give you ten minutes to get ready, then I'll walk in."

"I won't need that long."

"I will," Svetlana said. She said it firmly. "Turn my fantasy into a reality. If you do that, I'll be the sex slave you've always fantasized about owning." She put a hand on his chest. "Imagine tying me up and fucking me whenever you want."

She took Mendoza's hand and placed it on her breast. As he buried his fingers into the tender mound, she rolled her head back on her shoulders as though lost in the sea of sensuality that Mendoza's caresses could create. He pinched her nipple, and she stifled the gasp of pain and the urge to insult him for being such an uncouth brute.

"Ten minutes . . . stay here for ten minutes and be very quiet . . . then you've got to tie me to the bed and ravish me. But you must wait until I walk into the bedroom. That's the way the fantasy works. Promise?"

"I'll be everything you've ever hoped for."

Svetlana took her purse and stepped out of the bedroom, closing the door behind her. For several seconds she stood near the closed door, listening carefully. She heard Mendoza chuckling softly to himself, then heard furniture moving as he pushed aside the bedside table. He was working on ways to tie the neckties to the heavy wooden corner posts of the bed. Svetlana smiled. Mendoza was doing everything she had told him to.

She glanced at her wristwatch. It was two-fifty. So far, her timing had been perfect and everything had gone according to plan.

Moving quickly and working efficiently, Svetlana went to the sofa, tossed her purse onto it, then kicked off her high-heeled shoes. She unbuttoned her dress and squirmed out of it, tossing the garment onto the sofa beside her purse. Her bra went next onto her dress. Finally, she shimmied out of her bikini panties, then unhooked her garter belt and pulled it down, stripping out of her thigh-high silk stockings at the same time.

Naked from head to toe, Svetlana picked up her purse. She pulled out the folded wad of paper money she had inside—it was mostly in Colombian currency, though there was also Australian and Mexican money in with the mix — and set it on the sofa. Also inside the purse were her passport and an Australian driver's license, two different tubes of lipstick, a small bottle of perfume, and a comb.

Svetlana emptied the contents onto the sofa, then reached to the bottom of the purse and found the small leather tab that was neatly hidden. She pulled the tab to open the hidden compartment at the bottom of the purse. Inside were two latex surgical gloves, which Svetlana put on quickly, stretching the latex tightly over her hands and fingers to make sure her grip would not be hindered.

Lastly, she pulled the final two items from the secret compartment. There was a small Makarov pistol, chambered for the internationally popular .380 round, and a silencer that was even longer than the pistol. With a deftness that displayed experience in such things, Svetlana removed the Russian-made pistol and quickly fitted the silencer onto the finely threaded muzzle of the Makarov.

She placed her cache of money inside the hidden compartment, then partially closed the trap door before putting the purse beneath all her clothing, as though it was the first thing she had put on the sofa and not the last.

Taking the Makarov with her, she crossed the room to the balcony, her bare feet soundless against the thick carpeting, her heavy breasts swaying tautly with each step. She eased the sliding door open. An evening breeze washed over Svetlana when she stepped outside. Her nipples instantly tightened.

The balcony wasn't large, perhaps only four feet deep and twelve feet wide. Svetlana leaned over the balcony railing and forced herself to look down. It was nine stories to the ground. If she fell, she'd have plenty of time to think about the reality that she would soon be dead.

A shiver worked its way up Svetlana's spine. She looked to her right. There was another balcony for the suite next to Mendoza's. Six feet separated the balconies. Svetlana looked at her wristwatch. It was two fifty-three. She was running out of time.

While holding the silenced Makarov in her left hand, she put a foot up on the top of the railing. With a little hop, she jumped onto the railing, balancing there precariously for a second. There was nothing to grasp onto for support, but her fingers clawed into the brick siding of the hotel anyway.

Do it now! the voice of courage, discipline, and duty said inside Svetlana's brain.

She jumped.

Though she was in the air only an instant, to Svetlana it had seemed hours. Her bare foot slipped neatly between the artistically curved iron bars that surrounded the balcony, and with her right hand she caught the top horizontal bar. Several seconds passed before she caught her balance, dangling outside the balcony, kept in place by one hand and one foot. To lose her grip now meant tumbling nine floors to her death.

A moment later, Svetlana was over the railing and onto the balcony attached to the rented suite of General Palmero.

Svetlana pulled back the Makarov's slide to ease a .380 round into the chamber. She thumbed off the safety, gave the silencer one last little twist to make sure it was attached tightly and properly, then eased open the glass door separating the balcony from the suite's interior.

Naked from head to toe, Svetlana stepped into the room. There was a single lamp aglow. It provided enough light for Svetlana to enter the strange room and see where she was going. She went straight to the bedroom door, which was open. Looking inside the room, she saw that the bed was messy, but empty.

Svetlana's heart skipped a beat. What if the general had

decided to go out for something to eat? The messy blankets indicated that he'd been there since returning to the hotel from the nightclub. A thousand half-formed fears exploded within Svetlana's heart.

It was the sound of the toilet flushing that clued her in. Svetlana wheeled around, turning and crouching as she raised the pistol with both hands to shoulder level in a move rehearsed a thousand times in training at the Omega Force secret base. Completely naked, holding the Makarov in both hands, Svetlana waited, hardly breathing.

General Palmero stepped out of the bathroom. He was wearing silk pajamas. His hair was ruffled and he walked heavily.

He looked up, blinking his eyes. At first he looked at Svetlana's plump breasts, naked beneath her outstretched arms. Their fullness seemed to amaze him . . . but she held something in her hands that seemed to confuse him. And there wasn't a smile on her lips.

"You've come for me," General Palmero said with a self-satisfied, somewhat sleepy smile on his lips.

"Just like I promised."

A few ounces of pressure on the trigger and the Makarov jumped in her hand. The weapon coughed. The noise was enough to be heard in the suite, but not enough to be heard out in the hallway. The hollow-point slug hit the general in the chest. He staggered a single step backward. He looked down at the small, seemingly insignificant red circle on his chest.

Svetlana quickly fired twice more. Rounds two and three also hit the general in the chest, both hollow-point bullets mushrooming on impact, driving through his heart. General Palmero fell backward, his legs straight, landing heavily.

As Svetlana advanced, she continued firing, sending more rounds through the prone corpse. She fired six times quickly, aiming for the broad, silk-covered chest. With the seventh and final round in the magazine, when she was standing nearly directly over Palmero, she put a bullet into his forehead and through his brain.

She placed the now-empty Russian-made assassin's weapon upon the corpse's bloody chest. There was no need for her to check for a pulse. No man could live with six bullets in his chest and one bullet a head shot. General Palmero's long and bloody life had come to a short and bloody end.

Svetlana looked at her wristwatch. It was two fifty-eight. She hurried out to the balcony. Once again, she had to make the leap, and just as before, she had to tamp down the rising fear that pooled up inside her before she could jump. She made the leap, nearly lost her balance when her foot didn't ease between the iron railing just right, and then was once more back inside Colonel Mendoza's suite.

Pulling off her latex gloves, Svetlana rushed to the bathroom. She flushed the gloves down the toilet. She looked at herself in the bathroom mirror. Her nipples were hard as little pebbles and her heart was racing madly. She unfastened the clasp of her wristwatch, set it on the bathroom counter, then walked into the bedroom.

Chapter Three

Sergeant Stefan Vasquez checked his wristwatch. It was two minutes after three, so he was a little behind schedule in making his rounds. He didn't much care. General Palmero had returned to the hotel earlier and would be fast asleep. And Colonel Mendoza had returned with a woman, so though Stefan intended to open the door to the colonel's room as duty required, he certainly wasn't going to venture very far inside it. Besides, everyone agreed that having this much security — multiple bed checks and everything else that went along with them — was taking a good idea too far.

It was unwarranted fears, the young sergeant figured. Nothing less than paranoia. Sure, foreign governments were still angry with his country for human rights violations and for the wink-and-nod approach to enforcement of drug laws, but that didn't mean the British or the Americans — or anyone else for that matter — were going to take active measures to retaliate.

He slipped the plastic key card into the electronic lock, waited for the little green light to glow, then opened the door to General Palmero's suite. Stefan stepped inside and saw the body on the floor. At first he wasn't sure what it was. But the closer he got, the clearer he saw what was on the floor . . . and though his life did not literally flash before his eyes, it seemed to him that it might just as well have.

The murder weapon had been left upon the general's chest. Stefan recognized the weapon as being Russian made. Did the Russians have their finger in on this assassination? It was an unsettling thought for a soldier. All the young sergeant was absolutely certain of, as he looked down at the bloody corpse that earlier in the evening had been a high-ranking war hero to almost every member of the military and to almost all civilians back home, was that there would be hell to pay.

Stefan was nearly in a daze as he left the room, stepping back into the hallway. He walked only a few yards down the hall and inserted the proper magnetic key card into the slot of Colonel Mendoza's door, waited for the green light, then entered. There was no expression on his face at all, and he seemed to be following his feet rather than guiding them.

He stood at the bedroom doorway. The door was open, and a bedside lamp was lighted. If the young sergeant had been given an enormous shock to the system when he found General Palmero's corpse on the floor, he was given another powerful shock when he saw the next highest-ranking officer assigned to this Colombian mission.

Colonel Mendoza was naked and in bed. Stefan Vasquez knew that he wouldn't be alone, but he hadn't figured he'd find this kind of scene. Beneath Mendoza was a beautiful blonde, her arms and legs outstretched. Colorful neckties were tied around her wrists and ankles, attached to the four corner posts of the bed. Another necktie was around her head, over her eyes so that she could not see. Colonel Mendoza was thrashing above her, mauling her big pale breasts as he speared himself into her. There was nothing gentle about what he was doing to her.

"Colonel . . . Colonel . . . something terrible has happened," the young sergeant said quietly.

There was murder in Colonel Mendoza's eyes when he suddenly realized that he was no longer alone with Svetlana. Stefan suspected that had they been back home instead of in Bogata, the colonel might likely draw his service automatic and start firing.

"Get the hell out of here!" Mendoza spat. "Whatever it is can wait!"

"Colonel, you don't understand," Stefan continued. "General Palmero has been murdered."

It took several seconds for the reality of what the sergeant had just said to sink in. Mendoza climbed off Svetlana, his cock still hard as iron. Another minute of pumping and he would have released his lust inside her.

General Palmero was dead. Murdered. It was disorienting news to receive while having sex with a beautiful woman who thought being tied up with silk neckties was erotic.

"Do we know who did it?" Mendoza asked, getting off the bed.

"No, sir."

Colonel Mendoza paused a moment, standing naked, his cock still hard and glistening with the slick evidence of Svetlana's excitement. He looked at her in bed, completely naked, arms and legs spread-eagled and those spectacular breasts trembling with her deep breathing, the succulent mounds spread out now because of gravity. She had the most amazing body he'd ever had the pleasure to feel beneath his own — and she was into bondage. What more could a sadist such as himself hope for?

"Wait for me in the other room," the colonel said, his logical reasoning returning as his ardor cooled. "I'll be with you in a moment."

When the young soldier exited, Mendoza went to his closet and withdrew a terry cloth housecoat. He slipped his arms into the sleeves. Standing at the foot of the bed, he looked at the pink lips of Svetlana's pussy and thought briefly of getting back on top of her. A few more plunges were all it would take for him to come.

"What's happened?" the bosomy blonde asked. "Please, Mendoza, untie me. Take off my blindfold."

"Later. Something bad has happened. As soon as I'm sure you're not behind it, I'll untie you . . . maybe."

"Wait! Don't leave me like this!"

"Keep quiet. If you raise your voice like that again, I'll take a belt to you." The notion of whipping Svetlana with his belt was altogether enticing to Colonel Mendoza's twisted sense of eroticism. Tied up as she was, there wasn't anything that Svetlana could do to stop him from doing to her whatever he wanted.

Mendoza inspected the crime scene first. It was never a good thing when a soldier's commanding officer was killed, but there could well be an upside to this murder. With the general gone, Colonel Mendoza was the logical successor in the power vacuum that would be created.

"Don't touch anything," Mendoza said, turning away from the bloody corpse. A dozen young men, some dressed in civilian clothes and others still wearing what they'd worn to bed had gathered. "Ask around. Find out if anyone saw anything."

Mendoza returned to his own room. In the suite, he looked at Svetlana's clothes. Slowly, one article at a time, he lifted her clothes off the sofa and inspected them. When he found her purse, he opened it and casually dumped the contents onto the floor. With a bare toe he pushed the items around, looking for anything that might put a suspicious light on her. Nothing drew his eye.

He turned his attention back to the purse. He quickly discovered a small leather flap in the bottom of the purse. When he pulled the flap, a trap door in the bottom of the purse opened. Mendoza's heart accelerated. He had found a secret compartment!

Inside the secret compartment was nothing but cash. It was

a smart move to make for a woman traveling alone to hide her money. Colonel Mendoza looked at the cash, thought for a moment of stealing it, decided it was worth taking, then closed the trap door and dropped the purse, now empty of all its belongings, back onto the sofa.

The colonel shoved the bills into the pocket of his robe, ignoring the looks from the young soldiers nearby.

He decided there was enough time to get another erection, have his pleasure with Svetlana, then throw her out of the hotel. She could find her own way to whatever hotel she was staying at. Thinking about the stolen money in his robe, Colonel Mendoza decided that Svetlana owed him at least that much for the good time he'd given her. After all, hadn't he made it possible for Svetlana to live out her secret, forbidden fantasy?

Colonel Mendoza simultaneously felt his heart accelerate as his cock once again began to elongate and thicken because of Svetlana.

She's like a dangerous drug, he thought. *She intoxicates, and that makes her dangerous. Women like that are always trouble. Big trouble.*

This awareness made his cock reach full extension. Nothing in the world quite aroused him as completely as a dangerous woman—and Svetlana was that in spades. The fact that her body was exquisite, with curves and planes, hills and valleys, added to the narcotic effect on Colonel Mendoza's senses. There wasn't anything about her that didn't arouse him.

He stood at the side of the bed, his arms hanging loose at his sides, his cock standing straight out from his body, his mind in a whirl of confusion and chaos. Svetlana was there in his bed, her arms and legs outstretched, bound to the bed's posts by silk neckties that the colonel himself had selected because he thought they would give him an aura of authority and power. He had never thought, when he bought them, that he'd use them to tie up a woman.

So beautiful, he thought. *So fucking beautiful.*

It wasn't a thought he'd had with any woman he'd been with in a long, long time.

He bent down enough to touch her face. He caressed her cheek with his fingertips briefly, then with casual sloth removed her blindfold. When he did, she blinked her eyes several times in quick succession before focusing her gaze directly on his.

"What's happening?" she asked in a whisper.

"Nothing that you won't enjoy." His tone was flat, nearly emotionless.

"Are you fucking kidding me?" she asked with a certain anxiety in her tone.

The sound of her marginally controlled panic added dimensions to his cock. He was never thoroughly aroused unless the woman he was with was frightened. For him, a woman's fear was like a drug that he couldn't walk away from.

"Untie me," Svetlana said, a small but discernible quiver in her tone. "This little game has come to an end."

"It doesn't end until I say so." There was no equivocation in his tone. He would have his way, no matter what it was or what Svetlana thought of it.

She has the most startling blue eyes in the world, he thought, then felt the breath catch in his throat. His gaze trailed down from her eyes to her mouth. *A man could lose his soul fucking a mouth like that.*

It was an unsettling thought. "Take me," she said quietly, turning her face away from the colonel. "Take me all the way."

A shiver went through the colonel. Those were the words he ached to hear.

The colonel realized that he would quite happily turn his soul over to the Devil if he had endless access to Svetlana's mouth. Though not a young man, and far from his sexual prime, he suddenly thought of himself — with her — to be supremely virile and handsome, a man worthy of sexual accolades. Women, he decided at that moment, should beg to be on their knees at his feet.

Such homage, he knew, was what he deserved. He decided at that moment that — going forward — he would never again tolerate *less* than what he deserved. From this point forward he would never accept anything less than top shelf champagne, and caviar with sliced bread toasted to just the right degree of crispness.

"What's going on?" Svetlana asked. "I could hear voices."

"All you have to concern yourself with is making me happy." He got onto the bed. "After all, isn't this your fantasy? To be tied up and ravished by a powerful man?"

He saw the momentary defiant anger flash in her eyes, and it appealed to his erotic impulses. He was using her fetishes to satisfy his own desires, and the fact that he had outwitted her elevated his sense of self-esteem.

"Do you want me to fuck you?" There was sarcasm and a touch of contempt in his tone. He was a man who liked to be in control. "It's what you wanted when this evening started."

Svetlana ineffectually turned her face aside, as though she could somehow ignore the fact that she was tied up in a bed and hadn't asked to be that way. There was nothing about this situation that didn't put steel in the colonel's erection. At that moment he knew that he'd never, ever wanted to fuck a woman as much as he wanted Svetlana right then and there.

Without prelude, he positioned himself between her widespread, shapely thighs, rubbed the head of his cock several times up and down over her entrance — then plunged. Full-length and deep, he powered every inch of his cock into her tight sheath on the very first invasion.

"Oh, God!" Svetlana gasped as she tugged with all four

limbs against the neckties that bound her to the bedposts. "Oh, God!" she repeated as the colonel withdrew, then hesitated with just the tip of his cockhead still separating the pink lips of her pussy. "Fuck me," Svetlana said, her hips moving slowly from side to side as the colonel powered his cock in and out of her cunt.

Oh, no! the colonel thought as he thrust full-length into Svetlana's tight, wet cunt. *Not yet!*

But the awareness had come too late. On Colonel Mendoza's next downward thrust, passion and lust overwhelmed him, and the cum rushed from his body into Svetlana's.

He had wanted to fuck her for hours, but instead, it had taken less than a minute for him to achieve supreme sexual satisfaction.

He was profoundly disappointed in himself, and he immediately blamed Svetlana for his loss of self-control.

You bitch, he thought, *someday I'll get even with you for this. You can't treat me like this and not get punished for it.*

As his cock dwindled in size inside Svetlana's body, he looked down at her. *Cunt, you are going to regret the day you didn't treat me right.*

Washington D.C.

Omega Force was born out of necessity. After it had become abundantly clear that allies within the United Nations were taking top secret information and selling the illicit knowledge to America's enemies—or simply giving it away—men and women at the highest levels of the American government realized that changes in the standard operating procedures in the intelligence community had to be made. And if an ally acting like an enemy wasn't bad enough, elected officials from both the House and Senate—as well as the FBI, CIA, and DOJ—had also leaked intelligence and top-secret information to the news media, knowing that when the news reached the streets it would shine an unflattering light on politicians of the opposing party. Members of the armed forces had lost faith in their elected—and therefore transient—leaders. Career military officers soon understood that personal and ideological advancement in the political arena for many politicians was more important than what was right or wrong for the country.

Since politicians were voted into office, and occasionally actually were voted *out* of office, a surgically-precise fighting unit that remained totally autonomous from the American political realm and was invisible to so-called friends—who were really enemies—of the United States was difficult to create. A small fighting force *within* the Central Intelligence Agency and yet *independent from* it had to be created. This was especially true after terrorism became more of a threat to American freedom than standard armies.

Jefferson Burke was chosen to head a small fighting unit known unofficially as Omega Force. His assignment was simple: recruit the best personnel within the military to act, of a fashion, as snipers behind enemy lines in wartime. Except the war these soldiers were engaged in was ongoing and without any foreseeable end. It was a war in which there were no uniforms or international boundaries. Instead of a Ghillie suit and hiding in a jungle, Omega Force snipers were more likely to wear a string bikini and be hiding in plain sight on the beaches of Mazatlán. But despite the display of flesh and shapely curves, the end result would be the same: a single, skilled field operative putting bullets into an enemy.

After the assassination of a drug kingpin who virtually owned a Caribbean island-nation—and the annexation of that kingpin's personal bank account, which was a bit more than $4 billion—Omega Force received its necessary funding. After that, the verbal orders to Burke were simple: *Do what is necessary to stop the enemies of the United States. Do it quickly, efficiently, and with as little bloodshed as possible—but the bottom line is to do the job. Find the enemies of the United States and neutralize the threat. Don't bother seeking official approval from the United Nations, or even the United States government. Don't expect countries that are doing business with and making a fortune from a despot to suddenly approve of the removal of that despot from his political position. Get the job done and stay under the radar while doing it.*

Burke was also told that should any soldier under his command get caught while acting in an "extra-legal" capacity, the official line from the government would be denial. A renegade, without sanction from the White House or any political or military leaders, had been taking matters into their own hands. Burke would be thrown to the wolves and devoured by the enemies of the United States.

For Burke, the potential good he could do far outweighed the dangers he faced. He accepted the assignment, created Omega Force, and kept his mouth shut.

With the assassination of General Palmero, Omega Force had destabilized the power structure that held the reins of a largely unskilled and untrained though well-equipped military, which possessed among other things two suitcases filled with enough biological warfare chemicals to devastate an urban center the size of New York City.

Over the Gulf of Mexico

Svetlana Simonov put her seat back and closed her eyes. It felt good to be in the air again, aboard a Boeing 757 over the Gulf of Mexico, headed back to the United States. Though her military records stated that she had reached the rank of captain in the Army, specializing in procurement auditing, she was more importantly a ranking field agent of an organization unofficially known as Omega Force. She suspected that Omega Force was actually a part of the Central Intelligence Agency, though she really wasn't certain.

The assassination of the mass-murdering war criminal, General Martino Palmero, had gone off exactly as Svetlana had planned. When she'd given him sexual gratification in the taxicab, she knew that he would return to his hotel room and go to sleep. With his lust satisfied, there was no longer any reason for him to be crawling from nightclub to nightclub searching for women. And since she had been found tied up hand and foot in Colonel Mendoza's bed, she couldn't possibly be responsible for the general's murder — or so the colonel believed.

The world was minus one war criminal, and Svetlana felt good about that. She could hardly wait to get back to Washington D.C., where she would be debriefed by her controller and the only person in Omega Force she had met, Jefferson Burke.

She'd probably get a vacation for this one. Where to? Svetlana had always wanted to go to Sydney, Australia. Perhaps now would be a good time to travel there . . . .

Washington D.C.

Jefferson Burke looked at the computer monitor. The information he read from the computer screen wasn't going to make getting a good night's sleep any time soon an easy accomplishment. Burke's gaze locked onto the computer screen as he thought bitterly, *I screwed up. I should have checked this out before I assigned the sanction of General Palmero. Palmero was a monster, but as least I knew him and could figure out what his plans were.*

Burke was not at all pleased with what he had learned. It seemed that General Palmero's underlings were driven not so much by political zeal as they were with greed. Any one of a number of senior officers — and there was really no telling who had taken command now that Palmero was dead — was willing to sell Syrian-made chemical weapons to terrorists.

The intelligence officer thought, *At least with Palmero, I knew he wanted the power the ZT-550 chemical weapons gave him. With the other men, they want the money. They'll sell mass death and destruction to anyone.*

Burke realized the greed angle was pure conjecture, but it had to be close enough to verifiable fact to use as a working hypothesis. Burke was not a military leader who acted rashly, but now he wondered if his personal contempt for the murderous General Palmero had affected his judgment. His next moves *had* to correct his previous actions and decisions. Did any of the men in line for Palmero's job have a weakness? And who was the most likely successor to General Palmero? These were the key questions dancing through Burke's brain.

Colonel Mendoza had to be in the running for the job. And Colonel Galiano? His fingers had been in a lot of dirty deals in the past, Burke knew. And Galiano was a man of mystery, though apparently a true-blue fanatic, if intelligence reports were correct. He was different from the other rather loud charismatic leaders that Palmero had surrounded himself with. Colonel Galiano's nickname from his troops was *Iceman*. He was utterly fearless in battle. He inspired incredible loyalty from his men. Intelligence reports stated that Galiano gave the impression of being devoutly religious and didn't approve of tobacco or alcohol or loose women. Burke smiled to himself, thinking that every military commander in the history of warfare has tried to keep his soldiers away from liquor and women.

Alone in his Pentagon office, Burke said, "Every man's got a weakness. So does Colonel Galiano. I've just got to find out what it is."

He tapped keys on his computer. Endless reports scrolled by. He typed in "search" and then refined the search with "weaknesses."

The computer whirred for a moment. A field report came up on the screen. It was the report of a rumor heard by a low-level double-agent. Burke began reading the report, and his face creased into a smile.

To himself, he said happily, "Girls, eh? Young ones at that . . ." The report stated that the colonel was trying to keep his sexual preferences private, of course, but keeping that kind of information a secret while operating within a typical military unit was next to impossible. Burke grinned. It was precisely the kind of weakness Omega Force was equipped to exploit.

Washington D.C.

Jefferson Burke felt his heart pumping in his chest. He always reacted that way whenever he was about to see the woman now known as Svetlana Simonov, especially when he hadn't seen her in a while. She was the one woman in the world who could tantalize every nerve ending in his body, and she could do it without even trying. It had been that way now for nearly a decade.

There were enough people in the hotel's lobby to inform Burke that he hadn't been followed by enemy agents. Omega Force operated on the principle that none of the agents knew more than they had to, and consequently, it was the *most* secret of all the top-secret agencies in America's intelligence community.

There would be no leakers in Omega Force. And if there were, those doing the leaking would have effectively signed their own death warrant.

Burke stepped up to the appropriate door on the penthouse level of the luxury hotel in Washington D.C.'s toniest neighborhood, just hundreds of yards down the street from the White House, and knocked on the door.

The door immediately opened, and Burke saw Svetlana Simonov standing there, wearing a simple black dress that buttoned in front, with a modest neckline, held together nicely with a slender white leather belt. She was blonde haired, blue eyed, pleasantly though not extravagantly curvaceous, and wearing stiletto heels that put her a couple inches over six feet tall.

There was nothing in Jefferson Burke's body and soul that didn't want to fuck her right then and there, pounding her into the floor until she couldn't walk without a limp. He had to rein in his baser instincts.

"Hello, Svetlana," he said, his tone modulated, his facial expression neutral. "We have a lot to accomplish. Shall we just get right down to business right away?"

"Yes, sir," she replied formally.

She appeared slightly nervous. That pleased him.

"Of course, sir."

Burke felt blood coursing through his heart and straight into the shaft of his cock. This wasn't the first time he'd reacted so immediately to her erotic allure, though the extent of his physical response to her beauty still surprised him a little.

As she turned her back on him and walked into her one-room luxury suite in one of the most expensive hotels in all of the nation's capital, she asked casually, "Can I get you something to drink, or is this going to be a strictly a business meeting?"

"Business," Burke answered, the tightness in his throat preventing him from giving a more elaborate reply. For several more seconds his lips moved as though he was saying something, though no sound came out.

Her king-size bed was to the right, and to her left, tucked conveniently into the corner, was a desk and chair. Burke, aware of his own weakness regarding the field agent renamed Svetlana Simonov, chose to sit in the chair near the desk. The bed was simply too tempting, and he was determined to be on his best behavior.

At least for now.

"You don't mind if I have a little libation?" Svetlana asked, already walking toward the wheeled liquor cart near the small sink and refrigerator on the opposite end of the room. She walked with purpose, and Burke's gaze never left her.

"Of course not," Burke said, watching the sweet undulation of her ass cheeks beneath the thin cotton dress as she walked away from him. "You're not on an assignment. You deserve the chance to unwind after a difficult and dangerous mission." He smiled roguishly. "Sometimes vodka isn't liquor — it's more like medicine."

"Thank you," she said with her back still toward Burke as she poured herself a flute of Bollinger's champagne, which she had extracted from the ice bucket. "I was hoping that you'd see it that way. This mission was a bit more than I had anticipated." She chuckled softly then, without mirth. "Of course, aren't all missions that way? Don't they always become so much more than what we anticipate?"

Burke's instincts went on high alert. Was this a trap being set for him? He didn't see Svetlana as the type to do such a thing, but he hadn't become an agent of Omega Force without his antennae being fine-tuned to danger, whether real or imagined.

"I read your post-assignment summary report," Burke said, his tone just slightly below a conversational level. It forced Svetlana to move a half-step closer to hear him. "It was quite detailed, though couched in euphemism." He made a sound of disgust in his throat. "I've always loathed such prevarication."

"Sir?"

"You wrote in your report that you gave the mark *fellatio.* Such a bland word for giving your mark a blow job in a taxi on a crowded street, isn't it?"

He watched as Svetlana closed her eyes for a moment. He watched without blinking as she squirmed in discomfort, and the lengthening and thickening of his cock continued unabated. His teeth were clenched, and his hands balled into fists.

"You did suck his cock, didn't you?" He knew the truth. There was only one answer she could give. When she said nothing, Burke felt both his anger and his lust elevate simultaneously. "Did you swallow his cum? This little detail was somehow overlooked in your post-mission analysis."

He watched as she once again closed her eyes, though this time she squeezed them tightly shut, and for a much longer period of time.

"Well?" he prodded. He was enjoying her discomfort.

"Yes," Svetlana said after several more seconds, her voice barely more than a whisper.

"Yes? Yes, what?" Burke could feel his anger rising. The possessiveness he felt toward Svetlana was overpowering his own sense of logic and reason, and he knew it . . . but was powerless to stop it. In a stern voice, he asked, "Did you, or did you not, suck his cock and then swallow his cum?"

Svetlana nodded in the affirmative, though she did not respond verbally.

"And there was the other man—the one you let tie you up and then fuck you. He came inside your cunt, did he not?"

Several seconds ticked by before Burke said "Well, at least you didn't have to swallow his cum . . . but that isn't the same as being blameless, now is it?"

Burke watched as Svetlana squirmed in emotional discomfort. The urge to grab her by the hair, shake her a bit, and then throw her to the floor and fuck her hard and fast was pounding through his veins. Only his great willpower prevented him from letting his baser instincts have free rein over his actions.

"But no matter how you write your report, the fact of the matter is that you fucked one man and gave a blow job to another . . . and you did this without my permission. Didn't you?"

In a tone of voice that was nothing more than a whisper, Svetlana replied, "But I thought you'd want me to." She swallowed drily. "It was for the mission."

Burke stood slowly, consciously aware that his erection was tenting the front of his trousers and that his balls were literally throbbing with the need to release their desire deep inside Svetlana's oh-so-receptive body.

Burke touched Svetlana's cheek lightly with the back of his right hand. He inhaled deeply, and when he did, caught the pleasing scent of Chanel No. 5. She was the only woman he knew who consistently wore that fragrance, and it never failed to arouse his libidinous instincts. Even with his eyes closed, he knew if she was near.

"What should I do with you?" he asked quietly. He watched as the pink tip of her tongue crept out between her lips very briefly, then disappeared. What pleasure could such a tongue give a man? It was a thought worth contemplating leisurely, over a glass of whiskey as he sat in an over-stuffed leather chair in front of a crackling fire . . . while looking down to watch Svetlana give a heart-felt, expertly delivered blow job.

"I must do something, mustn't I?" he asked in the most reasonable of tones. "After all, I am your superior and you are my subordinate. Surely your behavior warrants some punishment, and the responsibility of meting out that punishment rests on my shoulders." He paused for several seconds, as though defying her to challenge his authority. "We can agree that you should be punished, can't we? The only question now is what the appropriate punishment should be. Am I not correct?"

He watched as Svetlana closed her eyes, then gave the briefest of nods. Burke's heart skipped a beat in his chest. Svetlana had surrendered to his control, his complete domination. His cock was so hard it hurt to keep it trapped inside his trousers.

"Turn around," Burke instructed, his tone much sharper than it had been seconds earlier. "Turn around and put your hands behind your back. Cross your hands at the wrist."

He removed his necktie quickly. In seconds he had the silk wrapped twice around Svetlana's slender wrists, then knotted tightly. She was breathing much more deeply now, and a blush had crept up her throat and to her cheeks. Burke took a moment to look at her hands tied behind her back. It was visual confirmation that this beautiful, erotic woman . . . was now completely helpless against him.

From behind, he combed the fingers of his right hand into Svetlana's silky blonde tresses. Very slowly, he curled his fingers until they were a fist in her hair. He pulled her head back on her shoulders, forcing her neck to stretch tautly. She uttered a short, soft sob.

With his lips so close to her face that his breath touched her ear when he spoke, Burke said, "I'm thinking that a spanking is what you deserve It seems to be the appropriate punishment to fit the crime." He used the tip of his tongue to draw her earlobe between his lips. He sucked on her lobe for several seconds, then used his teeth on her—lightly, to arouse, not to inflict pain. He heard her sharp inhalation.

He walked around Svetlana, then sat on the foot of her bed. As he looked up at Svetlana, who remained standing, he took off his suit coat and casually tossed it on the chair he had just been sitting in. The full extent of his swollen erection was clearly visible in the crotch of his trousers, and he made no effort to hide it.

"On your knees," he said, "then crawl over my lap."

"But my hands . . ."

"Are going to remain tied until I believe that you have satisfied the punishment that you deserve." He sighed, as though talking to a young child who didn't understand the trouble she was in. "Don't procrastinate. It'll only make your punishment that much more severe. You know it's true. And what you get is only deserved, don't you agree?"

Svetlana nodded, moved to the proper position so that she was standing parallel to the foot of the bed, then got down onto her knees on the plushily carpeted floor. Burke moved his hips forward slightly, shifting his weight so that he was just barely sitting on the mattress, but now there was more of his thighs for Svetlana to stretch over.

He watched, hardly able to breathe, as she leaned out over his thighs, then squirmed the toes of her stilettoes into the carpeting for better purchase so that she could crawl over his lap. He felt the firm fullness of her bosom sliding against his rigid cock, and no matter how many layers of clothing separated his arousal from her breasts, the sensation was still electrifying. She kept inching her way across his lap until the cheeks of her ass were lifted and the flat surface of her abdomen was pressed down against his captured, erect cock. Her face was only inches from the floor.

"Very good, my dear," Burke said, looking down at the luscious, captive feminine treasure that was now his to do with whatever he wanted. "It always pleases me whenever you follow my instructions to the letter."

He waited for her to say something — perhaps a whispered plea for leniency — and when she didn't, he put his right hand on her ass and rubbed back and forth, caressing her through the fabric of her dress and panties.

Using both hands, he reached down, grabbed the bottom hem of her black dress, then raised it slowly, leaning to the side so that he could watch the feminine perfection that he was revealing.

First there were the tapering thighs, sheathed in silk stockings. After that, there was the elasticized straps of the garter belt that held her stockings, then the pale, white flesh of her upper thighs, in stark contrast to her ebony lingerie. Burke paused a moment. At times like this, it was better to dally than to rush. Drawing out the pleasure enhanced it, whereas gulping from the glass diluted the nuances of ecstasy.

Finally, when he could wait no longer, he raised Svetlana's dress even farther, pulling the fabric up high enough that it rested on the small of her back, and the rounded globes of her ass, lovingly caressed by lace-trimmed bikini panties, came into view.

The breath hitched in Burke's throat, and he felt himself losing control of his willpower.

"Shameless," he said.

Without hesitation he raised his right hand high over his head, then brought it down with significant force. His broad-palmed hand connected solidly with skin as soft as silk. *Smack!*

Svetlana arched her back, and a strangled sound came from her throat. As she squirmed on Burke's lap, her abdomen rubbed erotically against his throbbing, aching erection.

"Bad!" Burke said, then spanked her left ass cheek, using just as much force this time as he had the first.

His blood was boiling now, his heart pounding furiously. He grabbed Svetlana's panties by the waistband at the small of her back, and an instant later, with a forceful tug, had the frilly lingerie down to her upper thighs to reveal her buns and the pink, moist lips of her cunt.

"Damn you!" Burke proceeded to spank both cheeks of Svetlana's ass quickly, striking one and then the other without stopping, turning her alabaster skin to a bright pink.

CHAPTER FOUR

Svetlana felt Burke's punishing palm strike her tush, and she writhed on his lap, intentionally grinding her stomach against the impressive dimensions of the bone-hard cock he had trapped inside the finely hand-tailored trousers of his suit.

Burke's really brought his A-game with him this afternoon. How long was this discipline going to continue? Sometimes he was patient, so the erotic hors d'oeuvres of spanking, domination, bondage, and submission could last an hour, or more. At other occasions there wasn't much time for games, and Burke got right down to the meat-and-potatoes entrée of melt-your-spine, rattle-your-teeth, bounce-off-the-walls hardcore sex.

She felt him grab her hair at the base of her skull once again, his hand tightening in an unforgiving fist, and pull up. He used just enough force to lift her head and shoulders and make the strands of hair pull against her scalp to hint at pain, but not so much that he actually physically hurt her. Her cunt clenched at the awareness of just how skilled the enigmatic Jefferson Burke was in the art of Dominance and submission.

"Oh, God!" Svetlana gasped, the words coming out with great difficulty with her head so far back on her shoulders and her neck stretched so tightly.

The spanking stopped, and Burke's right hand moved slowly, caressingly, back and forth over her tush. His touch was infinitely soft and soothing. Svetlana felt his fingertips slip between her thighs, then move upward slowly. A fresh burst of fluids moistened the lips of her pussy, and the tingling in her clit became infinitely stronger. She thought of begging him to touch her clit, but she knew she mustn't. That would be a violation for a sub, and rules had to be followed.

"Sometimes I think you misbehave," Burke said softly, with a teasing quality to his voice, "just so that I'll feel obligated to punish you. Is that the truth of it? Is that why after every mission I've got to put you over my knee?"

"No," Svetlana said, with some difficulty since Burke was still holding her hair. "I only do it because of the mission."

The wild D/s fucking you throw into me after a mission is just a spectacular, unintended consequence.

What she spoke about and what she thought privately were both completely accurate.

Burke suddenly stood, and when he did, Svetlana rolled off his thighs and fell to the floor. With her hands still tied behind her back, she was unable to catch her fall . . . though she did notice that Burke had put his feet forward just before he stood so that she rolled down his legs rather than falling straight down to the floor.

A Master Dom, Svetlana thought with appreciation as she came to a stop on her stomach on the floor of the luxury suite that had probably never before had such a sexual romp played out within its walls. *I'm the luckiest submissive in all the world.*

"Get up" Burke said sharply.

Svetlana felt his fingers once again combing through her hair, and she quickly wriggled—as best she could with her hands still tied—until she got her knees beneath her. Her panties were still around the tops of her thighs, which made spreading her knees wider apart for better balance somewhat more difficult. She tested the necktie around her wrists, found that there was no yielding in it, and felt a little more cream ooze to the entrance to her cunt.

"I want you to be at least as skilled and enthusiastic with me," Burke said as he unbuckled his belt, "as you are with our enemies." He shook her head by the hair. "That's not asking too much, is it?"

Svetlana got a bit more settled on her knees as she watched Burke slowly, almost leisurely, unbuckle and unfasten his belt, open the closure at his waist, then pull his zipper down. She saw that he was wearing navy blue boxer-briefs once he opened his trousers. He pushed his pants down to the middle of his thighs. His underwear was bulging, the cotton struggling to constrain an erection that was fighting like a caged animal to be set free.

Svetlana tried to turn her gaze away from the solid, manly flesh that Burke had for her, but she could not. She knew what pleasures were hers when Burke decided to unleash all his considerable sexual charms on her. And those charms were especially evocative when he was adopting his Dom persona and unleashing his prodigious cock.

Svetlana almost started to lean forward so she could kiss Burke's cock through the cotton, but at the last moment she stopped herself. After all, she was his submissive, and she was only supposed to do whatever he commanded of her. And wasn't that what made the whole role-playing game so multi-climactically fucking erotic? Her submission to his Domination?

Burke again pushed his fingers into Svetlana's hair, only this time at the top of her head. He tilted her head back, looked down into her eyes, then smiled wolfishly.

"I'm yours," Svetlana heard herself whisper. It was as though another woman had spoken. She was embracing her role as a submissive. "Do with me what you will."

He pulled her closer. Svetlana kissed his cock through his underwear. It seemed somehow more lewd to put her lips to his cock *through* his underwear. It was as though she was paying his manhood homage somehow.

After several seconds, Burke hooked the thumb of his left

hand into the waistband of his underwear and brought them slowly down, stopping until his cock at last—finally and gratefully—sprang free. When it did, Burke gave out a low groan of relief.

This time Svetlana couldn't contain herself. Rather than waiting to be ordered to give pleasure, she leaned forward and planted a kiss on the head of Burke's cock, then took the plump crown between her lips without another second's hesitation. Her cheeks caved inward as she drew a moist, tight suction.

"Awww!" Burke groaned, his hips driving forward.

Svetlana tightened her lips around the shaft of her lover's cock as it forced her tongue down in her mouth and simultaneously rubbed against the roof of her mouth, moving deeper with force and determination. When the plump head of Burke's cock collided with the opening of her throat, Svetlana's head snapped backward, and for a moment she sputtered.

Immediately, Burke put an end to his forcefulness, and once again Svetlana was eternally grateful that she had fallen in love with such a skillful Dom, one that could always push her to the edge without ever going beyond that boundary.

For several seconds Svetlana simply inhaled through her nostrils while holding Burke's cockhead in her mouth. She recovered her senses quickly. It wasn't long before she began moving her tongue in a circular motion against the underside of the crown of Burke's erection—where experience had taught her that he had a high concentration of nerve endings—and he groaned his approval. *Time out's over. On with the game!*

With a little less ardent enthusiasm than he had displayed earlier, Burke began fucking Svetlana's mouth with forceful but not brutish thrusts of his hips. He soon reached down with both hands to hold her by the hair, and while still on her knees, Svetlana trembled softly, pleased beyond words that her lover knew *exactly* what she wanted of him when he was playing full-on, hardcore Dom to her oh-so-grateful sub.

"Suck," Burke said, then gave her a firm shake that rocked her on her knees. "Down your throat! All of it!"

Burke pushed the crown of his cock against the back of Svetlana's mouth. She squirmed on her knees, fighting against her gag reflex. Burke's cock was simply too large for her to fit it down her throat . . . but the struggle to keep from choking against the erotic pressure added to the tightness and sensitivity of her nipples, and made her clit burn with anticipation of pleasures soon to come.

"Oh . . . oh, yes," Burke said, though this time he spoke much more quietly than before.

Give it to me. Let me take you over the top.

A moment later Svetlana heard a rumbling sound of primal ecstasy get ripped from Burke's soul. His hands tightened in her hair, and as he pulled her closer, he bent at the waist so that he was hunched over her.

"Svetlana!" he cried out as the rich, pungent thick cream erupted from his balls and splashed against the roof of Svetlana's mouth.

Svetlana nearly choked on the volume and flavor of Burke's orgasm. She swallowed as quickly as she could, because she knew that there were always several powerful streams that exploded out of him, and after those, then less forceful eruptions. He held her tightly throughout his climax, his body flinching as cum raced through the length of his cock to be deposited straight into Svetlana's mouth and then down her throat.

When the last of the eruptions had ceased, Svetlana continued to nurse on his cock, siphoning any cream that might remain. She continued sucking until he took a step backward.

Still on her knees with her hands tied behind her back, Svetlana looked up at Burke and did everything she could do keep from smiling. To smile would be a *very* unsubmissive thing to do, and she wasn't certain what punishment he might dole out for it. The cheeks of her ass were still tingling because of the spanking she'd received prior to the nearly intoxicating face-fucking he'd just given her.

"I'm not done with you," Burke said after several seconds, and Svetlana's heart did a summersault in her chest. "That was just the beginning of what I have in store for you."

Svetlana let Burke fuck her mouth slowly, and though initially his erection had lost some of its rigidity after he'd climaxed, in less than a minute he started his recovery, his cock hardening, thickening, resuming its impressive stature. Svetlana moaned softly, then reminded herself that she was supposed to remain silent. The game dictated that she pretend she wasn't as aroused as she really was.

"That's it. That's perfect," Burke said, looking down as Svetlana worked her oral magic on his cock while he unbuttoned his shirt. "Keep sucking, and don't stop until I say you clan."

That's my Dom, Svetlana thought with gratitude for the man who had taught her that she was a natural-born submissive. Though she hadn't known it initially, she had been looking for Burke her entire sexual life. *Take control. Make me do what you want me to do.*

Burke kept his trousers, socks, and shoes on. He always did whenever he was with Svetlana, no matter how intimate they were with each other. She knew the reason, though she didn't accept it, or at least didn't like it in the least.

She did, however, understand if not accept that she had little control over Burke's life.

Bending at the waist, Burke grabbed Svetlana by the upper arms and lifted her to a standing position. He unbuttoned her dress and unbuckled her belt, then he unfastened the clasp of her bra between the cups to free her breasts.

"Damn," he said softly, his pupils dilating as he visually drank them in. "Fuck. So beautiful. So . . . perfect."

He cupped her breasts from the underside and lifted them, his fingers squeezing lightly. Svetlana felt the tingles going from her nipples to streak throughout her trembling body.

Burke captured her nipples between his forefingers and thumbs and pinched softly . . . at first. Then he pulled at her nipples, tugging on them as his grip tightened. Svetlana let out a small sound, one prompted by discomfort. She never really knew how far Burke was doing to take her . . . and that was just one of the facets of the man that made him so fascinating. She watched as Burke smiled, obviously pleased with the response he had drawn from her.

"Did those men you were with treat you this way?" Burke asked as he pulled on Svetlana's nipples. She raised up on her tiptoes, but Burke only pulled upward more on her nipples, so she really had accomplished nothing. She uttered a small gasp, and Burke chuckled softly, a Dom in complete control of his submissive. "I asked you a question, and I insist that you give me a complete and truthful answer."

"No, they didn't treat me this way."

"Did they make you come?"

Svetlana shook her head vigorously, sending her blonde hair swirling around her face and shoulders. "No!" she said quickly, a bit more sharply than she had intended. "You . . . you're the only man who has ever made me come." She was speaking the truth.

"Are you sure? Are you telling the truth, or is this another one of your silly lies?" Burke's grip on Svetlana's nipples tightened, and he pulled upward another inch, making her gasp in pain. "Tell me now, because I'll know if you're lying."

"I'm telling you the truth." Svetlana squirmed and raised up onto her tiptoes again in an effort to lessen the pressure. Her nipples were burning. "You're the only man who can make me come. I promise. I swear it."

Burke released Svetlana's nipples, and she sighed softly as

the discomfort came to an end, though her nipples continued to tingle furiously. She stood flat-footed. Her clit by this time was literally aching to receive some attention from this barbarian Dominant who had so completely captivated her heart, soul, and body.

"Let's make sure it remains that way," Burke said. He took Svetlana by the arm, turned her around, then tossed her face-down on the bed.

Svetlana could do nothing to cushion her fall onto the mattress. With her hands tied behind her back, she was powerless to present any credible defense against Burke, and the awareness of her own vulnerability caused a fresh burst of fluid to moisten the lips of her pussy.

An instant later, she felt Burke get on the mattress, then grab her by the hips, pulling her up so that she was on her knees, though her face was still against the bedspread.

Her dress was lifted to the small of her back. Her panties were still around the tops of her thighs. Svetlana felt totally exposed. She closed her eyes and trembled softly. This was her favorite position. Getting fucked by Burke doggie-style while he had tied her wrists behind her back was about as erotic as anything that Svetlana could imagine.

Several seconds passed before Svetlana felt Burke's cockhead being rubbed up and down over the lips of her cunt. Even though he had just unleashed a torrent of cum against her tongue and down her throat, his cock was once again solid as stone, throbbing with lusty life, and across the surface of her mind she wondered if this was going to be a three-climax encounter with Burke — which was the norm — or just a two climax bout of high-energy afternoon fucking.

"Oh, God," Svetlana whispered when she felt her sex lips being pried apart as the crown of Burke's cock pushed forward. A moment later she felt his plump flesh pushing deeper into her cunt as her pussy lips surrounded the shaft of his cock. "It's been so long. You're so big."

Burke paused then, allowing her a few seconds to get accustomed to having his cock inside her body. She held her breath, waiting with anticipation for what was about to happen next. When she felt the crown of Burke's cock sliding backward, retreating from her body, she sighed softly . . . but she knew from experience what was about to happen next. Burke wasn't the kind of man who did *anything* in half-measures.

Spank me, Svetlana thought, when just the tip of Burke's cock was still separating the lips of her cunt. *Fuck me hard.*

She felt Burke's fingers tighten on her hips, and a moment after that, felt his cock start its second invasion into her sheath.

"Oh, God," Svetlana gasped, her body opening to the solid male thrust, feeling her clit tighten and tingle as Burke's cock rubbed so close to it. "Fuck me," she said after a moment, then several seconds later added, "me."

She felt his fingertips push into her hair once again, his fingers sliding against her scalp before tightening into a fist. He pulled her head back as he withdrew his cock from her velvety embrace. He gave her head two hard shakes.

"You've bewitched me," Burke said, then pulled her head farther back on her shoulders, his cock nearly sinking full-length into her cunt at the same time. "I can't get enough of you, and when I know you've been with another man, it nearly drives me out of my mind."

With the next thrust of his hips, Svetlana felt his pelvis strike the cheeks of her ass and his cock get buried full-length in her cunt. Svetlana was knocked forward, her face pressing into the pillow at the head of the bed. She tested the necktie surrounding her wrists, and once again was reminded in the most erotic fashion that she was in bondage and would continue to be so until Burke decided to free her.

Burke ground himself against Svetlana's ass cheeks and pulled just a little harder on her hair. Svetlana could feel his fury and his lust for her, and felt the passion pooling up inside her body. Her next climax would be soul-searing and spine-wrenching. And it wasn't far off. Svetlana had no doubts whatsoever.

While continuing to hold Svetlana's hair with his right hand, Burke began spanking her ass with his left. His hand came down fast and hard, and the sound of his palm striking her flesh echoed off the walls of the hotel room.

"Oh, yesss," Svetlana whispered, her ass stinging from the spanking she was getting, her scalp burning as Burke tugged harder and harder on her hair, fucking her with steadily increasing fury.

She started to say something more, but then Svetlana felt her insides begin to tighten, and she knew that she was only a few strokes of Burke's cock away from having her next jarring climax.

"Come!" Burke said, pulling on Svetlana's hair as he spanked her ass. "Come for me and only me!"

The myriad of wildly erotic sensations going through Svetlana was more than she could take. The next time that Burke's thick cock buried full-length into her cunt, she started to climax, her overheated libido unable to take any more pleasure without responding accordingly.

Svetlana felt the long, thick length of Burke's cock driving into her cunt, stretching the lips of her pussy, plowing deep and hard into her.

"Oh, God!" she whispered as the hard, manly cock drove full-length into her cunt. "Fuck me. Oh, yes!"

The sensation of silk surrounding her wrists was an aphrodisiac that she could not ignore. The weight of Burke's body pressing down upon her added fuel to the inferno that his passion had ignited.

"You're my drug," Burke said. "I'm powerless without you."

He drove his cock into her pussy until his pelvis collided with the cheeks of her ass. The low, rumbling groan of pleasure he emitted was one of pure ecstasy, and though she hadn't intended it, Svetlana's cunt tightened around the cock that filled her so completely.

"Yes!" Svetlana whispered. "Oh, yesss!"

She felt every nuance of his cock sliding into her cunt, tugging at the lips of her pussy, rubbing so close to her clit that she could hardly breathe. Every move he made, every subtle change of his forceful thrusts changed the friction against her body and heightened her arousal.

"Oh, God!" she gasped, then followed it up with, "Oh, no!"

An instant later she shivered as powerful contractions gripped her body and an orgasm ripped through her with all the subtlety of a sledgehammer smashing a chicken egg.

"Fuck!" Svetlana screamed as her body convulsed through a series of harsh contractions that went through her with a force that bordered on violence.

Svetlana felt her body cooling in her post-orgasmic lassitude, and she uttered a long, warbling sigh as her emotions descended from the heights that Burke had taken her to.

"More," she said, her face against the pillow. "Fuck me more." She could hardly believe the words that had come out of her mouth. Prior to Burke's entrance into her life, she never would have believed that she was capable of saying such bold words. "As hard as you can."

She had hardly finished speaking before Burke began pounding into her with even greater intensity, driving his cock hard and deep into her receptive body.

"Oh, God," Svetlana said softly as she felt yet another climax approach. Burke had the unique ability to turn her into a multi-orgasmic woman, and he could do it with a consistency that literally made her shiver, even when she was far away from him and wouldn't see him for days or even weeks. Knowing that he was there, waiting for her, made all the difference.

"Damn . . . you," Burke said, the words coming out between thrusts as he fucked Svetlana doggie-style.

Harder, Svetlana thought. *Fuck me harder. And pull my hair.*

As though Burke could read her mind, he did precisely what she had just thought.

"Oh, God!" Svetlana gasped as she felt strands of her hair being sharply pulled against her scalp. She uttered another word that might or might not have been "fuck," since because her head was so far back on her shoulders, the word itself was indistinct.

The pounding continued, hard, almost punishing. Burke drove his cock again and again into Svetlana's body, slamming himself against her ass with all the strength in his body.

"Oh, God!" Burke said through gritted. His cum raced through the length of his cock and into Svetlana's welcoming, receptive body.

He groaned, and his body went lax, all his weight against Svetlana, pressing her into the bed's mattress.

It was the lightest burden she could imagine.

"You bewitch me," he whispered into her ear.

Sometime later, Svetlana was in a twilight emotional state, not quite asleep but not truly conscious, either. Her hands were no longer bound. Burke's chest was beneath her cheek, and his breathing was even and slow. Was he asleep? Svetlana couldn't tell, and she really didn't care. She cherished these brief moments of post-coital torpor with the man she loved. They were short-lived, but they meant everything to her.

Burke cleared his throat. "I've got to take a shower, then

I've got to tell you something. I have to leave soon."

"Already?" Svetlana tried to keep the disappointment from her tone, but she did not succeed. Her time with Burke was always shorter than she desired. She wanted to protest, but she knew she shouldn't.

"I have to. Obligations. I can't shirk them," he said.

"I understand," Svetlana replied, but she wished like hell she didn't.

Burke started to get out of the bed. His trousers were still on, his belt now buckled. He was clothed properly from the waist down.

"Can I help you?" Svetlana asked, her voice little more than a whisper. "You could lean on me."

Burke shook his head, his lips pursed into a harsh, thin line. He kicked his feet over the edge of the bed. He was still wearing his oxblood wingtips.

"No. I must do this alone."

"At home . . . wherever that is . . . what do you do?"

"I use aluminum crutches, and I have a plastic stool that I keep in the shower." Svetlana watched as he closed his eyes. She knew she was sailing into dangerous emotional waters with this man. When he turned his head and then smiled at her, it was without warmth. "One learns to adapt."

"But couldn't I help?"

"No," Burke said coldly, in a tone of voice that suggested his attitude would never change. "What's so fascinating about seeing a stump? It's really nothing anyone wants to see."

Svetlana closed her eyes then. She had been making love with this man since she was eighteen, yet she knew almost nothing about him. Not even his real name. Whenever he talked — and that was a rarity under even the best of conditions — he said very little about himself. All she knew was that his first name was "Burke," not his last. The Jefferson part was an alias. She knew that he'd lost his left foot, just above the ankle, to an improvised explosive device while on assignment in Afghanistan. After surgeons amputated his foot, he became a controller for Omega Force instead of a field agent. Svetlana suspected he wasn't in the least bit pleased with his change of responsibility with Omega Force.

"I'm sorry," Svetlana said. "I know I'm not supposed to ask personal questions. But sometimes . . . I wonder. You can't blame me for that."

"No. I can't and I don't." Burke got to his feet and headed for the shower, then stopped. "I'm sorry I can't be more open with you. I'm sorry I can't be more . . . forthcoming." He kept his back to her, and his tone dipped precipitously. "You'll never see my stump. Never."

After he walked into the bathroom, he closed the door behind himself.

Svetlana felt unutterably alone. She felt alone on the planet. She refused to let herself cry.

Svetlana looked at her wrists and smiled coyly. Burke had *really* brought his A-game for this encounter. Around her wrists were the marks of the silk necktie that he'd used to tie her. The marks wouldn't last until the next day, but she wore them as a badge of honor now.

She heard the shower turn off and wondered whether Burke was sitting on the floor of the shower to wash himself or standing on one foot.

She wanted so much to help him, but he refused to let her. *He's so damned stubborn,* she thought, then wondered why she wanted so much to see his wound. In her heart she knew he had the right to keep personal secrets to himself, but it still irked her that his wound, which was so important to him, was something he wouldn't share with her. It must have scarred him in ways she could hardly imagine.

Knowing that he would be coming out of the bathroom

soon, Svetlana pulled on her silk stockings quickly, then attached them to the straps of her garter belt. Burke had made it abundantly clear over the years that he appreciated fine lingerie. It pleased her to please him.

After putting on her bra, she decided that going without panties would make her intentions a bit more obvious than she wanted, so she stepped into her bikini panties, but then put on her stilettoes, because she knew they made her legs look longer, and Burke had said he though her sexy in heels. Those were the kind of words she thought about . . . *especially* when she wasn't with him.

Burke opened the bathroom door and stepped out. He was fully dressed, and the necktie he had used to tie Svetlana's wrists behind her back was now casually and securely tied into a Windsor knot around his neck. He had the appearance of a prosperous man, secure in his employment, who understood precisely who and what he was, and what his role was in the United States' government.

Svetlana felt her cunt awaken when she looked at him, and she was glad now that she had consciously chosen to not get fully dressed in his absence.

He always wants me three times, Svetlana thought, more than slightly unnerved that Burke was going to leave her before she'd satisfied his lust once more. Was he leaving to meet another Omega Force agent? The agent might be significantly younger than Svetlana, and very beautiful, and oh so willing to satisfy his every desire. Svetlana tried to not be insecure, but telling herself something wasn't the same as truly believing it, not deep down in her heart of hearts.

"I thought you'd be dressed," Burke said quietly. He smiled. It wasn't a rebuke. "I can't say that I'm disappointed that you're not."

Svetlana rose slowly to her feet, particularly pleased that she had chosen to put on her stilettoes. She'd noticed when

Burke's gaze had gone down to her feet, and she saw his instant appreciation in the expression in his eyes. She didn't mind getting a little trashy, so long as it was for Burke. The stilettos were subtle, not overt, but Burke had noticed it, and because he had, cream moistened the lips of her pussy, even though she had no intention of entertaining Burke with that part of her body again on this afternoon.

"You're leaving," Svetlana said, her voice a sultry purr of carnality. "And I haven't showered yet." She made a motion with her hands as though to cool herself. "Being with you is always a sweaty experience." She put up a hand, palm outward. "But don't get me wrong. I'm not complaining." She walked slowly forward until she was standing directly in front of Burke, her head tilted back on her shoulders to look up into his eyes. "Will you think of me when we're apart? I always tell myself that you will, but I'm never really sure." She touched his cheek with the tips of her fingers. "I'm always insecure whenever you're involved. I should hate you for that . . . but I don't." She closed her eyes for a moment. "I don't think I could ever truly hate you, no matter what you do to me." She looked him directly in the eyes, trying to see through the facade he put up to hide the man he truly was. He was standing near the door to the suite, looking just as gorgeous as he always did. She'd never seen him in anything other than a suit and necktie, his shoes always brightly polished, his hair always combed, his breath always smelling minty.

There were times when Svetlana wished that Burke wasn't quite as perfectly in control of himself as he always seemed. Sometimes she wanted him to be a little vulnerable — not fearful, but just a bit uneasy with the way that things were going — though that never seemed to be the case with him. For his arrogance, she disliked him . . . at least a little. It was difficult to not resent a man with such supreme self-confidence.

"You're not leaving me without coming one more time," she said quietly as she approached him with a hip-swaying stride. "You always want me three times, and I'll admit to being insecure." She caught her bra between the cups, pinched the hook-and-eye closure between her forefingers and thumbs. "There isn't anything you have to do. Just stand there and enjoy yourself. I'll take care of everything else."

She watched as the fire of lust ignited in his eyes. This was something he hadn't anticipated, and Svetlana congratulated herself for her impromptu excursion into sexual impropriety.

"You can leave soon," she whispered, "but not before I swallow your cum. If you think I'm going to let you leave, and possibly go to another woman, with so much as a single drop of cum left in your balls, then you simply don't know me nearly as well as you think you do."

Svetlana sank to her knees, her hands sliding from Burke's shirtfront to the buckle of his belt. Her gaze never once left Burke's. Very slowly, consciously aware that he was watching her every move, she unbuckled his belt, opened it completely, unsnapped his trousers, then lowered his zipper. His underwear were boxer-briefs, white, and were bulging while trying to contain the hard cock that was straining to be freed.

Three times, Svetlana thought with confidence. She knew her man.

There were a thousand things in life that she didn't understand, but she did know Burke and his libido . . . and there was no way on this earth that she was going to let him leave her hotel room without being sexually drained.

Not if he might be leaving her to see another woman.

She tugged down his boxer-briefs, and his cock sprang out, not quite fully erect, but still distinctly impressive in both length and girth. Svetlana, sitting on the backs of her heels, consciously took a moment to look him over.

She made a point of not thinking too much about the fact

that she might not be the only woman to entertain herself with Burke's sexual prowess. There was so much about him that she didn't know and couldn't even ask about.

"Do women often sing the praises of your cock?" Svetlana asked. The censure was thick in her tone as she remained on her knees, looking at an erection that literally made her mouth water as though she was starving, and anticipating a delicious steak cooked to medium-rare perfection. "No, I don't want to know the answer, so don't say anything. The truth is, I don't really want to know how many women you fuck. The fact that you're willing to fuck me is good enough." She closed her eyes. "I'm such a sub . . . but I never used to be until you came into my life. You being a Dom changed me . . . changed everything about me." She shivered. "I never saw that coming, but I can't deny it now."

She curled her fingers around the base of his shaft and felt his cock throb in response. Whatever flexibility had remained in his cock vanished the moment she touched it. She leaned forward and planted a rather chaste, almost polite and even a bit demure kiss to the crown of Burke's cock. As she did this, she cupped his balls in her left hand and gave them a firm squeeze. She knew what they had for her, and she caressed them with affection.

"One more climax," she whispered, her lips nuzzling the head of his cock as she spoke. "That's not asking too much of you, is it?" She licked the tip of his erection. "You make me greedy for your cum."

In response, she received a rumbling groan of desire, and Svetlana knew that she was doing precisely what she should be doing. Burke wasn't just *literally* in her hands, he was *psychologically* in her hands . . . and she knew it. He might be her Dom, and she might be on her knees, but the power rested with her, and at that moment both she and Burke understood this.

"Come," she said softly, her lips nuzzling Burke's sac as she spoke the single word. For several seconds she sucked one of his balls between her lips. "Come for me one more time." She brought her tongue from the base of his cock all the way up to the underside of his cockhead, then licked his slitted tip slowly and sensually. "Let me swallow your cum one last time before you leave me." She pushed her lips over the crown of Burke's cock, then released his flesh with a somewhat loud slurping sound. "You always love it when you come in my mouth. I always see it in your eyes. You like it when I swallow your cum."

She conveniently omitted the fact that she found the taste of cum abhorrent, though she did like the look in Burke's eyes whenever she sucked him off and swallowed his sperm.

It seemed a very small price to pay for satisfying the man she loved so completely.

CHAPTER FIVE

Cartagena, Colombia

Colonel Mendoza leaned back in his chair and puffed his cigar contemplatively. Things seemed to be working out nicely for him, yet he had the feeling that something was slightly amiss. Mendoza had been living a life of treachery and duplicity long enough to know that whenever he got that eerie feeling it the pit of his stomach, it was a good idea to listen carefully to what his gut instincts were trying to tell him.

As it turned out, the murder of General Palmero hadn't put a bad light upon Mendoza. His job in Bogota had been to assist the general in the purchase of weapons on credit, not provide security. As such, Mendoza was certain that heads would eventually roll because of the general's murder, but one of the heads that got lopped off wouldn't be his own.

Perhaps the best part of what had happened—aside from Svetlana, who had such an amazing body and was secretly into bondage—was that now Mendoza was in control of the ZT-550 chemical weapons. The general had been keeping the two suitcases containing the canisters of chemical weapons close, intending to use them against anyone who presented a credible threat to his power structure. Now that the general was gone, Mendoza saw no reason why the weapon shouldn't be used for a more positive purpose—like stuffing the colonel's own Jamaican bank account to the rim with money.

Colonel Mendoza had put the word out that morning on

the international market, using secure channels, that there was ZT-550 nerve gas available to the highest bidder. His contacts had said there had already been a few feelers out, parties interested in using the deadly gas against an enemy. But the potential buyers were also leery of becoming targets, knowing how the international community was beginning to go after even the smallest cells of freedom fighter factions.

Before Mendoza was willing to part with the nerve gas, he'd have to find just exactly the right third party to negotiate the transfer of money for weapons. The colonel couldn't do this himself. He was already on too many lists at the United Nations as a suspected war criminal. His face drew too much attention in the wrong circles. So he'd have to find a third party who could be trusted, and paid, to provide the necessary services.

As Mendoza sucked on a Churchillian cigar, he began imagining what he would do with the fortune he figured the nerve gas was worth . . . .

Barranquilla, Colombia

Colonel Galiano bent over the sink, cupped the icy cold water in his hands, and once again splashed his face. The cold water helped to fight off the fatigue which had gripped him.

He was in Barranquilla in search of weapons. His men were down to rationing their bullets. Artillery was almost non-existent. All the stockpiles of ammunition that had once been in his command had been used up in various exercises and battle simulations. And there was also the problem of his men selling their weapons on the black market, and then deserting the ranks.

As he thought about this, a savage, ugly smile curled his lips. It if wasn't for the United States, his country wouldn't be in the abject condition it was in now. His home country could be powerful and strong if not for the United States, with its imperialist policies, and desire to control the lives of people in other countries.

Colonel Galiano sighed, cupped his hands with water and slowly put his face into his palms again. He was exhausted to the bone, but he felt good about the day's activities.

A knock sounded on the hallway door. The colonel pulled a towel from the rack—he discovered the towel was thin as paper as he dried his face—and walked to the door. He saw that it was Stefan standing in the hotel's hallway. Galiano opened the door.

"Yes, sergeant?"

"Colonel, sir, I have a message for you."

"Yes?"

"Colonel Mendoza is in Caracas. Apparently he's found a buyer. At least he's found someone interested in buying."

"Where did this information come from?" Colonel Galiano felt like he had just been kicked in the stomach. This was vital information.

"From your man inside his network. That's all he'd say. The information came over the telephone."

Colonel Galiano said, "Thank you, sergeant. You've done very well. How long ago did this information come in?"

"Just now, sir."

"Book passage to Caracas on the earliest possible flight." Colonel Galiano turned away from the door, and in a distracted voice added, "There might still be time after all . . ."

Washington D.C.

Svetlana Simonov's eyes narrowed as she looked at Burke. This had to be some kind of a joke. It simply had to be! This man was too competent, too experienced in the ways of the intelligence community, to think that she'd ever go along with something like this.

"Ask your question, Simonov," Burke said, his voice low

and not terribly respectful. "I can see you're just dying to get the answer."

"What I need to know," Svetlana said softly, her anger just barely being held in check, "is just whose idea it was to turn this eighteen-year-old Tatiana, whatever her last name is, into a field agent."

"It was someone else's idea, but she wasn't against it. Of that I can assure you," Burke said quickly. "You mustn't hold her back. She's an extremely capable young woman. She's dying to become a field agent."

"I don't want her to *die* a field agent!" Svetlana looked around her hotel room, shaking her head slowly in utter disbelief. "How could you have thought I would go along with this?"

Burke said quietly but forcefully, "It's not just what *I* want, it's what *she* wants. Don't kid yourself into thinking that I talked her into this. If anything, I'm sure someone tried to talk her out of it. She's a young woman who just wouldn't be denied." He chuckled and added, "It sort of sounds like you, doesn't it?"

Svetlana thought about Tatiana for a moment. She could picture Tatiana arguing to be given her first field assignment. Svetlana thought back to her own beginnings with Burke and Omega Force, and though she was younger than Tatiana when she first started, she hadn't been *much* younger when given her introduction into the murky world of black ops.

Svetlana could still remember her first assignment. Her mark was a French communist spy. He was nearly sixty. Svetlana had seduced him, and in the middle of having sex, while he was inside her and pumping away, she held her breath and broke a small capsule beneath his nose. The deadly fumes went deep into his lungs. The chemical was inert within five seconds. An instant after inhalation, his heart exploded — quite literally *exploded* in his chest. The coroner's report listed heart attack while having sexual relations as the cause of death. There wasn't a soul in the communist party who had the slightest suspicion that he'd actually been assassinated because of his role in naming a double agent working for the British Secret Service.

Svetlana asked quietly, "You're sure she's ready for it?"

"The truth?" Burke asked.

"Of course I want the truth!"

"No, I'm not sure," he answered. His tone was calm, measured. "As a matter of fact, I'm never really sure about something like that. But I do my best. I get all the information I can on our own agents, then decide to either send them out, or turn them away." He looked straight into Svetlana's eyes. "I was thoroughly insecure in my decision to put you in the field. But you've turned out well, haven't you?"

Svetlana hadn't expected the ball to get thrown back into her court. For the very first time since she'd heard that she was going to have a field agent she'd have to look after, she tried to detach her emotions from her thoughts and look at the situation clearly and logically. Coldly, with her emotions stripped from the equation, she thought about what had been presented to her. When in the field, she had always only been accountable to herself. Having someone else in the line of fire that she had to worry about was something she had never had to concern herself with. Until now.

"You're right," Svetlana said, staring at the floor in front of her. "I'm sure she's perfect for the assignment. She's young and she's smart. She's resourceful. I'm sure she's pretty. She'll twist that self-righteous bastard of a colonel around her finger, and when it's all over he'll never know what hit him or where he went wrong." She looked up, and when she did, the expression on her face said without words that she was deadly serious. "But I'm in on the assignment, too. I know Colonel Mendoza. He likes me. He trusts me. He's fucked me, and I'm sure he wants to fuck me again. From what you've told me so far, there are three possible men who have control of the ZT-550. They are Colonel Mendoza, Colonel Galiano, and General Jorge Ragga. I'm too old to trigger Colonel Galiano's fantasies, I suppose." Her expression twisted into a scowl. "I can't tell you how pissed I am to think that I'm considered too old when I'm only twenty-eight."

Svetlana pushed out of her chair. She was suffering from jet lag, post-mission depression, and the shock of learning that she was about to work with another field agent. And she was hungry, which made her cranky. She hated the fact that decisions were being made without her foreknowledge, but she also realized that upon becoming a member of Omega Force, she had willingly opted to lose control over huge segments of her life. It came with the lifestyle of an Omega Force operative. At least, she guessed it did. She knew very little about Omega Force, and there was very much to know.

"I'm going to get something to eat. Then I'm going to take what might well be the world's longest shower. When I'm done, I'm going to crawl into my own bed — alone — and when I wake up, I'll figure out what to do next. Until that time," Svetlana said, pausing to look Burke directly in the eyes, "I'd appreciate it very much if I wasn't disturbed, and Tatiana wasn't tempted with any new assignments."

Svetlana Simonov, agent of Omega Force, left the man she adored but sometimes was furious with. She never once looked back.

Washington D.C.

The young woman, now known as Tatiana Simonov, stepped into the lobby of the five-star hotel and tried to tell herself that she wasn't as nervous as she really was.

The hotel was everything she'd been told it would be. It was filled with people who were clearly society's one-percenters, if one judged by their clothes. But even more importantly, it was their attitude, bearing, and demeanor that marked them as people who couldn't and wouldn't be messed with by anything or anyone. There was something about every one of them—both male and female—that said "I'm at the top of my game, and I intend to stay there. If you think you can take me off my tower, go ahead and try—but prepare to suffer for your efforts . . . and don't expect any mercy."

Tatiana paused a moment and looked down at herself. For this important meeting with a woman she'd never met, she had chosen a lightweight cotton sundress of navy blue that was belted and came down to just slightly over the tops of her knees. She had done her makeup carefully, though she had under-emphasized her mascara, and had forgone the false eyelashes she usually wore. They highlighted her eyes, which were crystal blue, and she had been told more times than she could count that they were beautiful, but she didn't want *anything* about her to be ostentatious for the woman she was about to meet.

When you meet the woman who is going to lead you into your first mission that could end your life, it's better to be generic than ostentatious, she told herself.

She glanced at her wristwatch. It was a Cartier, and new to her. When she had agreed to become an Omega Force agent, all sorts of things had suddenly been purchased for her, and the diamond-encrusted Cartier was one of them. The bejeweled hands told her it was two o'clock.

Tatiana inhaled deeply, exhaled slowly through her nostrils, then looked around the hotel's crowded lobby. She saw the usual assortment of middle-aged men in expensive suits that had been tailored to hide the fact that they were twenty pounds heavier than they had been twenty years ago, and women of the same age who had spent a small fortune purchasing pantsuits that tried to hide the fact that they were *also* twenty pounds heavier than they had been twenty years ago.

Looking at them, Tatiana suddenly felt very young, very inexperienced, and very *under*-trained for whatever mission she was about to embark upon. Her handlers at Omega Force had warned her that this would happen, but somehow that hadn't made much of a difference.

Then, at the bar, she saw a woman in her late twenties who was beautiful in the classic Nordic-Teutonic sense, with blonde hair and blue eyes, a demeanor that said she knew she was beautiful but didn't want to be approached, yet wasn't being a rude bitch who thought she was "too good" for ordinary people.

That's got to be her, thought Tatiana. It was her unspoken attitude more than anything else that convinced Tatiana that she had just met her superior. *There aren't a thousand woman like her in all the world. She looks . . . regal.*

The woman turned her head, and their gazes met and held for several seconds. Tatiana suddenly felt inadequate, as though she wasn't up to the assignment that Omega Force had assumed she was qualified to handle.

Seconds that seemed more like minutes passed, then the blonde woman smiled. The woman crossed her legs at the knee and turned on her stool toward the bar. Tatiana watched as the woman took a sip of her drink from a martini glass.

It was an unspoken invitation to sit next to her. Tatiana noticed that a half-dozen men instantly began rising from their seats.

Tatiana didn't hesitate. She knew she couldn't. She crossed the room, taking bold strides, put a wide smile on her face, and approached the woman while holding her hand out.

"Hello," she said while still several feet away from the woman she had yet to meet. "I'm Tatiana." She paused a moment before reaching the outstretched hand of greeting. "I'm really hoping you're expecting me."

The blonde woman rose to her feet. She was wearing

stilettoes, which made her five inches taller than she really was. Tatiana had worn flats for the initial meeting, and barefooted, she stood just five-foot-one. The woman was over a foot taller, and Tatiana felt small . . . and insignificant.

They shook hands, and at the contact of their skin, Tatiana felt an almost electric charge go between them. At that moment, she knew with certainty that she had met the woman she had been assigned to meet . . . and that this woman would change her life irrevocably.

It was a sensation she had never before experienced, and which she knew with granite certainty that she would never experience again.

"I am," the woman said, then squeezed her fingers a little tighter around Tatiana's hand. "I'm Svetlana. Let's have a drink, and then we can get down to business."

Tatiana noticed that a half-dozen men returned to their seats. She smiled. She knew they'd been dismissed . . . and so did they.

This beautiful woman was waiting for me, not you, she thought, aware that her thoughts were both catty and petty. Under the circumstances, she didn't care.

She turned toward the room, issuing a Mona Lisa smile toward all of them in general, but none of them in particular. She suddenly felt far more beautiful than she generally did . . . though she didn't know why. But she strongly suspected that the woman she had just met was playing a prominent role.

"What can I order for you?" Svetlana asked, her smile pleasing and cordial, but nothing more than that.

Tatiana noted that Svetlana had immediately taken the dominant position. She wasn't going to let Tatiana order for herself; she was going to order for her, immediately establishing where they were on the power totem pole.

"I'll have whatever you're having," Tatiana said as she took her seat, deciding that she couldn't go wrong with deferring to the woman she now had to consider her superior in every way one could imagine. When Svetlana gave her a questioning look, she added, "I'm really not fussy."

"I'm having a gin martini, very dry, with a twist of lime. Will that do for you?"

"Yes, very nicely."

For a second or two Tatiana felt disoriented, and then she told herself—with more certitude that she felt—that she had been chosen for this assignment because people who had plenty of experience regarding such things thought she was capable, so there was really no reason for her to be insecure.

"I want you to know," Tatiana said softly, "that I've never before met an Omega Force agent other than the man who runs me, so this is kind of odd." Tatiana watched as Svetlana's breasts rose and fell with her sigh. She felt a momentary pang of envy because she felt that the woman's breasts were nothing less than perfect—a D-cup, which was neither too small nor too large. *Just frickin' perfect. Unlike my itty-bitty B-cup titties.*

Tatiana felt herself inadequate, and she resented Svetlana for it, though she tried to pretend that she really didn't.

Don't be petty, she thought. *She might be the one to teach you how to not get killed on your first assignment.*

The sobering thought emotionally grounded Tatiana. And from that point forward, she knew she could concentrate on the things that really mattered, and not the silly ego-driven shit that really meant nothing at all.

"Everyone's looking at us," Tatiana said as her martini was slid onto the bar in front of her.

"Only the men are," Svetlana said, a smile on her lips. "And the women who are looking are wondering whether or not you're going to be competition. There isn't a woman in this bar who isn't looking to meet a rich man. I'm not saying they're prostitutes. I'm saying they're shrewd women who have no intention of hitching their wagon to a man who may or may not have a career record of something less than being stable and high-paying."

Tatiana picked up her martini, tasted it, then sighed softly.

"Nothing less than perfection," she said quietly, using a voice that only Svetlana could hear. "I'm serious. It's that good."

"Good., I've always been a big fan of perfection." Svetlana's tone was low enough that only Tatiana could hear her. "But getting down to business, there are certain things we have to do, things we have to buy, and though these martinis are delicious, there's a salon that we've got an appointment at that's already got two bottles of Tattinger's champagne on ice waiting for us, and I guarantee you that a Tattinger's buzz is the best buzz in the world." She laughed softly. "Especially early in the afternoon."

"This feels decadent."

"At Omega Force, decadence is status quo."

Burke was right. She could be my sister, Svetlana thought, though not without a certain amount of resentment. It still pissed her off that at the age of twenty-eight she was considered too old to be a honey trap for a man the American government considered a serious threat. It made her feel unattractive and a touch insecure, and those were emotions she didn't like to dwell upon.

I'll protect her, Svetlana thought.

The awareness made her sense of responsibility heighten exponentially in Svetlana, and for a moment she resented Burke . . . though that didn't make her love him any less.

Tatiana cleared her throat softly after taking a sip of her martini. Svetlana could tell that she was drawing attention to herself, though only for Svetlana's benefit.

"Everyone's watching us," Tatiana said, holding the

martini glass close to her mouth so that only Svetlana could read her lips. "Is that something we should be concerned about?"

Svetlana felt a small thrill go up her spine. Tatiana was deferring to her without her having to make it clear that she was the superior officer, and that made her breathe a sigh of relief. She felt her heart open to the young agent who looked so much like herself.

"The men are trying to figure out whether or not they should try to make a move on us," Svetlana said, her voice a whisper. "I know just how to end their doubts."

Svetlana felt her clit tighten just a little, and as that happened, a fresh dribble of slick honey moistened the lips of her cunt. While looking into Tatiana's eyes, she placed her hand on the young woman's thigh, then moved it upward, pushing the hem of her skirt with it. She didn't stop until the edge of her palm was two inches from the leg seam of Tatiana's panties. "If you kiss me now," Svetlana said quietly as she leaned toward Tatiana, "there isn't anyone in this room who won't believe that you're spoken for

Svetlana knew she had backed Tatiana into an emotional corner she couldn't get out of, but there was still a certain amount of resentment that she felt for having a co-agent foisted upon her.

It's all part of the mission, Svetlana thought as she leaned toward Tatiana. *I'm only doing what Burke would want me to do.*

She wondered what kind of spanking she'd get from Burke if she gave cunnilingus to Tatiana. No matter how she looked at the conundrum, it seemed like a win-win situation for her.

As her lips came in contact with Tatiana's, even Svetlana understood the stunning, glaring hypocrisy of what she had just thought.

Svetlana felt Tatiana's hesitation from the first moment that their lips touched . . . but this didn't stop her. She angled her face slightly to the right to be at a more advantageous angle to kiss Tatiana, and when she eased her tongue forward, she was delightfully surprised to feel Tatiana's lips separate invitingly.

An instantaneous charge of erotic electricity went from Svetlana's mouth to her nipples, and from there to her clit. For the briefest moment Svetlana tried to tell herself that she was kissing Tatiana only because it would keep other men in the saloon from approaching them, but this delusion — which was really more of a *self*-delusion — lasted only a couple seconds. Svetlana understood almost immediately that she was kissing the young blonde woman named Tatiana because she *wanted* to, and the fact that her clit was throbbing was not because of the mission. Her clit was throbbing because of Tatiana's kiss.

Svetlana danced her tongue against Tatiana's, and when she did, she felt her nipples tighten and become just a little bit more aroused and sensitive.

I've proven my point, Svetlana thought, feeling the gaze of every man in the saloon watching her as she kissed Tatiana. *I can stop now.*

But she didn't. In fact, she did quite the opposite. She brought her right hand around to the back of Tatiana's neck to hold her securely, then pressed her lips even more tightly against the girl's lips and thrust her tongue more deeply into her mouth. The kiss that had started out theatrical was now nothing other than surreal.

"Fucking fuck! Would you look at that!"

It was as man who had spoken, and when he did, his words were slurred with alcohol.

That was exactly what Svetlana had wanted . . . though having to end her kiss with the young woman who was pretending to be her younger sister wasn't something she really wanted to do.

"Well, I think we've proven that neither one of us are looking to pick up a guy," Svetlana said, taking her hand off

Tatiana's thigh, though she could still feel the gaze of everyone in the room upon her. "How about you and I get to work?"

When Tatiana said, with a somewhat shaky voice, "I think that would be a good idea," Svetlana paused a moment to remind herself that the purpose of the mission wasn't to seduce a young, attractive, very inexperienced woman who had recently been in the Army. Still . . . Svetlana wondered when next the opportunity to kiss Tatiana would present itself.

Svetlana stood at the receptionist's desk at the spa that Burke had told her to go to, and which she had been instructed to take the rookie agent to. "We have an appointment."

The young woman at the receptionist's counter hardly glanced at Svetlana's black credit card. The color black meant that there was no limit to her credit. That was all the woman behind the desk needed to know, and she behaved accordingly.

"Your people have called ahead," the receptionist said in a quiet, dignified tone. She was nothing if not professional. "We've champagne and caviar on ice for you. The bread will be toasted upon request. We have two assistants."

"Two?" There was mild censure and a lifted eyebrow from Svetlana.

"For each of you," the receptionist said quickly. "I'm sorry if I didn't make myself clear."

"Not at all," Svetlana said. This wasn't the first time that she'd been to this spa. "The misunderstanding was all my fault. There isn't anything for you to apologize for." For a moment longer than necessary, her gaze met and held the young woman's. The messages Svetlana's gaze sent were ambiguous. She was a woman who always kept her options open.

For the next ninety minutes, Tatiana and Svetlana were

massaged, given a full body wax, drank champagne out of a straw because they were on their stomachs or their backs but most certainly weren't sitting up, and were basically treated as though they were princesses of one of the more significant and prosperous countries of Europe.

"I *sooo* could get used to being treated like this," Tatiana said softly as a masseuse gently worked her thumbs in a circular motion against her temples.

Svetlana, who had been an agent of Omega Force for a decade, and therefore was in possession of a fistful of credit cards that simply could not be "maxed out," merely smiled at her protégé's comment. But after several seconds, she said, "Get used to it. This is your life now."

The assistant asked, "Is there anything else you'd like?"

Svetlana wondered if the woman was being intentionally ambiguous, then realized this was not something she should intellectually or emotionally pursue. Nothing good could come of it.

"We'd like to have our hair and nails done now," Svetlana said. "Identical cuts, shades, and nails."

"Yes, ma'am," the young woman replied. "We've already been given those instructions."

CHAPTER SIX

Caracas, Venezuela

Colonel Galiano sat in the overstuffed chair of his hotel room. He thought about how he didn't need to travel in such splendor and how few luxuries his men had. They were squatting in fox holes or sitting in sweltering, hot barracks without air conditioning, wondering if they'd get fed a meal that day. Colonel Galiano didn't like the lavish accommodations that he traveled in, but he accepted them because he knew that if he didn't travel so comfortably, he would present an image of poverty, and his people had sent him to procure weapons — on credit — on a truly grand scale. A man who looked like he needed credit couldn't get it on the international arms market, but if a man who had the appearance of having all the money in the world, then he didn't need to do business cash-in-advance.

The perverse irony of it was not lost on the colonel. He loathed capitalism with all his heart and soul.

There was a solid knock at the door. Colonel Galiano knew it was Stefan. Without waiting to be beckoned, Stefan opened the door and entered.

"Good evening, Colonel Galiano. I have the latest report for you." He crossed the room with long, confident strides, and handed the colonel a manila envelope.

Colonel Galiano pulled the string on the envelope, breaking the wax seal that indicated it hadn't been tampered with. When he looked at the documents inside, he felt a rush of adrenaline go through him. He'd assigned a team of very competent men to tail Colonel Mendoza to find out what he was doing. The pages of information that Colonel Galiano received were a litany of squalid behavior. Everything he read indicated moral weakness, and to Galiano, that was the worst weakness of all.

Colonel Mendoza had been to a whorehouse in Caracas. He stayed there for several hours. Upon leaving, he was seen staggering slightly. It could reasonably be assumed that he left the house of ill repute quite intoxicated.

Colonel Mendoza had been to several whorehouses in Maracaibo. Once again, he stayed several hours. Whether he was intoxicated upon leaving the establishments had not been verified.

Colonel Mendoza had been seen talking with an arms merchant in Caracas. This wasn't damning in and of itself, since the colonel was supposed to be on a mission to purchase weapons for the militia. What *was* damning was the fact that the arms merchant was a man known for purchasing weapons from disgruntled generals of the former Soviet Union countries, then selling those weapons to terrorists and so-called freedom fighters from every possible political fringe group. The arms dealer had an international reputation that was known at Interpol. That made him precisely the kind of too-visible weapons merchant that Colonel Mendoza and Colonel Galiano knew to stay away from.

Besides, how old were these weapons now? Were they any good at all? Did they even function? And how could they be tested without actually using them and making them no longer of any use to a militia?

Colonel Mendoza had also been seen entering one of the finest, most posh restaurants in Valencia. He dined there in the company of a "working girl" he had met earlier in the evening. The tab for the bill came to more than six month's wages for the typical soldier.

As he finished reading the pages, Colonel Galiano felt his personal pride swell. He made a conscious effort to tamp down the feelings. Hubris, he knew, was a sin. Just like intoxication. Just like laziness. These were weaknesses in a man's soul, and when he was able to spot an enemy's weakness and know in his heart that he did not possess the same weakness, he did not fight the urge to feel superior.

The day would come when he would crush Colonel Mendoza. It might take some time, but the day would dawn when Colonel Galiano would look into the blood-shot eyes of Colonel Mendoza, then squeeze the trigger and kill the dissolute colonel. The execution in front of his men would serve two perfectly necessary functions: it would rid Colonel Galiano of an enemy, and it would show the soldiers that weakness was a sin that would not be tolerated. The punishment for weakness was swift death without mercy.

Colonel Galiano was a man without weakness.

Almost.

Rio de Janeiro, Brazil

Svetlana Simonov stood in the luxury suite hotel room, looking down at the city of Rio de Janeiro. It was a beautiful city. Possibly one of the most beautiful in all the world — provided one didn't look too closely, or looked at it from anything other than a luxury hotel from the penthouse floor. Salzburg was close to it in beauty, Svetlana suspected. Vienna was gorgeous, too. But there was simply something special about Rio de Janeiro that had always appealed to Svetlana. She wondered if it was the beaches with all those gorgeous men and those beautiful women wearing barely-there bikinis . . .

She felt tired, but she knew she couldn't sleep. Not just yet. Not until she had emotionally come to terms with recent events.

The first great shock had been learning that Tatiana would be working on the damnable assignment of finding out who was selling the ZT-550 chemical weapon, and who intended to buy it. And it was one hell of a blow to her ego to be told that, at twenty-eight, she was considered too old for a man like Colonel Galiano. An eighteen-year-old plucked out of the Army was what was needed. The thought of being considered "too old" galled the hell out of Svetlana.

Pushing thoughts of Tatiana away, Svetlana considered her present position, and wondered whether the anonymous army of men and women who worked behind the scenes for Omega Force had really done their jobs. Svetlana didn't have all the details, of course. Nobody at Omega Force had all the facts except for the one man who ran the whole show — Jefferson Burke. Field agents, intelligence analysts, and all other personnel only knew what it was necessary for them to know. Svetlana had no idea how many men and women were members of Omega Force. She'd never met anyone other than Burke, with the exception of the two men and one woman who put her through what for Omega Force was "boot camp." She had no idea how many other "field agents" there were. She'd once tried to get some answers from Burke, and he'd brusquely told her, "Don't ask."

The plan had all been quite simple, though, once it was explained to Svetlana. There was an arms dealer in Brazil — Rio de Janeiro, to be specific — who was over-extended financially. His financial dealings had taken a decided turn toward the better once he signed an agreement to sell a stolen shipment of Exocet missiles to a small but rather savage and well-financed group of "freedom fighters" operating out of Sierra Leone. The contract, with the help of someone from Omega Force, was cancelled. That meant that the Brazilian, a man named Sigmund Dornan, wouldn't make the sale, though he was already extended financially, since he had already agreed to buy the Exocet missiles from the thieves who had stolen the weapons from the British Navy. On the international arms market, a man simply did not go back on a deal. Not if he intended to live long enough to see another sunrise he didn't.

That meant the Brazilian needed to move the missiles quickly. He'd put the word out on the international market that he'd sell the Exocet missiles—carefully neglecting to mention that if he didn't sell them for cash very soon, he was a dead man—to the first person capable of meeting "reasonable financial requirements."

Such a lure could not fail to catch the attention of Colonel Mendoza. He'd go for it. And should Svetlana happen to be in Rio de Janeiro even before he got there, then her cover would be double-sealed. He'd never suspect a thing. How could she have known where he'd go before he himself knew?

It would work.

It *had* to work.

If it didn't work, the chances of some insane America-hating terrorist getting his greasy hands on the ZT-550 became significantly greater.

That was something that Svetlana couldn't allow.

Not while there was still a breath left in her body.

She looked at Tatiana, who was moving about in the room, looking at this and that, but really not seeing anything.

The telephone buzzed, and Svetlana reacted quickly. She paused a moment after picking up the receiver, then asked, "Yes?"

"A call for you, madam," the Brazilian receptionist said, speaking English with almost no accent whatsoever. "A *Mister Jones*. Do you wish you speak with him?"

"Yes, please put him through," Svetlana replied, trying not to sound nearly as excited as she really was. Mr. Jones was Burke.

There was a series of clicks as the long-distance call was

put through, then Svetlana heard the familiar voice she had long ago learned to trust, even love, though she sometimes despised it as well.

"Hello?" The voice was deep, distinctly commanding. It was American alpha male through and through. There were parts of Svetlana's body that reacted positively to the sound of that voice.

"Hello, Mr. Jones. How have you been?"

"My feet have been bothering me," he replied, speaking in the code that he and Svetlana shared. "As you know, I'd been hoping for a couple new pairs of shoes. I've got them now."

"Really?"

"Yes. And they've both just arrived today. I think you'll like to see them."

"Perhaps I will," Svetlana replied.

"Shoes" meant Colonel Mendoza and Colonel Galiano, and that they had arrived in Rio de Janeiro. Their arrival was quicker than Svetlana had anticipated. Burke said Svetlana would *like to see them,* which meant it was approved that she should do whatever was necessary to make initial contact and carry on with the mission.

The rest of the conversation between Svetlana and Burke was little more than inconsequential small talk. The critical information had been relayed in very few sentences from Burke to Svetlana, and she had understood every coded word. They continued to talk for several more minutes only to baffle anyone who might be listening in on the conversation.

When the conversation ended, Svetlana replaced the telephone to the cradle, turned to Tatiana and said, "We're in business!"

Colonel Mendoza entered the lobby of the hotel, took twenty

steps toward the front desk, then stopped dead in his tracks just ten feet from the night manager, who was waiting anxiously and obsequiously to help him.

What had stopped Colonel Mendoza so quickly and completely was the vision of a blonde-haired woman with tanned features and an extraordinary bosom striding hurriedly toward the door that the colonel had just passed through. Colonel Mendoza blinked his eyes several times to focus his vision, just to make sure that he hadn't been imagining things. Then he shouted, which was a profoundly uncommon action for him in a public place.

"Svetlana! Svetlana!"

It was the disorienting fact of seeing her in a hotel in Rio de Janeiro that had caused Colonel Mendoza to doubt whether he was actually seeing the same woman that he'd had such extraordinary sex with back in Bogota. It was the wide-spaced, sea-blue eyes and that magnificently curved physique that set Svetlana Simonov apart from all other women in the world. Her English-Russian ancestry gave her an exotic allure that the colonel—and countless other men and women in the world—found impossible to resist.

When she turned toward him, her blue eyes registered alarm. She took several steps backward, as though the sight of the colonel frightened her.

"Wait! Please!" the colonel said, rushing forward.

The young soldiers with Colonel Mendoza instinctively moved out to encircle the stunning blonde. One of them even hurried toward the hotel doorway to cut off her possible escape.

The men moved in coordination without having to be told, like a pack of hungry wolves all knowing what their individual duties were to see that a deer was brought down and devoured. Svetlana was the woman that the colonel had set his sights on, and he used his men to make sure that she could not escape. They knew what to do without having to be told.

"What are you doing here?" the colonel asked as he rushed forward. "I thought you'd be back in Sydney by now."

"I . . . I thought of going home, but then I just didn't feel like it," Svetlana replied. She stammered slightly, giving the impression of being as surprised to see the colonel as he was to see her. Her Russian accept, he noted, was slightly thicker than normal. He attributed this to nervousness. "What are you doing in Brazil? I thought you were in Bogota."

"That was before," Colonel Mendoza said. He reached for Svetlana's hand, but she pulled away. "I'm here now," he continued, his tone lowering seductively. "And so are you. That's all that matters. We'll figure out the particulars later."

Colonel Mendoza saw Svetlana Simonov melt inside. She had thought she would never see him again, he could tell. He guessed that even though she didn't want to admit it, her time with him in Bogota had been the most erotic experience of her life. She had lived her bondage fantasy with him, he believed, and that was an experience she couldn't forget. No matter what else happened, she had trusted him to tie her up properly before ravishing her in the manner which she desired. And the colonel believed that he had lived up to any and all erotic expectations, even though it was a considerable turn-off to learn, in the midst of getting laid, that a superior officer had been murdered in the next room. The timing of that murder couldn't have been worse.

"How often in life can history repeat itself?" Colonel Mendoza asked, continuing to hold onto Svetlana's hand, though she was trying to pull away. The hotel's security had begun to notice what could become a confrontation between himself and Svetlana. "Please, can't we just talk?"

Colonel Mendoza watched as Svetlana's willpower dissolved. He was absolutely confident that it wouldn't be long before he had Svetlana Simonov, the beautiful traveler with the body to die for, on her knees once again, looking into his eyes as she gave him pleasure. Memories of what it had felt like to feel his cock sliding between her soft lips and into her warm, wet mouth slithered through his consciousness, affecting him like a narcotic.

"With you it's never just talk," Svetlana replied quietly. She tried once more to pull away, but the colonel had no intention of letting her get free. "I'm not going to your room," Svetlana whispered as the colonel pulled her to the elevators.

"I don't even *have* a room yet."

"I'm not letting you into my room."

The elevator doors opened. The colonel waited until the passengers got out, then he stepped into the elevator, pulling Svetlana in behind him. The three young soldiers, wearing identical nondescript suits, stepped into the elevator. When a middle-aged man tried to enter, one of the soldiers smiled but put his hand up to push the intruder back.

A moment later the elevator doors closed. The instant the elevator doors closed, all three young guards for Colonel Alonzo Mendoza turned their backs to him.

"Where are we going? Where are you taking me?"

The soldiers moved so that they were standing directly in front of the elevator doors, their broad backs toward Svetlana. She was standing with her back to the rear of the elevator. Only Mendoza faced her, and the smile on his lips said he couldn't wait to kiss her again.

"Where are we going?" Svetlana whispered.

A metal railing ran around the elevator at waist-level. She put her hands on it, gripping tightly to the steel.

For Mendoza, the image of her seductive vulnerability was electrifying. Nothing made his cock harder than a vulnerable, defenseless woman who could do nothing to stop him from doing to her whatever he wanted to. Power was everything to him. It put the steel in his cock.

"We're going all the way," the colonel said as he closed the distance that separated himself from Svetlana. He could feel the blood racing through his veins. No woman in the world affected him quite like she did. The fact mystified him but didn't worry him. He understood that sometimes these things happened. They simply occurred, and there was really no explanation for them.

Mendoza kissed her hard on the mouth, pressing his lips tightly against Svetlana's and forcing her backward against the wall of the elevator. His left hand came up so that his fingers slipped behind her neck, beneath the thick fall of her silken blonde hair. His right hand cupped her breast, his strong fingers burying deeply into the lush mound. He clenched his hand into a fist, hard enough to make her moan in pain though her mouth never left his.

When she felt Mendoza's tongue touch her lips, Svetlana opened her mouth. As she began French kissing him, she heard one of the young men tell someone outside the elevator, "Sorry, we're full up." Then the elevator began ascending. Svetlana sucked Mendoza's tongue deeper into her mouth, letting him explore however he wanted to. His fingers found her nipple through her lacy bra and blouse. Tingles began passing from her nipple to ooze throughout her body.

Colonel Mendoza finally ended the kiss, and when he did, Svetlana pretended to nearly swoon with lust. She knew what it was Mendoza wanted from her.

"You're a barbarian," Svetlana whispered.

She raised her hands and placed them upon the colonel's chest. She made no effort to push his hand from her body. She felt the elevator come to a stop at a floor. The doors opened, but once again one of the colonel's young soldiers politely explained to whoever was trying to get in, "Sorry, we're full up" in only slightly accented English.

"But your men," Svetlana said, whispering now. She knew what it was he wanted to hear. "Not in front of your men. I can't. Not like this."

"They're very well-trained and disciplined soldiers. I'm the one who trained them," Colonel Mendoza said with a bit of boastful swagger in his tone. He stepped to the side so that Svetlana could see the men. They were turned away from Svetlana, facing the elevator door, which they'd completely blocked with their bodies. "They know what their job is," the colonel continued. He unfastened the buttons of Svetlana's bodice quickly and effortlessly. He then unzipped his trousers and brought out his awakening cock. "And you know what your job is." He smiled, touching a fingertip to Svetlana's chin. "You do a great job. Possibly the best."

"No," Svetlana said quietly, looking at the pale cock sticking out through the fly of the colonel's trousers. "Not like this. It's so . . . public."

The colonel pulled her close again, slanting his mouth down over hers. As he kissed her, his deft fingers unfastened the bra's hook-and-eye closure between the embroidered cups. Svetlana's heavy breasts were quickly bared. As the colonel's tongue danced with hers, she felt his fingers capture her nipples. Heady tingles zipped through her body, and as Mendoza's tongue probed deeper into her mouth, Svetlana could feel the lips of her cunt becoming dewy. Her response didn't surprise her, though she knew he could never bring her to climax. Men like him never did, and never could. He was capable of stimulation, but never satisfaction.

What was particularly appealing to Svetlana, though she really didn't want to admit it to herself, was that three handsome young men were standing so close, and the elevator was going up and down from floor to floor. Each time the doors opened, the young men explained that the elevator was "all full up." But did the people see what was happening behind the hulking bodyguards? Were the soldiers occasionally looking behind themselves at her lewd public behavior? There was a naughtiness to it that fired up Svetlana's passion and made her juices flow.

It wasn't the men she was with that aroused her, it was the situation, and Svetlana understood this . . . with gratitude and enormous relief. She had long ago accepted the fact that within her lurked an exhibitionist, and it was something that she had come to emotional terms with. The thought of being turned on by an odious, murderous man would have appalled her to the marrow of her being. But taking pleasure in exhibitionism . . . that was another thing entirely, now wasn't it?

The awareness of it made her suck the colonel's tongue just a little deeper into her mouth, and when she moaned, it was a little louder than it otherwise would have been.

The colonel placed his hands upon Svetlana's shoulders. He ended the kiss and for several seconds simply looked into her eyes. Then he began pushing downward, exerting enough pressure on her shoulders that Svetlana had to struggle to remain standing.

"On your knees," he said quietly, commandingly, though. his Spanish-accented English was becoming more difficult to understand. But his actions, and more importantly his intentions, were unmistakable to Svetlana. "You know what your job is."

He didn't say it, but the word "bitch" seemed to hang in the air. She could hear the word, even though it hadn't been spoken.

Svetlana resisted. The colonel pushed downward with greater strength. A fire in his eyes was ignited. The fire was lustful, but mixed in with the lust was marginally suppressed sadistic violence that would be given free rein unless Svetlana got down on her knees. He was a man who would not be denied. He had no qualms about using violence to get what he wanted.

Svetlana slowly began to descend, her ice blue gaze never leaving the colonel's face.

"Why am I so helpless against you?" Svetlana asked as she settled on her knees in the elevator. She knew the words that a man like Mendoza wanted to hear. It was one of the skills that made her so deadly as an agent.

Colonel Mendoza leaned closer to Svetlana. He rubbed the head of his cock against her lips, cheeks, and chin while she looked unblinkingly up at him. She knew it was exciting to him to be rubbing his cockhead against her face as he stared into her eyes. In almost no time at all he had grown until his cock was fully engorged and fiercely solid. Svetlana was impressed with the cock, but not with the man who possessed it.

"Kiss me," Mendoza whispered. Much of his swagger was missing now. Desperate need was gnawing at him, eating away at his self-poise. "Damn it, you know what I need!"

Yes, she knew, and she understood the power she had over Mendoza . . . and it gave her supreme confidence. She *owned* him, and she was certain that he didn't have a clue regarding how much power she had over him.

He was too arrogant to realize that she owned him.

It was the warmth of the colonel's cock pressing against her face that shocked Svetlana. It was as though she could feel the heat of his blood going straight from him into her own blood stream. Svetlana had, all along, planned and hoped that she would run into Mendoza in the hotel. But never had she thought she would be having a sexual tryst with him this quickly after seeing him again. She certainly hadn't planned on having a public sexual encounter with the colonel in an elevator with an audience present.

When he pushed his cock against her lips, Svetlana smelled

the masculine aroma of his flesh. Then, slowly, she let the crown of his cock force her lightly painted lips apart. A moment later, the colonel was filling her mouth with his lusty flesh, and her lips had formed a tight, erotic circle around the shaft.

Colonel Mendoza hissed a string of obscenities in Spanish. He put his hands on his hips and watched as Svetlana's lips, red against his pale cock, slipped back and forth over his knob and a short way down his shaft while she bobbed slowly. Her tongue, working against the underside of the head of his cock, continually moved, caressing, tasting, adding fuel to the lusty fire in his senses. Looking lower, the colonel watched Svetlana's amazing breasts jiggling tautly as she delivered the blow job with skill and apparent enthusiasm. The large, round, luscious tits were magnificent to look at, and even more impressive to hold and caress. Memories of tying Svetlana's arms and legs to the bedposts with silk neckties in his hotel bedroom in Bogota came to mind, and when they did, Colonel Mendoza felt a fresh wave of heat enter his veins.

Had there been a more erotic moment in his life than watching her squirming beneath him with her arms and legs tied outstretched as he held her breasts tightly together, then worked his throbbing cock through the cleavage? The colonel had thought at the time that it would be interesting to release his cum on her tits, or perhaps all over her beautiful face. He'd decided against it because Svetlana had a blindfold on. If he ever did erupt on her face, he wanted to do it while looking into her beautiful blue eyes.

"Deeper," the colonel demanded.

Svetlana's lips traveled slowly down the shaft of his cock. She placed her hands lightly on his hips, using only her lips and tongue to give pleasure. The elevator came to a stop at a floor and the doors opened, and just as before, the colonel's men politely but firmly explained to the people wanting to use the elevator that it was "all full up."

Had anyone noticed the woman on her knees in the back of the elevator? It was a tantalizing question for the colonel.

Reaching down, Colonel Mendoza grabbed Svetlana by the biceps. He hauled her to her feet. His cock slipped out of her mouth with a moist, popping sound. Still holding her by her arms, he pushed her firmly against the back wall of the elevator, and then kissed her hard on the mouth briefly before bending his knees to feast on her breasts.

"Ouch!" Svetlana gasped when the colonel bit her nipple.

It seemed he always went too far with her. She suspected he really didn't give a damn.

Svetlana was ready to receive Colonel Mendoza's cock, he knew. She was wet, the lips of her pussy faintly swollen with passion. It seemed her entire body was tingling with anticipation. As the colonel sucked on her nipples, turning his attention from one to the other and then back again, Svetlana shivered with obvious building excitement.

As the colonel remained bent over to feast on her heavy breasts, the elevator doors opened, and once again the new passengers were not allowed entrance. But this time there was a man waiting to use the elevator who was tall enough to see over the shoulders of the young soldiers.

"What the hell's going on in there?" the man asked. "What the fuck? Are you kidding me?"

The elevator doors closed in the man's face. Colonel Mendoza continued to feast on Svetlana's breasts, sucking on one nipple, then the other.

Colonel Mendoza released the grip he had on Svetlana's arms. He reached down, grabbed her dress, and raised it high above her waist as he continued to nibble upon her breast. He reached between her legs. He touched Svetlana's pussy through her tight-fitting bikini panties. Pulling the crotch of the panties to one side, he touched the lips of her pussy with fingers that had been made clumsy with desire. The colonel stood up straight, his body close to Svetlana's, holding her dress up. He looked into her eyes and said something in Spanish, but his lust was racing so furiously that his diction was dismal.

He made himself clear a moment later when he pulled her panties even farther to the side as he slipped his hips between her thighs. He guided his hard cock to her wet lips, then thrust forward and upward. He forced the delicate lips of her pussy to separate as he drove upward into Svetlana.

She felt the colonel's cock spearing into her. She hadn't anticipated taking such pleasure with such a brutish man, but she understood that much of the pleasure was because of the situation. Exhibitionism played a strong role in the excitement she was experiencing. She trembled at the thought of the pleasure she would be enjoying had it been Burke who was now fucking her inside an elevator, with other men there quite capable of watching her obscene behavior, and a whole host of citizens outside the elevator doors waiting to watch.

Looking over the colonel's shoulder, she gazed at the three handsome, well-built young soldiers and wondered whether she would ever be in a situation where she had to have sex with them. The idea was not an altogether disagreeable one to Svetlana, especially not when she had the colonel's cock pumping into her, and she was capable of drawing pleasure from sources other than the colonel. Still, she knew the type of men they were, and that dampened her ardor significantly when she gave it some thought.

She immediately tried to block all such thoughts from her consciousness. Nothing good could come from them. She was on a mission, and the mission was all that mattered.

For her, there was Burke. And then there was something *less than* Burke. Some men were close to Burke, and some where significantly less than Burke. But only Burke was Burke, and that was just the way it was. It was a truth that Svetlana had learned she just had to live with.

But at least she alone had Burke. And that was something no other woman could say.

She stroked the back of Mendoza's head as he tossed his hips between her thighs. He slammed her against the wall of the elevator each time his pelvis collided with hers. It was as though he wasn't merely trying to push *into* Svetlana, he was trying to spear his fiery cock completely *through* her.

Svetlana whispered into his ear, "Take me, colonel! Fuck me!" She knew what he wanted to hear. And then she uttered an expletive of the coarsest nature. "I love it when you fuck me hard."

She hardly ever spoke so crudely, but she understood the role she was playing. He rammed into her even more vigorously after that, driving her backward so furiously that the elevator creaked and shook. Svetlana's breasts were crushed against the colonel's heaving chest. He pummeled her with every bit of strength he possessed, pounding her body without any concern that he might be hurting her. His own pleasure was clearly paramount. His lusty selfishness didn't surprise Svetlana. She had no illusions regarding her enemy.

Svetlana heard the elevator doors open. She looked over the shoulders of the soldiers. There were half a dozen men standing in the hall just outside the elevator. Though they could not see much of Svetlana, the instant the men looked at her face over the colonel's shoulder, they realized immediately what was being done to her. A roar of approval came from the men, and when they tried to enter the elevator, they had to be literally pushed back by Colonel Mendoza's soldiers.

"I'm going to—" she whispered, conscious of the soldier's unspoken wishes. "Oh, make me come!"

Svetlana tightened around the colonel's thrusting cock as she shivered. She trembled, her legs spread wide. She did not climax. She only pretended to. Only Burke could bring her to the top and then beyond. Only Burke could make her come. But she was certain the colonel didn't have a clue. She was certain he never realized, or even considered the possibility, that she was only pretending.

Svetlana was teetering on the throes of a climax that she knew would never happen, her responsive body flexing and squeezing the solid flesh that filled it, when the colonel growled and erupted. She heard his moan of desire as he released his sperm inside her.

She held tightly onto him as he pumped into her. When he was completely drained, the colonel kissed Svetlana on the mouth and took a step backward. Svetlana's dress fell down her legs, but she had to reach it to properly adjust the crotch of her bikini panties. Then she hooked her bra cups together again and began buttoning her dress.

She had been on the brink of climax but had not reached it. She was pleased that he hadn't made her climax, but it was not something that occurred to her without conflicting emotions. She thought about Burke. He was the only man who could make her come . . . and she liked it that way.

"Why do I always give in to you?" she asked, her body still tingling with the afterglow of erotic sensations caused by a South American mass murderer.

Svetlana watched as the colonel tucked his dwindling cock back into his trousers and zipped up. She knew her cheeks were pink with passion and embarrassment. She wondered just how far she was willing to go for Omega Force, and just how far her fetish for exhibitionism would take her.

The colonel merely smiled at Svetlana, then turned his back on her. To his men he said in his native language, "Back to the lobby."

He was as calm and casual as if Svetlana wasn't even there.

CHAPTER SEVEN

Rio de Janeiro, Brazil

Tatiana looked over the wardrobe she had arrived with in South America. All of the clothes were new, though many had been made to look as though she'd had worn them several times. The styles weren't necessarily typical of her. Sometimes, not in the least.

Tatiana enjoyed dressing in the latest fashions and liked wearing clothes that made her appear sleek and professional, stylish and a bit upscale, even though until she had joined Omega Force, finances had always been an issue. The clothes that had been provided for her from Omega Force reflected her youthful age, but nothing made her look older than she was, nor younger.

"How much time do we have?" Tatiana asked Svetlana, who was standing in the hotel bathroom putting on fresh eyelashes. Her makeup was a lot more dramatic and sensual than Tatiana's much more subdued style.

Svetlana glanced at her gold wristwatch. It had diamonds to indicate the hours. "The colonel was expecting me five minutes ago. We'll let him wait another ten minutes, then leave the room."

"Fashionably late?"

"I want him dangling a bit. If we're going to find out where the ZT-550 is, and who intends to buy it, we'll have to keep everyone just a little edgy, a little off balance."

"Understood," Tatiana replied.

She paused a moment and looked back through the bathroom doorway at her superior officer. Svetlana was leaning over the sink, her face just inches from the large mirror as she applied her makeup. Svetlana wore matching black bra and panties, along with a black lacy garter belt and black silk stockings. She was the personification of sexy sophistication. Tatiana wished that she could look that way, but her desires weren't important — all that mattered was the mission she was on. Still, she understood that she wasn't nearly as sophisticated as Svetlana . . . and she knew it showed.

Taking a pair of simple white cotton panties, Tatiana shimmied into them, then slipped her arms into the straps of a white B-cup bra. The bra was unadorned in the extreme, without even the slightest bit of frill or embroidery to make the undergarment a pleasure for masculine eyes. The bra held the teenager's breasts securely, though not in the least bit romantically. Tatiana made a face of disdain as she adjusted her firm young breasts properly in the cups.

Tatiana brushed her hair straight back, then secured the ponytail with an elasticized ribbon. She wore no makeup whatsoever. No eyeliner. No mascara. No lipstick at all. She stepped into a cream-colored knee-length skirt, then pulled a black sweater over her head.

When Tatiana looked at herself in the mirror, she smiled. Though she knew what pleasures could be had by having a man in her mouth or between her legs, she certainly didn't give that appearance now.

"I'm ready," she called out.

"That was fast," Svetlana replied as she stepped into her own black dress that showed off much more of her legs than Tatiana's skirt.

"It's quick without makeup," Tatiana explained. Her expression transformed from pleasure and amusement to serious and thoughtful. "We're not sure that Colonel Galiano will be there?"

"No. The call I got said that he'd arrived in Rio de Janeiro, and Burke thought he was in this hotel, but they didn't have anything more than that."

"I just wish we had some guarantees."

"If you want guarantees in life, then you've gotten yourself involved in the wrong profession. When you work for Omega Force, you get almost everything you could ever want . . . but no guarantees. Never any guarantees. That's something you don't want to forget."

"I won't."

"Good. Let's go downstairs and see if we can find out what's really going on in this shitty place."

Colonel Mendoza looked at Tatiana walking beside Svetlana. The girl was in many ways an equally beautiful though diminutive version of Svetlana. And though she was certainly pretty enough in a teenage sort of way, the colonel wished she had stayed in her hotel room. Colonel Mendoza wasn't in the mood to let anything or anyone dampen his lust, and if he suspected anything, it was that Svetlana wouldn't be nearly as affectionate and passionate when her younger sister was nearby.

"You're late," Colonel Mendoza said sternly but quietly to Svetlana when the women reached him.

"Not even a word about how I look?" Svetlana asked sweetly, doing a slow pirouette to show off the evening dress she had selected for their dinner engagement. The dress was a simple black number that sported a wide leather belt which made her waist look more slender and her breasts even larger than they actually were.

Colonel Mendoza was standing with his three bodyguards just outside the hotel's restaurant. Introductions were made quickly. Tatiana didn't hold the colonel's hand any longer than necessary. All it took was one look into his eyes for her to conclude that he was a dangerous man that she would do well to avoid. The three young soldiers with the colonel looked like men who had killed in the past and would kill again.

Tatiana made a quick inspection of the layout. Colonel Mendoza had selected a large rear booth for himself. The three young soldiers had booths flanking the colonel's. To get to Colonel Mendoza, assassins had to get past the three soldiers who protected him, and Tatiana suspected that wouldn't be such an easy thing to do. And even though the young men wore European-style business suits, it didn't take more than a few seconds for her to conclude that they were battle-hardened soldiers. The fact that they were wearing civilian clothes was inconsequential. They moved like soldiers, and their gaze darted around like soldiers.

They slipped into the booth. Svetlana was in the middle with the colonel on one side of her and Tatiana on the other. Even before menus had been passed around by the unsmiling waitress, the meal was interrupted with a call to the colonel's cellular telephone.

He spoke quietly, tersely into the telephone. In less than a minute, he ended the connection.

"I'm afraid this meal will have to be postponed," he said. "There's a man who has just arrived in the hotel. He's out in the lobby now, and I must talk to him."

"I'm starving," Svetlana said quickly. "Why not invite him to have a meal with us? That way you can kill two birds with one stone."

Colonel Mendoza looked at Svetlana for a moment, then over at Tatiana, studying them both. Several seconds passed before he turned his attention away from the women and toward one of his men.

"Ask Colonel Galiano if he's hungry. If he is, invite him over," Colonel Mendoza instructed his aide.

At the sound of the name, Tatiana's heart began racing. It was the man she was supposed to lure into a honey trap was in the hotel! The young woman crossed her legs at the knee and forced her breathing to become natural, even. She couldn't appear nervous without arousing Colonel Galiano's professionally suspicious nature.

Moments later Colonel Galiano, with his own entourage of three young soldiers, walked into the hotel restaurant and headed toward the back booths. The moment Colonel Galiano's gaze met Tatiana's, the soldier known by his contemporaries as *Iceman* appeared to nearly fall over.

Tatiana knew that she had presented herself to him in the right way.

The atmosphere during dinner was tense. Though Colonel Mendoza and Colonel Galiano put forward a pleasant front — or at least tried to — the contempt the two powerful men had for each other was evident in the way they looked at each other, even if the words they exchanged were cordial. Every time the men had something important to say, they switched to Spanish, and though Tatiana was not entirely fluent in the language, she did speak it well enough to understand the controlled fury the men showed toward each other.

"You two are talking business," Tatiana complained when the meal had been finished and after-dinner cognac was passed around. Svetlana and Colonel Mendoza had cognac while Tatiana and the abstemious Colonel Galiano declined alcohol. "Let's not talk business on such a wonderful night."

"Then you like Brazil?" Colonel Galiano asked. His accent was more pronounced than Mendoza's. During the entire time he'd been sitting next to Tatiana, he'd hardly looked at her.

"I'd love to see the city, but we've been so busy that we haven't had the chance to do any sightseeing, any walking around Rio de Janeiro. It's just not fair."

Tatiana pouted, her lower lip sticking out prettily. To look at her then, her hair in a ponytail and pouting so petulantly, she knew no one would ever guess her true age. Nor her deadly profession.

"Perhaps, sometime, I might escort you," Colonel Galiano said. His tone was casual, but there was a shimmering intensity in his dark eyes that hadn't been there a moment before.

It was Svetlana's turn to jump in, and she did so smoothly. "It's just six-thirty. That isn't too late for you to take a walk, if you like." She glanced flirtatiously over at Colonel Mendoza, doing it in such a manner that it appeared as though she was interested in having some quiet, romantic time alone with him.

Tatiana turned toward Colonel Galiano, her mood bubbly, her body practically bouncing in the booth.

"Would you mind? Would you really take me around?" she asked, her voice rising as a girl's would at the prospect of getting a special treat.

The *Iceman* melted beneath the allure of Tatiana's youthful enthusiasm. His great willpower was no match for her exuberance. Tatiana could feel her confidence growing by the second.

"Be careful now," Svetlana dutifully said. "And behave. I want you to listen to Colonel Galiano and do what he says."

"Yes, of course," Tatiana said, rolling her eyes in teenager fashion.

The colonel got out of the booth first. Tatiana slid out after him. As she did, her pleated skirt rode very high up her legs, showing much of her slender thighs before she got to her feet. He'd seen her legs, just as Tatiana had wanted him to.

Rio de Janeiro, Brazil

Raoul Santiago got out of the taxicab and turned the collar of his jacket up. He was always leery of the possibility of someone taking pictures of him from afar. He knew he wouldn't be in Rio de Janeiro long enough to catch Interpol's interest. Not if he was successful, anyway. Success, in this instance, meant buying the greatest number of weapons for the least amount of up-front money. This was critical if he was to liberate his island country of St. Lucas from its capitalist-imperialist oppressors. There were guerilla soldiers back home who were counting on him to get the assault rifles and ammunition they needed to spread terror through the existing government of St. Lucas. Shoulder-fired rockets and missiles would be a big plus, especially since the government's helicopters had a nasty way of coming down seemingly out of nowhere in the mountainous terrain of St. Lucas and unleashing their terror.

Raoul paid the driver without tipping him. The driver scowled and sped off, leaving Raoul standing in the street with his battered, much-traveled suitcase.

Another angry worker being abused by the system, Raoul thought, conveniently ignoring his own role in the taxi driver's suddenly sour mood. *In five years, maybe ten, he'll be a guerilla soldier, fighting for the cause of justice. He'll be a brother soldier. Then he'll thank me for not giving him a tip. It's only then that he'll understand.*

Raoul picked up his suitcase and headed for the hotel that was across the street. He had already been told that the rates were reasonable and the rooms were clean. That was as much as he could hope for, considering the amount of money he was allowing himself to use on food and hotels. What money he had was necessary for *The Cause*. Every assault rifle purchased carried with it the possibility of another imperialist's death. Every shoulder-fired rocket purchased was a multi-million-dollar jumbo carrier plane destroyed on the runway.

The possibility of getting Stinger missiles, which could take a Boeing right out of the sky, was too much to hope for. But still, a revolutionary could dream . . .

As soon as Raoul negotiated a favorable deal with the Brazilian arms dealer, Sigmund Dornan, then he could fly back home and once again enjoy the warm Caribbean breezes that gave him such a sense of contentment. Until then, nothing would avert his concentration.

Svetlana felt Colonel Mendoza's hand on her thigh. She tried to ignore it. She had satisfied his lust earlier that evening in the elevator, when he had ravished her so savagely against the elevator wall, so she hoped he was still sated. She wanted him feeling content. Experience had taught her that sexual contentment had a way of loosening a man's tongue.

"What were you and Colonel Galiano talking about?" Svetlana asked quietly, taking a sip of cognac. "It seemed very important."

"Nothing," the soldier replied. His hand slipped higher up Svetlana's thigh, caressing her through her silk stocking. "Nothing for you to concern yourself with."

"Maybe if you talked about it, you'd feel better."

The colonel looked closely at Svetlana, his eyes narrowing. "You're asking an awful lot of questions."

Svetlana smiled and patted the back of his hand, making no effort to push it off her leg. She spread her knees a little wider apart. It was a subtle invitation, but the move couldn't be ignored, either. As he eased his fingertip beneath Svetlana's skirt, Colonel Mendoza seemed to forget all about the probing questions she had asked.

Svetlana smiled and moistened her lips with her tongue.

Colonel Galiano turned to the young woman and said quietly, "Stay here." To the soldier, he said, "I don't want Colonel Mendoza going anywhere without you following him." The lieutenant began to protest, exactly as Galiano knew he would. "I'll be safe," Colonel Galiano explained, silencing the protests before they gained momentum. "There's no one here who wants me dead. I know your assignment is to be my bodyguard, but I need you and the others to stay with Colonel Mendoza."

"At least let one of us stay with you," the lieutenant said quietly. He was a dutiful officer, and always concerned for Colonel Galiano's safety.

"I'm going to see what the girl knows. Her sister was in Bogota when the general was murdered. Perhaps there's something more to it than I had first thought."

Colonel Galiano actually didn't have any suspicions of Svetlana, and certainly none of Tatiana. He was overjoyed that Colonel Mendoza seemed utterly enraptured with Svetlana Simonov. It was the younger woman that Colonel Galiano craved. The girl had triggered erotic fantasies in him from the first moment he set eyes upon her. His lust for young women was a guilty secret the Iceman had to keep hidden. Should the rumors begin to swirl, he'd be ruined within days — or maybe even just hours.

Colonel Galiano waited until his men took up positions outside the hotel, where they could see everyone coming or going. Then he turned toward Tatiana and smiled warmly.

"There, now we can go for that walk you've wanted," he said, his English thickly accented. "Is there anywhere in particular you want to go?"

Tatiana smiled openly, shrugging her shoulders. Her pert breasts jiggled tautly inside her bra and lightweight sweater. The colonel's gaze went down to her breasts, then crawled slowly back up to her face.

"Wherever you want is fine with me."

The colonel smiled in the same way a lion in Africa would smile upon seeing a young antelope suddenly start to limp.

Ten minutes later, at six-fifty, Tatiana was walking into Colonel Galiano's hotel room. He said he needed to get something from the room, but she didn't believe him. She knew he simply wanted to get her somewhere alone so that he could make a pass at her. In the time that they had been together, she had gently been trying to get information from the colonel on what he was doing in Rio de Janeiro. She couldn't dig too hard without triggering the soldier's suspicions.

He'd said very little about the reasons for his activities. Tatiana knew she had to be especially careful.

Tatiana sat on the colonel's bed. She crossed her legs at the knee, letting her pleated skirt ride up her thighs a little. She watched as Colonel Galiano picked up something from the dresser and put it in his pocket. When he turned toward her again, his eyes went to her exposed knees. He walked closer slowly. His eyes were practically glowing.

"You're very lovely, my dear," he said softly, seductively. "Has anyone ever told you that before?"

Tatiana nodded. Her heart quickened its pace. Colonel Galiano was standing directly in front of her, his crotch almost level to her face. She knew that wasn't an accident.

After several seconds, she finally said, "Sometimes."

"I'll bet you've got lots of boyfriends."

"Some," Tatiana answered quietly. "Nobody special." She rolled her eyes expressively. "They're just *boys*."

Colonel Galiano smiled tightly. "You don't need boys. What you need is a man. A man to show you the things that you should know." He paused a moment as though choosing his words carefully. "You need a man to teach you the things you do not yet know."

"Oh?" Tatiana raised her eyebrows innocently.

"Let me show you something." He chuckled softly and added, "Your sister did say you were to listen to me, didn't she? I believe the word she used was *obey.*"

Colonel Galiano caressed himself through his trousers for several seconds before he pulled down his zipper. He eased his growing cock out slowly. He smiled when Tatiana put a hand to her mouth in shock, though her gaze remained locked onto the stiffening and growing erection he had for her. She understood the role she was to play, as well as the importance to national security of what she was now doing.

"Give me your hand," the colonel said. "I'm going to teach you things."

Tatiana watched as his cock got harder, longer. She waited until Colonel Galiano grabbed her wrist, guiding her right hand to his erection. She wrapped her fingers around the shaft. She felt the heat of the colonel's lust going through her palm and into her blood.

"Stroke it," Colonel Galiano said in a tense whisper. Holding Tatiana by the wrist, he brought her hand back and forth over his cock. He quickly grew to full extension. "That's right. See how big you're making it?" He smiled. "I'm a very big man."

Tatiana nodded in agreement, her focus locked onto the flesh that filled her fist. *Big? Not really. So-so at best.* As she watched the colonel's cock literally pulsing with lust, she reminded herself that she was playing a role, like an actress on a stage. She would disappoint Colonel Galiano if he discovered that her supposed naïveté was an act to weaken his willpower. The urge to tell the colonel that he really *wasn't* very well endowed was nearly overpowering.

His ego was colossal, but his cock surely wasn't.

"Am I doing this right?" Tatiana asked quietly. She knew

she was, but it seemed to be the right thing to say.

"You're doing fine," the colonel said. He stepped a little closer to her. Barely fifteen inches now separated the crown of his cock from her pink mouth. Tatiana had made a point of not wearing lipstick. Her learning curve as an Omega Force agent was steep.

Tatiana uncrossed her knees but remained seated on the side of the bed. She continued stroking Colonel Galiano while he unbuckled his belt and let his trousers fall down around his knees. As she worked her hand back and forth, the colonel grabbed her fist and began rotating it around his cock.

"I see what you want," Tatiana said. She began twisting her hand round the colonel as she continued pumping back and forth.

Tatiana never looked up. She simply stared at the hard flesh as though mesmerized by its appearance. The colonel quickly removed his jacket, necktie, and shirt, and then stepped out of his trousers without ever taking his cock out of Tatiana's fist.

"Give me your left hand," Colonel Galiano said.

There was a commanding quality to his tone now that hadn't been there earlier. Tatiana felt her confidence surge.

When Tatiana raised her left hand, he took her by the wrist, then guided her hand to between his legs.

"Squeeze them gently. Later on, they're going to give you something special."

"Cum?" Tatiana asked, her tone sweetly innocent, but with an undercurrent of sauciness. She couldn't pretend to be too naïve or he'd know he was being played.

"That's right, my dear. That's absolutely right. Do you know what that is?"

"Yes." Tatiana gave the colonel's testicles a firm squeeze. They both understood now that they were definitely playing a silly game that had sexual consequences which both of them were willing to pay. A certain level of falseness had been stripped away, and Tatiana was grateful for that. She had been growingly concerned with just how long she could convincingly play being utterly naïve. "I've done this to two boys before." Her voice was very soft, like the touch of a butterfly's wing. It was a barely audible caress. "They liked it, but they wanted me to do more." Her eyelashes lowered for a moment, but she allowed herself to let the corners of her lips curl upward into a sly smile. "Much . . . more." She looked into his eyes. "With my mouth."

She was pleased with her performance.

"Do you want to kiss it?"

Tatiana shook her head. She continued staring at the cock and watched as a drop of opaque fluid formed at the tip. She smoothed the pre-cum over the head with the pad of her thumb. He let out a low groan, clearly pleased.

Colonel Galiano bent over at the waist as he reached down for her breasts. He touched her through her sweater and bra, catching her erect nipple and giving it a pinch and twist. Then he put his fingertips beneath Tatiana's chin and forced her to look up into his face.

"Beautiful girl," he whispered, looking into her eyes. "I've never seen such beautiful eyes. Such a beautiful, innocent girl."

Tatiana let the colonel push her onto her back on the bed. He followed her quickly, half laying atop her, his cock still in her hand. When he brought his lips to her mouth, she let him French kiss her immediately, his tongue sliding between her lips. She felt his hands on her breasts through her sweater. Moments later she felt his palm against her stomach. It wasn't long before he had her sweater over her head and her bra off to expose the small mounds of her breasts.

Colonel Galiano reached between Tatiana's, slightly parted thighs, then eased his hand into her panties. She did not have much pubic hair. The curls were soft as silk, yet apparently displeasing to the touch, because the colonel groaned with frustration.

Tatiana felt a finger slide over her clitoris, then slip between the lips of her pussy. She trembled softly. She forced herself to remember that no matter what she did, it was for the United States. This man with the skilled fingers was a fanatical murderer who gave speeches exhorting his men to kill Americans wherever they were found. She loathed him, though she couldn't let him know her true feelings. He was a war criminal whose idea of mercy was to kill prisoners of war quickly rather than slowly. Tatiana reminded herself that her controlling officer, none other than Burke, had commanded her to gain the colonel's confidence and interest however possible, then use whatever means necessary to find the ZT-550 and destroy it before it could be used against the United States . . . or anyone else, for that matter.

As the invading caresses became more intense, Tatiana moaned softly and spread her legs wider apart, surrendering herself completely. She squeezed her eyes tightly shut and tried to pretend that Colonel Galiano was a young lover that she was giving herself to for the first time, not a sadistic killer who deserved nothing more than a bullet in the back of the head.

Colonel Galiano crawled onto Tatiana, his pants still around his ankles. He shivered with excitement like a boy. He pushed her skirt up to her stomach, pulled her panties aside, then reached between their bodies to guide the crown of his cock to the slick lips of her pussy. Tatiana gasped when she felt him enter her. The colonel thrust down hard, driving nearly the entire length of his cock into her. He instantly pulled up, then stabbed downward a second time, not bothering to give Tatiana time to adjust to his invasion.

She hated him in her heart and was pleased with herself

that she could think of such things while he was thrusting into her. She was unimpressed with his dimensions.

"Tight," Colonel Galiano whispered through clenched teeth. Then, coarsely because it apparently pleased him to be demeaning, he added, "You're a tight little cunt."

Tatiana suspected that this was how he liked it best. With a young woman beneath him, her slender body being crushed to the mattress as he pounded into her with everything he had. She knew of guys who only liked having sex with a woman for the first time. After that, the women were disposable playthings that they were no longer interested in.

Shoving a hand between their bodies, the colonel grabbed Tatiana's breast and squeezed it cruelly, his fingers burying painfully deep into the firm, tender flesh. A squeal of protest was ripped from Tatiana's throat.

"Not so hard," Tatiana finally managed to say. She was practically bouncing on the hotel bed beneath Colonel Galiano. "You're hurting me."

Colonel Galiano said nothing. He silenced her protests by kissing her hard on the mouth and shoving his tongue between her lips. Tatiana sensed instinctively that he was trying to punish her, though she didn't understand what crimes she had committed. But as he thrust into her pussy time and time again, she could feel his hatred, feel his fury. It was a frightening thing to be aware of.

Tatiana twisted her face away to end the kiss. Whatever pleasure she might have taken in the colonel's caresses had ended. She thought of fighting him, pounding his face with her fists until he stopped abusing her, but she quickly abandoned this notion. She was an agent for Omega Force, after all, and she was doing exactly what Burke expected of her. Hadn't she been selected for the mission precisely because she was *cute?*

Colonel Galiano thrust his cock into Tatiana and groaned

loudly as his passion exploded from his overheated balls. He had hardly finished coming before he rolled off Tatiana and pulled his trousers back up.

CHAPTER EIGHT

Rio de Janeiro, Brazil

General Jorge Ragga leaned forward just enough to guide the tip of the Havana cigar to the burning match that Colonel Mendoza held out. Once the cigar was glowing nicely, General Ragga leaned back in his chair and inspected the cigar, then the colonel.

"You're more ambitious than I had thought," the general said slowly. There was a touch of contempt in his tone, but it was laced with respect, too. "Perhaps too ambitious for a young country such as ours."

Colonel Mendoza shook his head slowly, his mouth turning downward. "Ours is not a young country, General Ragga. My family had lived in Treloone for six generations. We've fought for our land honorably for many years." His tone softened slightly. "But they are all gone. You see before you all that is left of my family. I am the last of my line." He took a sip of whiskey and made a mental note to always have plenty of Tennessee whiskey on hand wherever he was living once the sale of the ZT-550 finally went through. "But let's not talk of families we no longer have. War has ravaged everyone. Let's talk of what is the best move to make next with the ZT-550."

Once again, the general smiled faintly and nodded. The colonel was utterly ruthless, driven by family pride, political pride, and a greediness that flowed in his veins like his blood.

"You said that Sigmund has negotiated these things in the

past?"

"Many times, from what I've learned. I've used him before to get what we needed."

"But this isn't just a sniper's rifle, and it isn't a pistol with a silencer, Colonel. This is enough nerve gas to kill a quarter of a million people if administered properly."

"He's aware of that."

"And he has the connections to find a buyer who can afford our price?"

Colonel Mendoza blew a stream of gray smoke toward the ceiling. "He knows everyone. Or, rather, all the international big-time players know him."

General Jorge Ragga looked at the glowing ember of his cigar, delicately twirling the tip against the smooth glass ashtray to knock off the ash. It still didn't sit quite right with him that the ZT-550 was going to be sold for personal profit. The weapon, which had been either a gift or stolen from the FSB by General Palmero years earlier — not many people had been told the story by the colonel, and over the years nobody had heard exactly the same story — could be used to threaten NATO nations should they decide to stick their nose into a civil war once again. And there were always the rebels in the mountains that simply refused to put their weapons down and give up. An application of ZT-550 to a rebel base camp would put psychological terror in every young man who thought of becoming a rebel. The story of the silent slaughter would be told for years to come. Rebel recruits wouldn't be quite so eager to take up arms after that.

The general felt a tightening in his gut, the way he always did whenever he was just about to make an important decision that, once made, could not be backed down from.

"All right, Colonel. Do what you must. The proceeds will be split evenly. I have a numbered account at a Jamaican bank. The Nationale."

Colonel Mendoza smiled. "I have an account there, too."

For the first time in weeks, Jorge smiled openly, without guile, and replied, "How convenient for us!" Jorge took another sip of his liquor and said, "Now tell me about this blonde I've seen you with. The one with the big chi-chis."

"From Australia, I gather, though originally I think she's from the United States by way of Russia. Beautiful, isn't she?"

"Extremely."

"And passionate. She can't get enough of me."

"You're a lucky man. Is there another one like her somewhere?"

Colonel Mendoza shook his head. When the general looked disappointed at the news, the colonel added slowly, "Yes, that is too bad . . . but she has a younger sister."

General Jorge Ragga looked away, and his gaze became distant and unfocused. "Isn't that an interesting development? Well, Colonel, I'd say our fortunes are definitely beginning to look up. A sister, you say?"

"Younger sister." He cleared his throat. "Significantly younger."

"You're sure you can handle him?" Svetlana asked, looking at Tatiana. They were sitting in the hotel room, preparing for the evening ahead.

"Colonel Galiano isn't as tough and hard-nosed as he pretends. Remember, he's a man with a weakness that's he's got to keep secret," Tatiana replied. "You go off and figure out what Colonel Mendoza's got cooking."

"You're sure?"

"Positive."

Svetlana checked her makeup in the mirror and forced fearful thoughts from her consciousness. About ten or twenty times a day she wished she had put her foot down and demanded of Burke that she be allowed to work alone, like she always had in the past. But every time she came to this conclusion, she also realized that if their positions were reversed—and Svetlana *had* been close to the same age as Tatiana was when she began her involvement with various shadowy branches of the American military—she would behave precisely as Tatiana was now.

"Just be careful." Svetlana looked at her wristwatch. "I'll see you as soon as I can."

Svetlana kissed her on the cheek and hurried out her hotel room. For superstitious reasons, she did not take a backward glance.

Rio De Janeiro, Brazil

Anni de Chevreaux looked at her reflection in the mirror and was reasonably pleased with what she saw. Looking back at her from the mirror was a twenty-three-year-old French woman with blonde hair, brown eyes, a mouth that made men beg for a kiss, and small breasts that were high and firm now, and would probably always remain that way. This was important to Anni, because her breasts were important to the man who paid her way through life—Sigmund Dornan, a Brazilian arms dealer whose legitimate business of selling military arms paled compared to the profit margin he made on his illegal sales.

"Hurry up in there," Sigmund said, knocking on the bathroom door. "I don't want you in there when they arrive."

"I'm almost finished, honey!" Anni called back brightly.

Her lover was in his sixties, though he was far from being old. He had kicked, clawed, and backstabbed his way into a fortune, and it was his opinion that as long as he was paying all the bills, his mistress should never talk back to him, and must always be bright and cheerful. And she needed to be passionate whenever and however he wanted her to be passionate.

For Anni de Chevreaux, who had an insatiable thirst for all the finer things in life, being an on-call, full-time, live-in mistress was a particularly easy burden to bear in order to live in a palatial mansion, being waited on hand and foot by two butlers and her own personal chambermaid. She also had spending cash she didn't have to answer for, a budget that was lavish, and virtually no responsibilities whatsoever other than to look beautiful, young, and sexy whenever she went out with Sigmund.

Bending down, Anni held her hair away from her face, and then inhaled the line of cocaine on the small mirror. Immediately, she felt the effects of the drug as it rushed into her blood stream.

I hope tonight isn't going to be too boring, Anni thought as she wiped the mirror with a towel. It was always best to get rid of any evidence. Sigmund didn't approve of her cocaine use. As the drug exploded in her brain, Anni thought, *Tonight's going to go just fine! I'm positive of it!*

For the evening, Svetlana had chosen a wrap silk dress of ruby red that highlighted her ripe curves, and since it cinched in tight at the waist, it did nothing to hide the fullness of her breasts. Quite the opposite, in fact. Beneath the dress, per Colonel Mendoza's instructions, she wore a red lacy bra she had purchased in Caracas that matched the garter belt encircling her waist. Her stockings came up to the tops of her thighs and were black and made of pure silk. To highlight the stark red-and-black ensemble, she wore brilliant ruby earrings and a gold necklace holding a large black onyx jewel, which rested gentle between her breasts. She was not wearing panties.

During the time that she had been with him, she had

learned that his requests were just politely worded commands.

The colonel arrived at the hotel's front doors in a rented long black Volvo sedan. He was in the back seat. One of his unsmiling young soldiers was behind the wheel, with a second young and unsmiling soldier, wearing civilian clothes, also sitting in the front seat. Colonel Mendoza was alone in the back seat.

"I'm on time!" Svetlana said, pretending to be a bit breathless as she hurried to the car. Her breasts bounced with her stride, as she knew they would. She saw the appreciation in the colonel's eyes when he looked at her. "See? I can be on time when I really try!"

The soldier in the front seat hurried out of the car to open the rear door for Svetlana. The colonel moved across the seat, making room for her as she got in. He appeared pleased that she appeared a bit breathless. She made it quite clear that she was concerned with being on time, that she did not want to disappoint the colonel. She suspected Colonel Mendoza was the kind of leader who liked to keep those men and women around him a little unsure of themselves and of their position with him.

Svetlana slid across the seat so that her hip touched the colonel's. She placed her left hand on his thigh as his right arm slipped around her shoulders. She expected the colonel to kiss her, but he did not. She wasn't disappointed that he didn't, though it did surprise her a little. His kisses weren't exactly something that she looked forward to with great anticipation.

The black sedan pulled swiftly away from the hotel, blending seamlessly into the thick nighttime Rio de Janeiro traffic. Svetlana watched the lights of the city going by outside as she waited for the colonel to speak. When he didn't, she asked, "Where are we going?"

"Tonight, I have to meet a man to discuss something that's

very important. There may be times when I'll need privacy. When that happens, you'll have to go elsewhere in the house. You'll have to amuse yourself."

"But I want to stay with you." Svetlana's left breast pressed against his side. The flirtatiousness of the move could not be ignored. "I don't want to be alone."

"What I have to do is important, and it requires privacy."

Svetlana felt a charge of excitement go through her like a bolt of lightning. Was tonight the night the weapon would be sold? Would the ZT-550 actually change hands tonight? The idea that the mission might be coming to an end was both exhilarating and frightening. She was without weapons, and didn't even know where she was headed, yet she might have to somehow gain control of a deadly weapon of mass destruction. Svetlana Simonov felt horrifically unprepared for this moment. Her mouth was suddenly really quite dry.

"Where did you say we were going?" Svetlana asked, looking out the side window of the Volvo, hoping the question sounded innocent.

"I didn't say. If I wanted you to know, I would have told you."

Svetlana thought then as she turned toward the colonel that she might well have done Omega Force, the United States, and the entire free world a service had she, when she had been in Bogota, not only put .380 caliber bullets through General Palmero's evil heart, but did the same to Colonel Mendoza. The world would probably be a safer place had she assassinated two war criminals on that fateful night instead of just one.

Hindsight is twenty-twenty. If I start looking backward, I'll never see what's coming.

"I'm sorry," Svetlana said softly. She tamped down her personal feelings for now, while hoping that the time would come when she would look at the colonel's face in the sights of a silenced handgun. "I just . . . if I'm going to have to spend time alone . . . I mean . . . I just want to be with you, that's all. Is that so bad?"

Colonel Mendoza pulled Svetlana a bit tighter against himself. "Business shouldn't take too long." For the benefit of the soldiers in the front seat, he added hypocritically, "Obligations and duty to my country must always come before everything else, my dear. You must understand that. I am a patriot. I always — *always* — think of my country and my men first and foremost."

"I understand."

Svetlana looked out the window again. The traffic was thinner now. The black sedan was headed westward, moving away from downtown proper. They were going out of the city, but where exactly, Svetlana still did not know. She began memorizing the lights of the city, neon lights from businesses, anything that might help guide her later, should she have to return on her own to wherever they were now headed.

Colonel Mendoza asked quietly, "You look lovely, but did you follow my instructions?"

Svetlana nodded, but continued looking out the window. There was an enormous neon sign for Jamaican-brewed Red Stripe beer. A smile touched her lips. It shouldn't be difficult to find that sign again later, she decided. Her confidence edged up just a little.

The colonel's right arm was around Svetlana's shoulders. He used his fingertips to push against her chin, forcing her to look away from the window and toward him. When he looked into her eyes, she looked back at him coolly, confidently, though she didn't let the confidence show in her expression. After several seconds, the colonel's gaze travelled downward. His eyes widened as he stared leisurely at Svetlana's breasts.

In a stern voice, he said, "I asked you a question. I need an answer."

"Yes, I followed your orders." Her gaze darted to the two men in the front seat. They were both facing forward, not appearing to pay any attention to the people in the back seat of the sedan. She doubted that appearances told the truth.

"I'm not sure I believe you."

"I followed your instructions to the letter," Svetlana replied. In a significantly softer voice, she said, "You know I always do whatever you tell me to."

Colonel Mendoza twisted so that he was facing Svetlana in the back seat. The fire of lust was in his dark eyes. He pushed the fingers of his right hand into Svetlana's hair and placed his left hand on her knee.

"Just the same, I'd better check," he said.

Svetlana reached down, catching his hand by the wrist. She looked at the two soldiers in the front seat. "Please don't, Colonel," she whispered. "Your men will see us."

"They only see what I tell them to see." Colonel Mendoza pushed his hand up beneath Svetlana's dress despite her efforts to the contrary. "They're trained to watch out for me, not to spy on me."

Colonel Mendoza bent his head to kiss Svetlana's mouth. She moderately struggled to keep his hand out from between her thighs, but when his mouth came down over hers, she could feel the suppressed violence trapped inside the man. She relented, opening her lips to let him French kiss her as she released the grip she had on his wrist. A moment later his fingers rubbed firmly against her pussy. And though she was not ready for him, he tried almost immediately to separate the sensitive lips with a fingertip. Svetlana flinched as she was pierced by a digit.

"What's wrong, baby," Colonel Mendoza growled, his diction poor now that lust was blossoming within him. "You were always ready for me before."

Svetlana spread her knees wider apart, giving the colonel

complete access. She tilted her face up to the colonel's. Once again, his mouth was immediately pressing against hers, his tongue entering her mouth. She thought about the fingers touching her intimately, but just as importantly, she thought about the two young soldiers in the front seat. Were they watching? The exhibitionist in Svetlana hoped that they were. The possibility of being seen while she behaved so lewdly with an audience was enough to get her juices flowing.

The next time the colonel tested Svetlana, his fingertip slipped easily between the lips of her pussy. He groaned softly as he French kissed her, pushing his finger two knuckles deep into her. While kissing Svetlana, he rubbed her clit with the shaft of his finger. Svetlana could feel her body heating up, warming to his kisses and caresses, and for that she was grateful. It was always easier when she was at least a little bit aroused by the man fondling her.

Svetlana twirled her tongue against Colonel Mendoza's, and as he worked his finger in and out of her pussy, she placed a hand between his legs and fondled his cock through his trousers. It wasn't long before she felt him growing long and hard inside his pants.

"Give me a little," the colonel said, putting a hand to the back of Svetlana's neck. He began to apply pressure.

The colonel was much too forceful, pushing down so hard against the back of Svetlana's neck that her spine bent at a painful angle.

"Easy!" she whispered. She slid her hips away from Colonel Mendoza so that she could put her face in his lap without contorting her spine. "Don't be so rough."

"Shut up! You know what I like!" For the benefit of the soldiers in the front seat who could undoubtedly hear every word spoken in the sedan, he added, in his native Spanish instead of English, "She's turned giving head into an Olympic sporting event!"

Svetlana didn't catch all of the colonel's last sentence, and the fact was, she really wasn't too concerned. The colonel was thoroughly enraptured with her, and that was what was important for her mission. She slipped far enough away from him so that when she leaned over in the back seat of the car, her face was near his crotch. She watched as he fumbled with one hand, trying to get his zipper down and his burgeoning cock out.

"Let me help," Svetlana said after a moment. She shoved her hand inside his trousers and, none too delicately, jerked his growing cock out through the opening.

"Easy, damn it!" Colonel Mendoza said sharply in English.

His shaft had scraped against the brass teeth of the zipper when Svetlana had jerked him out. Svetlana knew it was fortunate that he couldn't see her face because when he flinched in pain, she smiled. It gave her pleasure to hurt him, even if she only hurt him a little.

When the warmth and wetness of Svetlana's mouth surrounded the crown of his cock, the colonel uttered a string of obscenities in his native language. Svetlana tightened her lips around the shaft and formed a firm suction on the cock. She would rather be sitting upright in the car so that she could pay attention to where they were going, but it didn't particularly bother her to have the colonel's cock between her lips now. She knew that every time she gave him a blow job, his suspicions of her, his wary nature of everyone and everything that could possibly be an enemy, diminished. It wouldn't be long before he couldn't possibly imagine her as being a threat to him . . . and it would be at that exact moment that Svetlana would be his most deadly enemy!

She felt his right hand slip around her body, reaching beneath her to cup a breast through her clothes. He pinched her nipple hard through her bra and dress. She moaned softly and theatrically, her mouth filled with the colonel's cock, letting the colonel think she loved everything about him. When he pinched her nipple too hard, drawing pain, she gasped and let her teeth scrape lightly against his cock's shaft as she bobbed up on down.

"Watch the teeth, goddamn it," the colonel growled.

From the front seat, Svetlana heard a masculine voice, speaking Spanish. "Colonel, we'll be there soon."

"Thank you," Colonel Mendoza replied in English. He lifted his hand off the back of Svetlana's neck. "That's enough for now, my dear."

Svetlana sat upright in the back seat of the sedan. Her dress was up to her waist, and with an annoyed brush of her hand she smoothed the fabric down over her legs. Looking into the front seat, she saw that both soldiers were looking straight ahead. She wondered whether or not they had been watching her behaving so lewdly. Had she been truly honest with herself, she would admit that their presence helped to turn her on, igniting the lusty exhibitionist that Svetlana struggled in vain to keep hidden from the world. On his own, the colonel didn't excite her at all. But when she had an audience . . .

"You can be a beast," Svetlana whispered to Colonel Mendoza. There was mock censure in her tone, as though to indicate that she really didn't mean it. Svetlana understood that this was what he'd want to hear. She never forgot that she was playing a role, like an actress. It was one of the things that made her so effective as an Omega Force agent.

From her purse she extracted a tube of lipstick and reapplied some to her lips. As she was putting the lipstick back in her purse, the Volvo sedan pulled off the road, easing between two large concrete columns, moving onto a long cobblestone driveway. The mansion at the end of the driveway was made of marble and was fit for a king — or for a man making a fortune illegally selling billions of dollars' worth of military weaponry.

When Svetlana turned her attention away from the mansion and back to the colonel, he had tucked himself back into his trousers and had zipped up, though there was still a prominent lump in the fabric.

"You're showing off," Svetlana teased, patting the colonel's bulge.

"Leave it alone now. You make me feel younger than I have in years." Colonel Mendoza gave Svetlana a pleased grin. "It'll go down if you just leave it alone." He kissed her temple. "You'll be sucking me again later. Your lips are like magic to me. But not now. I know you love having my cock in your mouth, but you've got to wait."

Svetlana pouted prettily, as though being deprived of some special treat. Colonel Mendoza's smile widened.

Raising a single eyebrow, Svetlana said quietly, "I know just what to do to get it up again. Think about that when you're trying to concentrate on other things." She held up her right hand, then sucked on her thumb for a couple seconds, the lewd pantomime unmistakable.

The colonel merely groaned his approval.

The Volvo pulled up to the double front doors of the mansion. Both young soldiers hurried out of the sedan to open the rear doors. As Svetlana stepped out, the front door to the mansion opened and a young blonde woman, impeccably dressed in a cream-colored evening gown, stepped out. There was a warm smile on her lips. When Svetlana's gaze met with hers, the woman smiled even more brightly and stepped forward.

"Allow me to introduce myself. I'm Anni de Chevreaux," she purred in refined, only slightly French-accented English. "I'm so happy you could make it here this evening."

Svetlana took the young woman's hand. She was slightly surprised when Anni leaned forward and kissed her lightly on the cheek. When Colonel Mendoza stepped around the sedan, Anni shook his hand and kissed his cheek. The two young soldiers silently disappeared back into the Volvo.

The colonel trusts whoever lives here, Svetlana thought as she watched the two soldiers getting into the sedan's front seat, settling in for what could be a long wait. The fact that the colonel felt safe enough to leave them outside said volumes about a man who was almost always in a semi-paranoid state of mind.

The colonel put his arm around Svetlana's waist as they entered the mansion. In the entryway, Svetlana was introduced to Sigmund Dornan. He was immaculately dressed in a jade green velvet smoking jacket. His dark hair was flecked with gray, and his eyes were steel gray. Introductions were made quickly, and then Svetlana and the colonel were escorted into a spacious dining room with a table large enough to seat twenty people comfortably.

"I thought you might be hungry," their host said as he held out a chair for Svetlana. "We'll eat first, and then we can discuss other matters afterward."

"Excellent," Colonel Mendoza said. His gaze drifted over to Anni. His eyes took on a warmth of appreciation. "I must say, you've got it pretty good here, Sigmund."

"I do enjoy my comforts," the arms merchant replied, smiling expansively. "I make no claims to the contrary."

Dinner was a four-course masterpiece made by a superior chef. On two separate occasions Svetlana tried to get the men to discuss business, but each time she tried, she was gently rebuffed. The men weren't going to talk openly in front of the women about anything as important as the sale of illegal weapons.

Once dinner was finished, Anni pushed her chair away from the table, smiled at Svetlana, and said, "Let's leave the men alone, shall we? We can have cocktails in the ballroom. Besides, I want the chance to show you around my home. I'm sure it's terribly vain of me, but I like giving tours."

Svetlana wasn't particularly interested in leaving Dornan and the colonel. The words that they were going to be said in her absence were the ones she most needed to hear. But to try to stay with them would be to invite suspicion, so she smiled at the hostess and hoped that during the "tour" she would learn something valuable enough to help crush the colonel's plans.

When Svetlana got in step with Anni as they left the dining room, she wondered how much the young blonde woman knew about Sigmund Dornan's business.

She can't be more than a couple years over twenty. Maybe, if her lover has a weakness for pillow talk, he's told her what he's up to. I might learn more from her than I would from listening in on the colonel and Sigmund Dornan.

The hotel room telephone buzzed, and Tatiana picked it up.

"Hello. Is this Tatiana?" the voice at the other end asked.

She recognized Colonel Galiano's voice immediately. "Yes!" Tatiana replied, faking joy. She had quickly learned that faking emotions was an integral part of her job duties as a field agent for Omega Force. "I've been waiting for your call." With a theatrical flair, she added in a breathless whisper, "I was afraid you wouldn't."

"Plans have changed slightly. I can't come to pick you up. I'm sending a taxicab for you."

"Why? Is something wrong?"

"Nothing is wrong. Just get in the taxi. The driver will take you to where you need to be."

Tatiana felt an empty stab in the pit of her stomach. She didn't like this. When she had been in training, she was warned over and over again against changing plans in the middle of an operation, and to never let the enemy have the upper hand in deciding what course of action was taken. She had been taught that, as a general rule, the original plan was the best plan. She knew Colonel Galiano was a murderer and a savagely duplicitous man. Only a fool would trust someone like him.

Tatiana was new to the world of espionage, but she was no fool.

What would Svetlana do? Tatiana asked herself. Svetlana was her touchstone.

A moment later, though she was not at all certain what action Svetlana would take, Tatiana decided she would get in the taxicab. Whatever happened after that, at least she would be with the colonel — and he was her key to finding out where the weapon was and how the weapon would be used.

CHAPTER NINE

Walking beside Anni as they returned to the men, Svetlana got the feeling the young French women had been
born and bred to be a mistress, like some Asian geisha who
got training from a very young age to be the perfect adorn-
ment to a man's arm and the perfect counterpart to a man's
passion.

Anni explained each of the numerous paintings in the
house, providing a brief biography of the painter and a short
history of the piece's origin. Svetlana wondered whether
Anni was impressed with the paintings or impressed with the
fact that her lover could afford them. It didn't matter either
way. Anni was fine companionship during the tour, and Svetlana soon believed that whatever nasty business her lover,
Sigmund Dornan, was involved in with illegal military arms
sales, the business was not directly tied to her. The conclusion
helped her find solace in enjoying her time with Anni.

The meal had been a scrumptious affair consisting of four
main courses, two involving meat dishes and two vegetarian.
The dishes for each course were removed by a team of efficient silent maids, all of whom, Svetlana noted, were at least
fifty years old. It seemed that Anni wasn't going to hire competition for Sigmund's affections. She didn't blame Anni in
the least. In fact, her respect for Anni went up a notch. Had
their positions been reversed, she would have done the same.

Sigmund suggested they move out of the ballroom to the
entertainment room. Svetlana and Anni led the way, while
Sigmund and Mendoza followed. Svetlana felt a tickle in her

stomach. Something was about to happen . . . she just didn't know what.

The entertainment room was small in comparison to the other massive rooms in the arms dealer's mansion. Two long, comfortable sofas were strategically located along with an assortment of leather, overstuffed chairs. On one wall was an enormous flat screen television. Speakers were discreetly distributed around the room. Beneath the television screen was an assortment of video equipment, including two digital video cameras. This was a room where people could watch a movie with the finest electronics money could buy — or make a home movie, should their lust and sense of exhibitionism turn in that direction.

"I'll put some music on," Anni said upon entering the room. She took Svetlana's hand and led her over to where innumerable music disks were arranged helter-skelter. "Do you have a preference?"

Svetlana was just about to answer when the men entered the entertainment room. They were discussing something heatedly but not angrily.

"I'm quite serious," Colonel Mendoza insisted, "that's just the way she is."

"They're beautiful," Sigmund replied, just as vociferously. "Don't get me wrong. I'm not saying they're not. I just think that I can spot the work of a surgeon. I have an eye for these sorts of things."

"What sorts of things are those?" Anni asked casually as she crossed the room to where an ice-filled sterling silver bucket and an opened bottle of Dom Perignon waited.

The opened champagne warned Svetlana that the move to the entertainment room had been decided in advance. She wasn't terribly surprised. The people she was with planned their actions to maximize success. She expected nothing less of them.

"Colonel Mendoza and I were just discussing you ladies," Sigmund explained casually. "I mentioned that Svetlana is extremely lovely."

"Yes, she is lovely," Anni replied. Her voice was low, silky. She looked at Svetlana, her gaze traveling slowly, appraisingly over feminine curves she herself did not possess. "Very, very lovely."

"And then I said that her cosmetic surgeon did a lovely job on her breasts. He didn't go overboard and make them mountains, like some women want their doctors to."

Svetlana felt the tickle in the pit of her stomach. Not altogether sure what the right response should be, she put her hands on her hips, puffed her ample bosom out just a bit, and said with mild indignation, "I'll have you know that what you're looking at is nothing but me! I didn't get my figure in a doctor's office!"

"Yes, yes, of course," Sigmund replied, his tone suggesting he did not believe Svetlana but was willing to let the subject drop. There was a smile on his lips and a lustful glow in his eyes.

"She's telling the truth," Mendoza said. He held out his snifter and let Anni pour in more brandy. "She's a natural D-cup. Trust me. I'd know if they weren't natural."

"So you say," Sigmund said quietly, his eyes on Svetlana's bosom, which was artfully displayed with the red dress's deep V-neck bodice.

"Well, there is a way we can find out one way or another . . ."

Svetlana laughed softly and sipped her champagne. The Dom Perignon was icy cold and delicious. She realized now that the discussion was just the arms dealer's way of getting the chance to feel her up. She looked at the men for a moment, reminding herself that they were both extremely dangerous and would kill her without hesitation if they knew she was a secret agent for the United States.

"You're just saying that because you want to touch me." Svetlana took another sip of champagne, her eyes bright and alive as she looked at Sigmund over the rim of the glass. "I know how you men think."

Sigmund shook his head, his expression mock serious. "No, my dear, I only want clarification, though it is a tempting notion to touch you. What the colonel and I need is an objective third party. Or so it seems. I promise I'll keep my hands to myself and be the perfect gentleman and host."

"That seems fair enough," the colonel said after a moment. "And since I am on one side of the argument, and Sigmund is on the other, we must either have Anni administer the test, or we can call one of your maids."

Sigmund chuckled. "No, not one of the maids. You can't imagine how difficult they are to replace, and Anni absolutely refuses to hire anyone under sixty."

"My rule is no maid under fifty," Anni corrected. "But in any event, there's no need for a maid. I can handle this myself." She chuckled then at her own double entendre. "Or should I say *handle* them *myself*?" Anni turned toward Svetlana. The men stepped much closer. Anni smiled at Svetlana and said, "Men can be such nuisances sometimes. No matter how old they get, they're still just little boys at heart."

Svetlana's mouth went dry when Anni casually raised her hands and placed them lightly over Svetlana breasts. Svetlana still held her champagne glass in one hand, and she took a big sip of it immediately. Gazing down, she watched as Anni's small, pale hands moved gently over her breasts.

"They don't seem to be enhanced," Anni said, removing her hands from Svetlana's body after only a few seconds.

"That was hardly a credible test, my dear," Sigmund said quickly. "It's not so much the shape as is it the firmness, the texture. That's how you can really tell."

"Oh, you're right, of course."

Anni again placed her hands over Svetlana's breasts, only this time she pressed her fingers deeper into the plush mounds.

"Are you certain this is necessary?" Svetlana asked, a faint smile touching her full-lipped mouth.

Warm tingles were coming from her nipples because of Anni's gentle caresses. Though this certainly wasn't the first time a woman had touched Svetlana's breasts, this wasn't the kind of situation she had planned on, and because it wasn't, there was an added element of excitement to it. Her nipples tightened a little more.

Mendoza had moved to Svetlana's right, and Sigmund to her left. Both men watched with unblinking, focused attention on the pale hands firmly massaging Svetlana's breasts.

"They're lovely," Anni said, her voice soft in the suddenly silent room. "Very firm, but naturally so. I think you're wrong this time, Sigmund. Svetlana's breasts are truly magnificent and truly her own."

"Wrong? I'm never wrong about these things!" Sigmund declared. He looked at Mendoza and asked, "Mind a more thorough examination?"

"Whatever it takes to convince you, Sigmund." the colonel said.

Svetlana asked, "Shouldn't someone ask me if I'm all right with this?"

Anni looked straight into Svetlana's eyes and said quietly and sincerely, "Don't worry. I won't hurt you, and I won't let Sigmund touch you."

"See how jealous she can be?" the arms dealer declared.

Svetlana slithered the tip of her tongue around her lips briefly, knowing it would make her mouth glisten invitingly. Her heart was pounding in her chest, and though she was try- ing very hard to not become overly aroused by the pale-skinned young woman's hands, Svetlana could feel her own blood heating and her passions coming to life. Her nipples had hardened visibly. Her clit had awakened and was tingling softly.

"You're lovely," Anni continued. She gently pushed the strap of Svetlana's dress off her shoulder, smiling as she did so. "There's no reason for you to be embarrassed or ashamed. You're beautiful." She closed her eyes for just a moment, then inhaled deeply through her nostrils. The inhalation seemed to refresh her. "So *very* beautiful."

Svetlana thought she should say something, but just exactly what that *something* should be was a complete mystery to her. When Anni took Svetlana's glass from her, she first began to complain, then silenced herself. Moments later, Anni eased the other strap off Svetlana's shoulders and pushed the red dress downward to expose the lace-trimmed red demi-bra.

"How convenient," Anni said, a slight sexual tension in her tone now. She touched her fingertip to the clasp between the cups of the bra. "I was afraid this might be in back."

Svetlana could hardly breathe as Anni eased her fingertips beneath the underside of the bra and pulled the garment outward slightly. With deft fingers she released the bra's clasp, then very slowly, as though opening an infinitely precious and delicate gift, eased the cups away from Svetlana's breasts. Both men sucked in breaths and then held them. Svetlana, too, inhaled deeply when her breasts were exposed. The move caused her bosom to swell out even more.

"No surgical scars that I can see," Anni said, looking carefully at Svetlana's exposed breasts. Seconds passed before she whispered, "My God, they're beautiful. Fucking flawless." Several more flattering obscenities passed between her lips, spoken very softly.

Svetlana shifted her weight uneasily from one stiletto to the other. The sense of exhibitionism that she almost always tried to keep tamped down was coming to the forefront of her consciousness, making the lips of her cunt dewy. Her nipples were hard and elongated with excitement. When Anni touched one nipple lightly with a fingertip, Svetlana uttered a soft, sensual moan.

The colonel didn't truly arouse her body, but Anni seemed to have a map that showed her how to go straight to Svetlana's libido.

"See? No scars," Mendoza said, standing so close to Svetlana that she could practically feel the heat of his gaze.

"Yes . . . yes . . ." Sigmund replied, staring at Svetlana's naked breasts as Anni placed her hands over them.

Anni smiled as she squeezed. The breasts more than filled her hands.

Another moan came from Svetlana, a bit louder than the first one. She wasn't acting. As an agent of Omega Force, she understood that she was expected to do things that she wouldn't otherwise do in civilian life. But still . . .

Sigmund cleared his throat with what seemed to be a certain amount of anxiety and said, "Anni, dear, see if you can make her nipples stand up a bit more."

Svetlana looked over at Mendoza. The colonel could be savagely possessive, she knew. She was still looking at the colonel when Anni removed her hands from her breasts, then bent down and kissed her left nipple.

The startled gasp that came from Svetlana was pure sensuality. She felt the warmth and wetness of the young blonde woman's mouth against her erect nipple, and as Anni began sucking tenderly upon the responsive nub, a shiver worked its way up Svetlana's spine. Svetlana looked down to see Anni's lovely face pressed deeply into her breast, her mouth open, her cheek hollowed inward as she sucked passionately. Svetlana's pussy was extremely hot by this time, and though she stood casually with her arms at her sides, she trembled from head to toe and could not control her rapid breathing.

"Now the other one, Anni," Sigmund quietly instructed. "You must distribute your kisses evenly."

Anni kissed her way slowly across the front of Svetlana's body. She paused a moment to look at the breast that she had not yet kissed.

"Her skin is gorgeous," Anni whispered, her breath warm against Svetlana's sensitive flesh. "Not too dark, not too light. I love the bikini tan lines. Just deliciously tanned and perfect." She opened her mouth and sucked Svetlana's nipple and much of the areola into her mouth.

Seconds passed slowly. Finally, with her arms still at her sides, Svetlana said, "I think I've proven beyond any doubt that my breasts are mine and not the work of a cosmetic surgeon."

"Yes, of course you have." Sigmund's tone was casual—the heat in his gaze was not. "Well, Anni, I think you can stop now. I must admit that I was wrong. Svetlana's charms are perfectly natural."

Anni straightened, releasing Svetlana's nipple from her mouth with a popping sound. Svetlana stood with her arms at her sides, her naked breasts exposed, her nipples glistening wetly from Anni's mouth.

She felt thoroughly disoriented by all that had happened. On the drive over to the mansion, she had gotten aroused. And now, once again, she had become extremely aroused without actually bringing the excitement to an orgasm. She found it profoundly difficult to maintain a professional detachment between what she was actually doing and what her mission was.

Mendoza tilted his head back, draining the last of his brandy. He said, "Sigmund, might I have a bit more?"

"I've been a terrible host," Sigmund answered theatrically.

"Anni, dear, would you be so kind?"

"Of course." Anni turned her back to Svetlana and crossed the room to where a crystal decanter of brandy was waiting. She behaved as though what she had just done to Svetlana was the most natural thing in the world. "Would you like some music as well?"

"Please. Pick something that won't drown out conversation," Sigmund replied.

Svetlana slipped her breasts back into the lace-trimmed cups of her bra and refastened the clasp. When she eased the bodice of her dress once more over them, another sigh escaped her. Her breasts literally ached with tension, and she could feel her own rapid heart rate pulsing in her clit.

Colonel Mendoza sat on one of the sofas. He patted the cushion and Svetlana sat down beside him, her mind reeling at the possibilities of what surprises the night held in store for her.

"We have some movies," Sigmund said, speaking to Colonel Mendoza, but giving Anni a sly, knowing look, "that I think you might find interesting . . ."

Svetlana wasn't in the least bit surprised that the movie selected was highly erotic in nature. It had been made in France, produced by a company from Spain, and the production values were extraordinary, far superior to any of the American-made fare she had sampled — and been disappointed with — in the past. The men in the video were all reasonably handsome, hung like stallions, and hard as a policeman's nightstick. The women were beautiful, willing, and took *money shots* to the face with a smile. There were very few tattoos, and only one actress had absurdly disproportionate implants. There were no rings in parts of bodies other than earlobes and belly buttons, and the director seemed to have a pretty good idea of where to put the camera for maximum effect.

But it wasn't the giant television screen that captivated Svetlana's attention and made her pussy wet and hungry. It was the young blonde who had been sitting beside her but was now kneeling on the thickly carpeted floor of the entertainment room.

After fifteen minutes of the movie, Anni—who had been sitting directly beside Svetlana—slipped off the sofa. She crawled between Sigmund's knees and unzipped him. Moments later, with her youthful countenance calm and serene as if she was watching a beautiful sunrise, she began sucking him, nodding up and down over Sigmund's cock, giving him a leisurely blow job as he calmly watched the wanton activities on the television screen.

You stupid, horny fool, Svetlana thought, angry with herself for her own passionate ways. *You're here on assignment! You're not here to get laid!*

She knew that wasn't entirely true, and the angry, self-critical thoughts did little to satisfy the itching in Svetlana's cunt. She tried to keep her gaze away from Anni, who was giving a slowly delivered blow job, taking the weapon merchant's most treasured possession deep into her mouth, then pulling up so that she could lavish the conical crown with swipes from her tongue. Svetlana couldn't keep her focus away from Anni. Beside Svetlana was Colonel Mendoza. He slipped an arm around her shoulders, then reached down and squeezed her breast.

"Get down on the floor," Mendoza whispered into Svetlana's ear. "Give me a little of what Anni's giving her man."

Svetlana didn't resist. She had no illusions about her role with Omega Force. When she eased between the colonel's spread knees and reached for his zipper, she noticed that her hands were trembling slightly. She paused a moment and looked to her right. She was only a little surprised to discover that Anni, though continuing to give her lover fellatio, was now watching what Svetlana was doing.

It turns me on to give a show, Svetlana thought as she reached inside Colonel Mendoza's trousers for the cock that she had become quite familiar with. *It always has been exciting to be an exhibitionist. It's just something that's hard for me to admit.*

Feeling the eyes of others upon her, Svetlana opened her lips and took the colonel's cock deep into her mouth. She nibbled down the shaft with her lips until she felt the crown throbbing hotly against the opening of her throat. She moaned softly but made sure the sound was loud enough for the others to hear. This wasn't just sex, it was live theatre.

"Before you do that too long, Svetlana," Colonel Mendoza said calmly, "why not give Anni a kiss for me?" He looked to his left at Sigmund and added, "You don't mind the women giving us a little show, do you?"

"A good host is supposed to provide entertainment for his guests," the arms dealer replied. "Anni, give Svetlana a kiss for us."

Svetlana had been with women before, of course. A woman couldn't be as sexually adventurous as Svetlana Simonov without having had at least some experience in lesbian pleasures. There even had been times when she initiated the seduction, though this wasn't the general rule. On a lesbian level, Svetlana liked to be the seduced, not the seducer. Nevertheless, when Anni turned toward Svetlana and leaned over Sigmund's thigh, Svetlana's pulse quickened considerably, and her heart fluttered as though she'd never before kissed another woman.

Closing her eyes, Svetlana waited. She didn't have to wait long. Anni's soft mouth was soon pressing against Svetlana's. The kiss was rather chaste. Tongues did not explore. The passion was held in check. They didn't know each other well, at all. And the circumstances made being adventuresome difficult, or at the very least, awkward.

Holding the passion in check didn't last long. This was a

fact that did not bother Svetlana in the least.

Svetlana soon felt the moist tip of Anni's tongue touching her lips. The soft, throaty purr signaling rising feminine passion drifted to Svetlana's ears. The sound surprised her, but only after she soon realized that the moan had come from herself. She swirled her tongue against the young blonde's. The men moved out of the way, and when they did, Svetlana slipped more tightly into Anni's embrace. While remaining on their knees, the women squirmed closer together so that their bodies were pressed together from the knees to where their mouths were joined in the passionate French kiss. Svetlana felt herself melting inside. Anni's kiss touched her to the core of her being.

"So beautiful," Colonel Mendoza whispered, watching the women kissing. "Damned good idea you had, Sigmund."

Svetlana quickly learned the rules of the game. It was expected of her to fool around with Anni and give the men a good show, but both Colonel Mendoza and Sigmund Dornan were far too jealous and possessive to let their women touch another man. Svetlana would satisfy the colonel and Anni would satisfy Sigmund. But the women were expected to give each other pleasure, and to do it in such a fashion that it entertained the men, who were spectators.

Men can be selfish bastards, Svetlana thought, though this realization did not linger long in her mind, because shortly after having thought it, she was rolled onto her back, and Anni was pulling Svetlana's silk dress up her legs.

CHAPTER TEN

Colonel Galiano leaned back in an overstuffed chair in his hotel room and told himself that soon he'd never again have to accept anything less than five-star quality, no matter where in the world he was. Yes, he'd still be the Iceman that he had been in his youth, but gone were the days when he would forego creature comforts — like the Tennessee whiskey on the rocks that he had in his hand at that very moment. He was aware of the recent psychological changes in him, and he embraced them. He now felt that the man he used to be was a bit silly, and not really much of an adult.

He looked to his left, toward the king-sized bed. The young and beautiful Tatiana Simonov was sleeping quietly, her blonde hair spread across the pillow in artful disarray, her face void of makeup. She couldn't have looked sexier if she had tried. And to the colonel, that made her much sexier. Not trying was *sooo* much sexier than making an obvious effort.

The slightest of smiles curled the colonel's lips. The more innocent she appeared, the more he wanted to defile her, to use her sexually in ways that he hadn't yet done. His lust for her had only increased from the first time he'd thrust his cock into her tender body.

I could fuck her in the ass.

Now wasn't that something to think about? The thought seemed to have come out of nowhere, but the logical part of his brain never liked the notion of coincidence.

Colonel Galiano was almost certain that Tatiana hadn't yet sexually taken the road less traveled, and that brought a feral heat to his libido. But he didn't want to fuck her ass—not just yet. He'd wait until he had her somewhere where she didn't have any friends or family who could protect her, a place where she was his captive and there was no one she could call an ally. He liked his victims powerless. *That* was when he'd take the virginity of her ass. That was when he'd teach her *precisely* how a submissive cunt was supposed to treat her master.

Just thinking about that day brought blood to the shaft of his cock, and he felt himself getting harder, slowly but steadily. He tried to forget that erections hadn't been coming to him quite as easily as they once had.

Looking at Tatiana, the colonel thought *not yet*.

It wasn't that he didn't want her as a man wants a woman, it was that the next time he took her sexually, he would do it with an audience, and he'd do it in such a way that every man in the room—all of whom would be wishing that they were him—would realize that he was in complete and total control and was master over his world, and *everyone* in it. He was done doing things in half-measures. From now on, people either did what he had commanded them to do . . . or they would die.

The colonel smiled.

It wouldn't just be sex with Tatiana, it would be a statement . . . and there wouldn't be a man in the room who'd have the slightest doubt as to what had just been said.

The colonel looked at his wristwatch. It was made out of plastic, and it was a reminder that the world hadn't shown him the respect that he deserved. It was nearly seven-thirty in the morning, and his soldiers that were to arrive were still an hour off. The colonel decided it would be best—for him, anyway—if he let Tatiana continue to sleep. Soon enough she'd be awake . . . and shortly after that she'd be glaringly, intensely awake . . . and when she was, then the colonel would prove that he had total mastery over everyone within his universe.

He looked once again at Tatiana, thinking her to be one of the most beautiful young women he'd ever had sleeping in his bed . . . and wondered whether or not she'd scream the first time he fucked her in the ass.

It was the kind of conundrum that he liked to leisurely ponder.

Tatiana awoke with the instant awareness that she was in enemy territory, that she was in bed, and that she was completely naked. She kept her eyes closed, and she didn't move a muscle—but every nerve in her body was instantly, vibrantly awake.

Colonel Galiano is nearby. He's watching me. She felt his gaze. Her body remembered the feel of his touch. It wasn't a pleasant memory . . . but that didn't matter. What mattered was that he wanted to touch her, and because of the mission, she was willing to let him.

Quite suddenly, she wished that Svetlana were with her so that they could talk over her possibilities.

Don't think about that. You knew from the very beginning that you'd be on your own when you're in the field on assignment.

With a theatrical yawn, Tatiana stretched her arms over her head, then kicked her feet just enough to ensure that the bed sheet moved low enough to expose her breasts. She knew that the colonel was watching her, and she knew that he loved looking at her naked breasts.

"Good morning," she murmured sleepily, sitting upright on the mattress, letting the bedsheet pool around her hips. She combed her fingers through her hair, then gave her head a little shake. She could feel the lusty heat of the colonel's gaze on her breasts, though she pretended to be unaware of it.

"Please tell me there's coffee on the way." She gave Colonel

Galiano a half-smile. "If not coffee, how about mimosas?" She watched as the colonel's brow furrowed in confusion.

"Mimosas?"

"Champagne," she explained, reclining back on one elbow, adopting a pose that she knew would appeal to Colonel Galiano's libido. While on this assignment, every move she consciously made. "Champagne and orange juice. It's like the most perfect drink in all the world to have the first thing in the morning."

"American decadence," the colonel said softly, with only a small measure of contempt.

"American ingenuity," Tatiana countered. "Who other than Americans would be sensible enough to team champagne with orange juice, and call it a breakfast drink?"

She watched as his jaws clenched, a muscle flickering high in his cheek, and Tatiana knew that she had pushed him about as far as she could without him either having an aneurism or unleashing his fists on her. She had no illusions about the man, even though she gave him sexual satisfaction. He was a cold-blooded killer, and he'd kill her the moment she no longer satisfied his desires or served his needs in other ways.

Tatiana got out of bed and walked slowly toward the bathroom, pretending that she wasn't flaunting her beauty, pretending she was still mostly asleep when in point of fact she was wide awake and her senses were attuned to every sensory input.

"Be a darling," Tatiana said, just as she was about to disappear into the bathroom. "Order coffee. I need an eye-opener." She gave him a sly smile. "You really exhausted me last night." She paused, stretched her arms over her head while yawning, then turned so that she gave Colonel Galiano an unhurried view of full-frontal nudity. "First coffee, then mimosas. After your performance last night, it's going to require some champagne this morning."

She looked into his eyes, and in that instant, she knew that she had said exactly what he wanted to hear.

I'm getting better at this secret agent stuff, Tatiana thought as she closed the door behind herself in the bathroom.

She turned on the shower and tried to not worry too much about what the day held in store for her. There was a certain gleam in Colonel Galiano's eyes that she couldn't make sense of, and though she was entirely new to being an Omega Force agent, she already understood in the very depths of her soul that what she *didn't* know could hurt her.

The unknown was always the demon in Tatiana's closet.

Tatiana sensed it more than actually felt it coming. It was Colonel Galiano, and he had something planned for her, and whatever it was, she wasn't going to like it. There was a gleam in his eyes — a feral gleam like that of a cat who had gone from being a house cat to being a barn cat and now killed his own meals and knew the taste of warm blood. *This isn't an animal who concerns himself about what can of pet food he's going to be fed. This is an animal who feeds himself on the flesh of other living beings.*

Tatiana suspected that Colonel Galiano was done begging. He was done asking for scraps from his betters. He was now going to take whatever he wanted. He was done asking for permission.

Tatiana stepped close to him as he sat in a chair and said in a quiet voice that only he could hear despite the closeness of the other military men in the room, "What is it? What's wrong?"

With a Cheshire cat smile on his lips, the colonel asked, "What makes you think something is wrong?"

Tatiana gave him a look that exaggerated her youth, which she hoped he'd like. "You know very well what I'm talking about. It annoys me when you act as though I haven't got a single brain cell in my head."

"I'm just thinking that it might be time for me to make a statement." He reached out casually with his left hand and placed his fingertips lightly on the back of her naked calf. When Tatiana flinched, the colonel's smile broadened fractionally. "You're in a position to help me make that statement."

His fingertips trailed lightly from Tatiana's slender calf up to the back of her knee, then to the back of her thigh. She felt her heart accelerate, beating stronger and faster as the colonel's hand moved higher, his touch more intimate. She knew that every man in the room could see exactly what he was doing, and she felt heat and color rush to her cheeks and throat.

How far is he willing to go? Is this about humiliating me, or about something else that I don't quite understand?

For a moment she desperately wished that when she had poured drinks for all the men, she had poured one for herself.

But an instant later she knew that such behavior would be wrong under the circumstances. She needed all her faculties functioning on high octane if she was going to survive this mission.

"Colonel, are you sure there's nothing I can get you?" she asked, thinking that maybe a Jack Daniels on the rocks might cool his ardor.

The instant this thought entered her head, she knew it was a foolish one. The only person she'd ever seen him drink liquor with was herself, and that was only when they were alone together, and in an intimate setting. He had spent decades building up the facade of the *Iceman,* and she knew he wasn't going to let it shatter to pieces now that he was so close to the fortune that he had lusted after many years.

Tatiana understood this, and it frightened her.

"Nothing, my dear," the colonel said after a moment, turning his attention back to the men in the room, all of whom were watching him with intense interest. "Please, just make sure that our guests have pleasant refreshments at all times."

Tatiana nearly breathed a sigh of relief, but at the next moment, Colonel Galiano's hand eased up beneath the hem of her dress, his fingertips grazing over her skin with a surprisingly delicate touch. Meanwhile, the colonel's entire demeanor was as though he was doing nothing more intimate than caressing the back of her hand at a dinner table while discussing the day's activities with close friends.

Needing desperately to find an excuse to step away from the colonel, Tatiana noticed as a major — wearing a uniform she didn't recognize — finished the last of his cocktail with a rather large gulp as he stared at Colonel Galiano's hand moving beneath the skirt of her dress.

"Let me get you another," Tatiana said quickly, moving so that Colonel Galiano's hand was no longer beneath her dress, and his fingertips were no longer caressing her flesh just a scant inch below the bottom seam of her panties.

She took her time refilling the glass with liquor and ice, her hands moving without needing any real direction from her brain. After several seconds, the men resumed talking, though she could tell from their tone of voice that they were all terribly distracted — by her, and by what Colonel Galiano had been doing to her.

She turned and served the drinks, then gave the colonel a questioning look. She still wasn't certain what this whole charade was all about, but she knew it couldn't be good for her when it all played out.

"Are you sure I can't get you anything, my dear?" she asked the colonel, as deferentially as possible.

"Ice water would please me," he replied, and again that cryptic smile curled his lips. "You do enjoy pleasing me, don't you?"

Tatiana felt her heart seize up for a moment, but then she forced herself to remain calm. She replied, "Of course, darling. You must know by now that there isn't anything I wouldn't do to please you." She smiled sheepishly, for the benefit of the other men in the room, and added, "Surely, I must have convinced you of that by now."

She saw the gleam in his eyes and knew that she had said the right thing.

"Then some ice water, if you please." The colonel leaned back slightly in his overstuffed chair, and there was an unspoken obscenity in how he pushed his crotch forward, to the edge of the seat cushion. Tatiana sensed the threat in the not-so-subtle move, but what was even more frightening was that she knew the other men in the room had caught the implication.,

She got the ice water and brought it to the colonel, and she could feel the gaze of the men in the room focused on every move she made.

This is theatre of the absurd, taken to an obscene level, and I'm the lead actress on the stage . . . whether I want to be or not.

After she handed Colonel Mendoza his water glass, she considered what her next move should be. In the forefront of her mind she realized that every move she made, every gesture, every utterance, could have the gravest of consequences.

She stood beside the colonel's chair, positioning herself so that she faced the men in the room and was directly at Colonel Galiano's side. It wasn't quite a move of open subservience, but it was close. Very close.

"Now, where were we?" the colonel said after taking the smallest, most abstemious of sips of his ice water. "Oh, yes, we were about to begin discussing the surface-to-air missiles that will soon be in my possession." He smiled at the men in the room at the same time that his hand slipped up the back of Tatiana's thigh, not stopping until he was cupping the half-moon of her ass cheek in his palm. "What's needed are state-of-the-art, modern weaponry . . . and they can take any commercial Boeing or Airbus out of the sky in just a matter of seconds, and that aircraft—fully loaded with commercial jet fuel that's virtually impervious to water from civilian fire hoses once it is ablaze — will come crashing down onto heavily-populated urban areas like New York City, London, or any other major metropolis you wish to name and want to destroy." He smiled up at Tatiana briefly. She realized he was bragging, and for a moment it was hard for her to accept the fact that there were people like him in the world. "You get three for one — the plane, the people in it, and the people on the ground."

The words made the bile rise in Tatiana's throat. What the colonel was proposing was nothing less than barbaric. In light of that it seemed insignificant that his fingers had just slipped inside the leg hole of her panties, and he was now squeezing her bare ass cheek while men whose names she did not even know watched him.

And there was nothing she could do but stand there and let him do whatever he desired. It was what the mission demanded of her.

This is what Colonel Galiano wanted all along. To show his power over me to these men, and in doing so, prove that he is more of a force to reckon with on the world stage than they. This isn't really sexual to the colonel. I'm just a pawn to be moved on the chessboard to best suit his narcissistic needs and selfish desires.

More words were spoken, some of them by Colonel Galiano, more by the other men in the room. Tatiana couldn't quite concentrate because she now had a man's fingertip lightly nudging her clit, touching gently but with steadily increasing determination, and it wasn't long before that fingertip was easing its way between the lips of her cunt, retreating briefly, then moving forward and upward once again.

"I can guarantee shipment of the missiles no later than three months from now," the colonel said as his finger slipped into Tatiana's pussy to the second knuckle. "And as with all of my transactions, it is a fifty percent deposit, and fifty percent on delivery. We can all agree on that, can we not?"

Tatiana heard a murmur of approving voices as she felt, simultaneously, the palm of Colonel Galiano's hand pressing against the cheeks of her ass while his finger reached full insertion into her pussy.

She tried to concentrate on the words that were being spoken regarding missiles and weapons of mass destruction, but this was nearly impossible when a man she personally despised with every fiber of her body and being was finger-fucking her while she stood in front of a group of men she had never seen before in her life.

"But we haven't discussed the price." The speaker was peeved. "You've spoken at length about everything but the price of the missiles.

He's a man who keeps his eye on the bottom line. He's not distracted by what he's watching the colonel do to me.

She found it odd that she *somewhat* respected him for that.

"If we're going to get down to the nitty-gritty" — Tatiana was surprised that the colonel had used an American cliché — "then let's do exactly that."

"It always comes down to price," said the military man who had been annoyed.

"Price," Colonel Galiano said after a moment. "And satisfaction."

A cold stab of fear went through Tatiana when she heard the slight inflection in the colonel's tone as he'd said *satisfaction.*

The colonel, still remaining seated while Tatiana stood beside him, looked up at her, his gaze meeting hers, his focus hard and unyielding. He looked into her eyes for several seconds, then he raised his right hand, and simply curled his index finger toward himself as though he was summoning a child who had been caught misbehaving. It was the gesture of a man who knew he had complete control over his subordinates.

Tatiana bent low so that she could put her ear close to his

mouth. She waited for him to speak, and when he hesitated, she brought up a hand to plug her other ear so that she could hear the softest of voices.

"On your knees," Colonel Galiano said after several seconds of weighty silence. Tatiana felt as though the floor had suddenly disappeared beneath her stilettos. "Keep your back to them. They don't actually need to see what you're doing . . . but they do have to *know* what you're doing. And trust me, my darling—" his tongue flicked out to glare against Tatiana's ear, and she flinched as though she just been given an electrical shock—"I want to be *completely* satisfied with your performance, or you will pay a very dear price."

"Now?" Tatiana asked in a very soft voice. The question was rhetorical. "You know I'll satisfy you any way you want when we're alone." The statement was superfluous. She'd already made that very clear to the colonel.

"The last thing in the world you want is to disappoint me," the colonel said.

When this mission's over, I really hope I'm the one that kills you, Tatiana thought.

"Yes. Of course." After several seconds, she said, "Sir." The words were bitter on her tongue.

"You're about to be the best distraction to the other men in this room that I can imagine. You're the distraction that's going to work in my favor."

Tatiana looked over her shoulder at the other men in the room. They were all silent. Even though they were all powerful men who undoubtedly commanded other men, what they were witnessing now was something new and shocking to them. It was a level of power over others they hadn't seen before—and Tatiana suspected it impressed the hell out of them.

Colonel Galiano was right, Tatiana thought, grudgingly having to credit gamesmanship to a man she hated but was about to give extraordinary pleasure to. *He knows exactly how to play this game.*

She moved so that she was directly facing the colonel in the corner of the room, and all the other men in the room were behind her, her body blocking their view of everything above her shoulders. Furthermore, her hair hung down, and that would obscure her face should any of the men move to the side to get a better view of what she was about to do.

You can do this, Tatiana thought as she put her hands on the insides of the colonel's knees, then pushed them apart to give her a little more room.

She heard Colonel Galiano clear his throat several times. He was trying to appear calm, but that wasn't his emotional state of mind—and it pleased Tatiana that she could knock him off his game when he'd always looked at himself the Iceman.

"How will the missiles be delivered?" one of the military men asked. Tatiana could hear the tension in his voice, too. "Ships are inspected. Ports are watched with a close eye by governments mine is not friendly with."

"You needn't worry about transportation," Colonel Galiano said, then there was a hitch in his breathing when Tatiana began unbuttoning the fly of his trousers. He regained his complete composure a second later. "I'll take care of that out of my share of the profits. I've handled the transportation of contraband successfully for more than a dozen years. I've got my connections in place, and they've all got money in Swiss or Jamaican bank accounts. Well, some are in Belize. Trust me, I can put those missiles into the American consulate in Beirut if that's where you want them."

Tatiana reached inside the open trouser fly and found his cock half-erect.

So far, so good, she thought, summoning up the courage to follow through with what she knew the assignment required of her. She pulled him out.

With her fingers surrounding the shaft of his cock, she

began stroking him, alternately tightening and loosening her grip on his flesh as she worked her hand up and down. She immediately felt his cock growing, getting longer and thicker as the lusty blood that flowed through his veins pumped directly into his cock.

Tatiana leaned forward and kissed the crown of his cock. Behind her, she could hear the military men all simultaneously inhale sharply. No matter what they had seen before in their life, nothing had prepared them for the shock of watching what was happening now.

Tatiana licked the head of Colonel Galiano's cock, and it stretched to full extension in a matter of seconds. Having him aroused, Tatiana felt more confident than she had just seconds earlier. Colonel Galiano wasn't the only one possessing power in this dynamic.

She decided to add fuel to the fire. This wasn't the time to do anything in half-measures.

"Oh, God," she said, loud enough that there wasn't a man in the room who didn't hear both words. "I do so adore your cock."

For several seconds she flicked her tongue against the slit at the tip of his cock, and even though he was known as the Iceman because of his great willpower, a low, throaty groan of sensual pleasured rumbled out of his throat, and Tatiana was certain that everyone in the room knew he wasn't as impervious to physical delights as he pretended.

With a slurping sound, Tatiana let the colonel's cockhead slip out of her mouth, then sighed as an actress would if on a stage when she needed to make the audience in the last row know what she was feeling.

"Don't let me disturb you," Tatiana said, her cheek against his thigh as she remained on her knees. "Keep doing business. That's what you do best." She kissed his cock with a moist sound that could be heard by every man in the room. "And

I'll keep doing what I do best." She chuckled softly. There was an element of youthfulness in the tone that she had used — with intention. "But give me as little warning before you come. You always come so much, it's hard for me to swallow it all without at least a little forewarning." She made a soft sound in her throat. "I'm half-afraid that someday you'll drown me."

Colonel Galiano pushed his fingers into Tatiana's hair and clenched his hand into a fist, then guided her face down to his flaring erection.

"Suck," he said with a commanding tone. The he said to the men in the room, "Now gentlemen, we were discussing the pricing options for the missiles I shall soon possess." He groaned, and said to Tatiana, "Fuck, that's good."

I've got him right where I want him, Tatiana thought as she began bobbing up and down over the colonel's cock with greater urgency, relieved that she knew he really didn't ejaculate that much, so swallowing his discharge wasn't much of an effort.

Svetlana was on her hands and knees on the carpeted floor. She was facing the long sofa. Behind her, Colonel Mendoza was driving his cock into her cunt with all the energy he possessed. In front of her, Anni was sitting on the sofa with her knees spread obscenely wide apart. Her lover, Sigmund, was standing on the sofa, watching Anni as she gave him fellatio. Svetlana, with her arms resting lightly on Anni's naked thighs, was also watching the young woman sucking cock. From the hardness of Sigmund's erection, Svetlana guessed that Anni was a master at giving pleasure to a man with her lips and tongue. It wasn't a revelation she considered shocking.

From behind her, Colonel Mendoza growled, "Don't stop!"

Svetlana knew what was expected of her. She dipped her face down once again, bringing her full-lipped mouth to Anni's feminine sex lips. She eased her tongue between the pink labia and then dragged her tongue upward, separating the lips delicately before reaching the small, partially hidden clitoris. Once there, Svetlana circled the clit with the tip of her tongue before capturing it between her lips. Anni squirmed on the sofa as she bobbed, sucking cock with noisy enthusiasm.

"You're insatiable," Colonel Mendoza said, his voice a hoarse whisper. Then he said, "You're my very own personal cunt, aren't you?"

Svetlana wasn't at all certain whether he was talking to her or to Anni. She didn't really *need* to know, and since she didn't, she didn't much care. This was not the first time she'd ridden a bronco in this kind of rodeo.

Each time the colonel's pelvis slammed against Svetlana's ass, she was forced forward, her mouth mashing tightly against Anni's hot sex. Svetlana felt pleasure, along with a twinge of guilt for this sensation. Work was work and pleasure was pleasure, and she made a point of always keeping the two separate. She knew who her heart belonged to. Omega Force owned her body, but not her soul, and most certainly not her heart. That belonged to Jefferson Burke.

She had no expectation of an orgasm. Experience had taught her that the only man who could bring her to climax was Burke. Burke, and his talented hands and devastating lips . . . and, of course, that extraordinary cock that took days to tire out. The only real man in Svetlana's world was Burke. He was in a league by himself. There were times in their past together when she had wondered whether or not he'd fuck her to death. After all, there were only so many climaxes a woman was capable of having . . . weren't there?

Svetlana turned off her mind in the same way that a

woman turned off the electricity to a computer, and the circuits all rather quickly went dead.

From there she went into autopilot, doing what others expected of her without thinking about her actions one way or another.

Experience had taught her that sometimes as an Omega Force field agent, turning off and tuning out was the best course of action to take.

Svetlana rocked on her hands and knees, impaling herself upon the colonel's thrusting cock. She knew she was going to be sexually unsatisfied with the way this encounter ended, but that was something she had learned to accept. She tongued Anni's pussy a bit more ardently, thinking that there was no reason Anni shouldn't experience a climax.

Seconds later it was Sigmund who exploded. Svetlana watched as Anni worked on his erupting flesh, satisfying his passion, milking him of his cum. And when he was drained and could give her no more, she swallowed just once and continued to hold him between her lips until he pushed her gently away.

Svetlana watched as Anni swallowed one last time, then licked her lips. Svetlana could tell that it was all just a show for her lover. Anni was an actress in front of the camera . . . only there was no camera around, and only Anni realized that she was in stage makeup.

She swallows her lover's cum. She does it in such a way that Sigmund knows what she's doing. Everything she does is dramatic. It's all theatrical gestures. It's all just part of the game she's playing in the role of Sigmund Dornan's insatiable mistress. Svetlana thought for a moment, then came to the conclusion that the truth was, Anni really didn't give a shit about him. It was all just a show because he had the money and she got her share of it.

"Baby, get me a drink," Colonel Mendoza said, still sprawled on the carpeted floor. "I'm exhausted."

Naked except for her garter belt, silk stockings, and high-heeled shoes, Svetlana got unsteadily to her feet and walked over to the tray where the open bottle of chilled champagne waited. As she poured champagne for the colonel, she made a point of not pouring a glass for herself. She couldn't lose her razor-sharp edge with champagne, no matter how delicious and icy cold it was. She intended to return later to sneak into the arms dealer's mansion. Somewhere hidden in this mansion were the answers countless questions Svetlana had.

All she had to do was find some way past the elaborate security system Sigmund Dornan had installed, and maybe she would finally be nearing the end to her latest mission for Omega Force.

CHAPTER ELEVEN

Washington D.C.

Burke was sitting in his office. He was reading for the third time the report that had just come onto his computer screen.

"The girl seems to be holding her own," Burke said. He was talking on a conference call with men he'd never met and did not know. They were superior officers, and though he answered to them, he'd never seen any of them. That was the way Omega Force worked. "She's already met Colonel Galiano."

"And Svetlana?" inquired an anonymous superior officer.

"Haven't heard from her in a while. I'm less worried about her. She's an experienced soldier. Probably the best covert agent we've ever had. She's got a real sixth sense when it comes to being in the field."

"Keep a close eye on this," another voice said. "The price of failure on this mission could be greater than any of us can now imagine."

"Yes, sir."

Rio de Janeiro, Brazil

Raoul Santiago looked at Sigmund Dornan's mansion. He was disgusted with the opulence. Raw, seething hatred gripped his freedom fighter's soul, and he had to resist the urge to kill Sigmund Dornan. Dornan represented the excessive wealth that some people had, and by being so una-shamed to display his wealth, he proved to others — to unsul-lied men like Raoul — that he was a plague upon the planet and deserved nothing less than a swift and bloody death.

"You're sure I can't get you anything to drink?" Sigmund asked.

"Nothing. Thank you," Raoul replied crisply.

It was early morning, but Raoul wasn't tired. He had learned that in the illegal weapons business, unusual hours for conducting business negotiations were the norm. Nine to five was more likely to mean nine PM to five AM.

Raoul had to consciously tamp down the hatred he felt for Sigmund so that he could concentrate on what he had come to Rio de Janeiro to accomplish: buying the best, most deadly weapons possible for as little money as was necessary.

Raoul could tell from Sigmund's expression that he was very tired and fighting against the fatigue that tugged at him. The man needed sleep, but he also needed money, so he was willing to do business even in the wee hours of the morning. Raoul felt this might give him some advantage, however small, and he was determined to make the most of it.

"You're not too tired?"

"I'm fine, *Senor* Santiago," Sigmund replied quickly. "You're sure I can't get you a drink of some sort?"

"Nothing for me." Raoul smiled. He decided that Sig-mund, like so many obscenely wealthy men, was essentially a weak man. Money had poisoned his soul. Could liquor and fatigue assist the cause of freedom fighters? "But don't abstain on my account."

"Very well." Sigmund sighed heavily. "Now you say you're in the market for weapons. What kind of weapons are you looking for? Remember, the more precise you can be with your answer, the more likely it is that I'll be able to find what you need at a price you can afford."

Raoul smiled and spread his hands out in a gesture of innocence. He decided to go about the buying negotiations slowly. Time — and Sigmund's fatigue — were on Raoul's side.

Rio de Janeiro, Brazil

The suitcase looked like standard piece of luggage, but it had been altered by Omega Force to be something more than just a piece of stylish luggage needed to carry clothes and belongings. Svetlana placed the suitcase on her hotel bed, flipped open the locks, then carefully pulled the hidden nylon zipper on the right side of the case. The trap door was invisible on quick inspection, and nearly impossible to see even on close inspection. Whatever was inside the secret compartment was invisible to airport X-rays, and the folks over at Research & Development at the Department of Defense weren't about to tell anyone how they'd invented that little trick.

Inside the small compartment were the things that Svetlana needed for her quickly concocted plan to inspect Sigmund Dornan's residence.

She pulled out her Mauser automatic, checked to see that the clip was fully loaded, then set the weapon aside. Though the Mauser had been designed prior to World War II, the German-made weapon felt good in her hand, pointed straight and true, and in .32 caliber — internationally known as 7.65 mm. — ammunition was easy to come by most anywhere in the world. The hollow-points packed a lethal punch, despite what proponents of high-caliber weapons insisted. The silencer made the seven-shot automatic a dispenser of whispering death. The silencer was six inches long, made entirely of composite materials, and brought the Mauser's roar down to a hissing cough.

Svetlana slipped the Mauser into the canvas clam-shell holster with the figure-8 harness, then tucked the extra two magazines into the holster's holding compartment under the right arm. The Mauser would rest comfortably beneath Svetlana's left arm, and she could draw and fire the weapon in the blink of an eye.

The bathroom door opened and Tatiana stepped out. She had a towel around her head to dry her hair, but other than that was completely naked. Svetlana tried not to notice that she looked nothing short of delicious. She made a point of not thinking too long about this, and she managed to do so, though not without difficulty.

Tatiana opened the secret compartment of her suitcase and pulled out her own sidearm—a Walther .380 automatic with silencer.

"When Anni was giving me the tour of the mansion," Svetlana said, stepping into a pair of black, form-fitting Calvin Klein jeans, "I got a pretty good look at how the security system works. Once we're inside, I want you to keep your eyes open for a secondary security system. The first one seemed a bit old-fashioned, so that might just be a ruse to fool thieves."

"Okay," Tatiana replied. "Do you think there will be trouble?"

"He's made a fortune selling arms to murderers, so we're not talking about the most reputable businessman in Brazil. Also, he's financially strung out, so he'll be edgy right now."

"How did Burke get the weapons sale cancelled?" Tatiana asked.

"Get used to not knowing much about how Omega Force operates." Svetlana sighed. "Shit happens behind the scenes. Sometimes it's nasty shit." She sighed again. "This is the time to learn to accept that there are a lot of things that are going to happen in your life that aren't explained and aren't going to make sense. This is your *get over it* moment. Welcome to Omega Force. And you'd better buckle up, because it's one hell of a bumpy ride."

Svetlana slipped her arms into the shoulder straps of a

black lace-trimmed bra. She eased the soft cups around her breasts before fastening the twin hook-and-eye closures between the cups. Then she slipped on a long-sleeved black cotton shirt and buttoned it. Lastly, she pulled on the figure-8 holster and adjusted it so the Mauser was comfortable under her left arm and the extra magazines were beneath her right.

"If the shooting starts," Svetlana continued, "the mission's off. Anni's a civilian, not a player, so she's off limits. If you see Sigmund Dornan and he's in the way, take him out." She paused a moment, then said, "Actually, if you see him, take him out. He's evil. Take him out if you can."

"I hope there's no shooting," Tatiana said as she shimmied into a pair of panties that were somewhere between bikini and thong. "But if there is, I'm ready for it."

"I know you are."

But in truth, Svetlana wasn't sure about Tatiana.

Svetlana knelt in the darkness and attached one end of the alligator clamp to the fuse and the other to the receptor. A small red bulb, midway between the two clamps, glowed when the circuit was completed.

"Bingo," Svetlana whispered.

She looked over her shoulder up at Tatiana. Tatiana's slender athletic body was perfectly built for black bag jobs. Svetlana motioned, and Tatiana was up and over the electrified fence in seconds. Svetlana, taller, heavier, and certainly more curvaceous despite her athleticism, took longer to get over the top and inside Sigmund Dornan's compound.

Svetlana led the way, moving at an easy trot, crossing the fifty yards of lawn to the base of the marble mansion. She was dressed in black, as was Tatiana, and she knew they blended smoothly with the shadows. Svetlana, with her back to the mansion, looked to the east. Sunrise wasn't for another hour. She planned to be in and out of Sigmund Dornan's mansion long before the sun came up.

From her back pocket she extracted a long, slender stainless-steel flashlight. She followed the east wall, moving toward the north. Hours earlier, when she had been shown the mansion by Anni de Chevreaux, Svetlana had surreptitiously unlocked the window. Provided the maids and butlers weren't looking for unlocked windows, it should make for an easy entrance.

She found the wall, and with a little pressure, eased the window silently upward.

"How did you know that was going to be unlocked?" Tatiana whispered.

Svetlana leaned her head and shoulders inside the open window, then gave a small hop. She crawled silently through the window, holding the penlight flashlight in her mouth. The room, an unused guest bedroom, was dark and empty, just as she had planned.

Colonel Galiano pulled the Ford van over to the curb and cut the engine two hundred yards from Sigmund Dornan's mansion. Though the colonel was still wearing civilian clothes, his men were in generic military uniforms. It gave him confidence to see them once again in uniform, looking like proud soldiers instead of soldiers pretending to be civilians.

"Take no prisoners," Colonel Galiano said. He almost trembled because the words tasted so sweet on his tongue. "There'll be servants inside. We can't allow them to talk to the police later."

"No witnesses," a soldier replied.

"Come directly back here."

"Yes, sir."

Colonel Galiano knew he should say something to the four men, but he didn't know quite what it should be. His men were armed with AK-47s, along with one extra magazine of ammunition. Each man also had on him two R5 high-explosive fragmentation grenades, a knife, a thirteen-shot 9 mm. automatic pistol, and two garrotes. They were equipped to kill silently or to make it sound like the four of them were actually an entire army. Colonel Galiano didn't care how his men killed the Brazilian arms dealer, so long as they accomplished their task and took possession of the ZT-550. Nothing was more important than that.

"Good luck, men," the colonel said at last. "Your country is counting on you."

The soldiers silently left the van, blending in with the shadows, heading silently toward the marble mansion like a pride of stalking lions.

Standing several feet from her, Tatiana watched as Svetlana, with the penlight flashlight once again in her mouth, deftly attached the suction cups to the wall safe hidden behind a painted portrait of Sigmund Dornan's mother. Attached to the suction cups were slender wires, which ran to a small metal box the size of a pack of European cigarettes. Svetlana touched a button on the small box, and a red light began to glow. She spun the dial of the safe and the red light blinked rapidly, once for each number that went past the indicator notch. Then Svetlana began turning the dial very slowly. Each number brought a blink of the red light.

Then it blinked green and held steady.

"I love working with good equipment," Svetlana whispered, flashing Tatiana a smile in the darkened room.

Each time she found the proper number of the safe, the glowing light switched to green. When the light flashed alternating red and green, she grabbed the safe's handle, paused a moment, then exerted sideways pressure.

The handle turned and the safe door opened soundlessly on its heavy metal hinges.

Stefan saw the open window and smiled. Wasn't it just like the wealthy to pay for a security system, then throw the money away by leaving a window open? He had hoped that it wouldn't be necessary to storm the mansion, and now it looked like the entrance would be silent.

Using hand signals, he motioned for his men to enter through the window. The men — each one a highly-trained professional mercenary — went through the open window hardly making a sound, despite all the equipment and weaponry they carried with them.

The room was a guest bedroom. *Just like the wealthy to have more rooms than necessary when so many people have no roof over their head at all*, thought Stefan.

He crossed the room, tested the doorknob, then opened the door. The hallway was dark. He stepped into the hallway, holding the Russian-made assault rifle in his right hand with the shoulder stock tucked between his elbow and ribs. He made a motion with his left hand. Tomas and Rico headed down the hallway in that direction.

Stefan turned and went the other direction, with Alejandro behind him.

Anni de Chevreaux was in bed, drifting in the half-world between sleep and consciousness. She had a bedroom to herself. Whenever Sigmund wanted her, he called for her. Anni didn't mind not having to share her bed on a nightly basis with Sigmund. At first, she had thought it odd that he preferred sleeping alone. Now she was pleased, because she, too, had learned to enjoy the privacy she got from having her own bedroom.

Her sleepy mind was wandering through erotic visions.

The orgasm that had ripped through Anni's senses earlier in the evening had been one of the most powerful ones that she'd ever experienced. She didn't think of herself as a lesbian, but the pleasures that had surged through her system because of the magnificent oral caresses bestowed by Svetlana caused Anni to question whether or not she wouldn't enjoy having erotic encounters with women more often. If they all gave pleasure as skillfully as Svetlana, then Anni wanted more!

Even though she was more asleep than awake, her right hand crept beneath the blankets. She was sleeping naked, and she touched herself with the soft pad of her index finger. A subtle heat began diffusing through her body. Her mouth curled at the edges into a gentle smile. Her finger, moving of its own volition, began caressing with a circulation motion.

She felt the knife touch her throat and it roused her from half-sleep.

Anni de Chevreaux opened her eyes in time to look into the intruder's eyes just before he slit her throat.

Tatiana looked at looked at the stacks of money in Svetlana's hands and tried to calculate just how much was there. Maybe half a million? Maybe more? It was hard to tell, and she wasn't up on the most recent value of South American currency versus American dollars. It really made no difference. The facts were that Sigmund Dornan had a small fortune in cold, hard cash in his safe . . . but he didn't have the ZT-550 there, which was what the Omega Force agent had been hoping for.

"What do we do with that?" Tatiana asked in a whisper, standing beside Svetlana. She was holding her Walther automatic in her right hand. The silencer was attached to the muzzle. When she had spotted all that money inside the safe, she'd instinctively drawn her weapon, though now she felt a little foolish standing beside Svetlana, holding the weapon pointed at the floor.

"We could put it back in the safe, make a quiet exit out of this place, and maybe Sigmund Dornan would never know that we were ever here," Svetlana replied. She looked at the two handfuls of notes she held, each one bound with a wide paper wrapper.

"What else could we do?"

"We could completely empty out his safe and piss him off beyond his wildest imagination."

"That's what I vote we do."

"Me, too!"

Svetlana began stuffing the stacks of money into the zippered shoulder bag that carried her burglary tools. The bag was made out of parachute material, and though the fabric was very thin, it was extremely sturdy.

Tatiana smiled. She was really beginning to *seriously* respect the way Svetlana made decisions under pressure.

"Listen to me very carefully," Raoul Santiago said, leaning forward, his dark eyes earnest as he looked at Sigmund. "If you have such a weapon, then I would want it. But I must be assured that the weapon is real, and that it will do as you claim."

"The only way to test the weapon is to kill people, and I'm not willing to do that," Sigmund replied. "Not without a sizeable, non-refundable down payment."

Sigmund fought down a yawn. Had the sun come up yet? He had, over the past hour or so, seriously considered telling this intense but annoying freedom fighter from the stinking, insignificant little Caribbean island of St. Lucas to buy his weapons from someone else. Not even the threat of death could keep Sigmund Dornan from fantasizing about the comforts his own bed and the blissful rejuvenation of many hours of dreamless sleep.

"I will not pay for empty promises," Raoul declared.

"And I will not kill unless I'm paid handsomely to do so." Sigmund rose to his feet, stifling the groan of fatigue that nearly escaped his lips. For more than a decade he had been dealing with freedom fighters — or terrorists, depending upon one's political viewpoint on any given issue — and though they were without exception intense fellows, they were often drastically under-funded, and as Sigmund looked at Raoul, he began to wonder if this drawn-out negotiation was simply a ploy to hide the fact that he didn't have any money at all in this alleged Caribbean bank account that would "pay for everything on demand."

"If you want a display of the ZT-550's capabilities, then I'm going to need a good-faith up-front financial offering from you," Sigmund said, looking down at Raoul, who remained seated.

"Perhaps I could see to it that fifty thousand pounds British sterling be transferred to your account."

Sigmund Dornan shook his head slowly. "I said good-faith, not a drop in the bucket. If you want to see the weapon at work, you'll need to come up with a serious offer." He combed his fingers through his hair. He realized that he had made a mistake dealing with this insignificant little man. Raoul was nothing other than a drain, costing valuable time and personal energy. "Listen, I've got a lot of deals in the works right now. I can't be wasting time and prospects that go nowhere." He looked down at the embattled freedom fighter.

"Well, what's it going to be?" Sigmund impatiently asked.

Raoul began reaching for the snub-nose revolver he kept in a holster on his right ankle. If the ZT-550 was as deadly — and portable — as Sigmund Dornan claimed it was, then he could steal the weapon much more inexpensively than he could buy it from the Brazilian.

Tatiana was in the hallway, with Svetlana a step behind her. Tatiana was the first to see the uniformed soldier holding the assault rifle. The Walther was in her hand, but she did not fire immediately. She hesitated a second, no more than that, but it was enough to warn the soldier that he had been discovered.

Svetlana, a step behind Tatiana, reacted spontaneously. Holding the silenced Mauser in her right hand, she raised the weapon and crouched as she squeezed the trigger. The move was fluid, made in a single motion. The small handgun coughed, jumping in her hand. A hollow-point bullet sped toward its target as the soldier squeezed the trigger of his assault rifle.

Svetlana's aim was true.

The soldier's was not.

The AK-47 roared, sending bullets into the floor several yards in front of Svetlana and Tatiana. Svetlana's bullet caught the soldier low in the abdomen, just beneath his belt buckle. He pitched forward, clutching desperately onto his rifle as the weapon screamed on full-automatic.

Svetlana's second round, delivered an eye-blink after the first one, silenced the assault rifle when it punched through the soldier's forehead.

"Remember, no civilians," Svetlana said to Tatiana.

A thousand thoughts raced through Svetlana's brain. Of all the potential trouble she had expected to find within the mansion, a fully armed soldier wasn't one of them. Furthermore, the soldier wasn't simply a guard who had overreacted. He was there looking to kill the home's occupants, not to protect them. Svetlana didn't doubt this for a second.

The women started running, with Svetlana in the lead. She had the bag over her shoulder and was holding her Mauser in both hands as she jogged down the hallway. A door opened behind her and Svetlana wheeled around. Even before she got the shot off, the soldier who stepped out was firing with his assault rifle.

This time it was Tatiana who put an end to the soldier, firing three fast shots with her Walther, punching holes in the big man's broad chest. The first shot probably killed the man, but Svetlana figured inexperience in gunfights had caused Tatiana to at first delay her reaction, then to overreact.

"Out the front door," Svetlana said, her tone hushed but nevertheless commanding.

Svetlana could hear footsteps from down the hall. More soldiers were in the house, and they had her and Tatiana blocked off. Escape through the same window that they had entered in was no longer an option. When Svetlana looked at Tatiana, she saw that her student's expression was one of intense concentration. Tatiana was young and scared and she had just killed her first man, but she was also courageous and trained, and she would not fold up easily under pressure.

As machine gun fire roared in the hallway, Raoul pulled the snub-nose revolver out of the ankle holster, thumbed back the hammer, and aimed at Sigmund.

"Don't be an idiot!" Sigmund shouted frantically. "You think they're after you? You little pissant, you're nothing! It's me they're after!"

Sigmund could hear the high-pitched crack of Russian assault rifles firing on fully automatic. The soldiers were down the hall, going room to room. For a moment there was a scream—that of an elderly woman—but her cry of fear was cut short with a four-shot burst of gunfire.

Sigmund Dornan looked at Raoul, and in that shining moment, realized that he had been a fool to think that the terrorist with dreams of grandeur could possibly afford the ZT-550. Raoul was standing, staring at the closed door, a .38 Special in his hand, a look of wild frustration in his eyes. He raised the weapon, aiming at the closed door.

The instincts that had enabled Sigmund to claw his way out of the gutter and into a life of wealth and comfort came back to him in a heartbeat. He took three silent steps backward and eased down to his knees. He crawled between the sofa and the wall before stretching out flat.

He heard Raoul say, "Sigmund? Sigmund Dornan?"

Sigmund heard the door burst open, swinging wildly on the hinges to bang against the wall. Raoul said something. Sigmund heard the first syllables, but whatever else was spoken was drowned out with the roar of an AK-47 being fired within the confines of a room.

Lying behind the sofa, Sigmund didn't even breathe. He heard the soldier take several steps into the room, then stop. Sigmund's senses, heightened with fear, distinctly caught the aroma of burned cotton. Clearly, the gunman had been very close to Raoul when the deadly rounds had been fired.

The sound of boot steps retreated out of the room. The Brazilian arms dealer allowed himself a shallow breath, but he made no sound at all, and he did not move so much as a muscle. He did not look over the back to the sofa to see what had happened to Raoul. He could imagine what had happened to Raoul, and the only reason that Sigmund himself wasn't lying in a bloody heap was because he was smarter than Raoul.

He was smarter than everyone. That was why he was rich, and that's why he was still alive. Sigmund Dornan believed this with the intensity of the Born Again. He believed, quite honestly and at that moment, that he was invincible.

And nearly God-like in intelligence.

The self-awareness of this simple yet inescapable fact made him tremble with almost orgiastic ecstasy.

As he lay on the thick carpet, Sigmund Dornan decided that he would sell the ZT-550 as quickly as possible, for as much cash as possible. Then he would disappear into the lush rain forest of Belize. It was a contingency plan he had devised long ago for just such a situation as this. A new identity, a modest lifestyle, and plenty of cash in his Caribbean bank accounts would keep him anonymous, safe, and happy.

Gunshots rang out, farther away, perhaps from the library. Sigmund couldn't be sure. He thought of getting up to his knees, then discarded the notion as a bad one. He'd wait. Retirement was just around the corner, and like a cat that had used up eight of its nine lives, Sigmund knew he had time, but only if he was careful. He couldn't live through another bad decision.

Tatiana ran out through the front door of the mansion two steps behind Svetlana. Neither one of them had any assurance that they weren't running into more trouble than they were running away from, but in the midst of a firefight, decisions have to be made and then followed without hesitation or question. There were times in life when there wasn't time for a leisurely deliberation of facts, suppositions, and opinions. Sometimes in life, decisions had to be made *now*.

How many shots had she fired so far? Five? Tatiana had been trained to always keep track of how many bullets she had remaining in the magazine of whatever weapon she happened to be carrying, but in the near-panicked chaos of the battle, that lesson had been forgotten.

Tatiana was running full-out, crossing the distance from the mansion's front doors to the front gates. She was three steps behind Svetlana, who was also running like the Devil himself was chasing her. The gun in Tatiana's right hand felt heavy. The silencer, attached to the muzzle, distorted the weapon's balance.

It was instinct—like a little clock inside her head that said time had run out—more than anything else, that made Tatiana look over her shoulder and to her left. She saw, almost completely obscured in shadow, a figure coming out of the mansion's window. The foot was booted, and the trouser leg—it was all Tatiana could see of the man—was clothed in a camouflaged uniform.

Tatiana stopped and, one-handed, thumbed the magazine release on her Walther. The nearly empty magazine dropped out of the grip even as Tatiana reached beneath her right arm for the extra magazines kept in the holster's twin pouches. She plucked out the magazine and, without looking, slapped it into the pistol. The soldier, by this time, had come out of the window, holding an assault rifle in his hands. Another soldier hurried out of the window as Tatiana raised her weapon.

CHAPTER TWELVE

"Forget about—" Svetlana began, nearly at the wide front gates, a full twenty yards from Tatiana and fifty yards from the shadow-shrouded enemy soldiers.

Svetlana saw what it was that had drawn Tatiana's attention, and instantly realized that had they allowed the soldiers the time, they would have been cut down by bullets. A small-caliber pistol was no credible match against a high-powered assault rifle.

Svetlana glanced at Tatiana. The teenager was on one knee, then dropped so that she was belly-down in the grass, her pistol held out straight in both hands. Svetlana saw the weapon jump and heard its hissing *pffft* as the Omega Force-designed silencer worked its magic. Svetlana dropped to the ground, her body hitting the grass hard. An instant later, machine gun bullets cut through the night air, copper-jacketed slugs clanging against the iron gate behind Svetlana.

The distance was too great for accuracy with a pistol, though well within range of the Russian assault rifles. The soldiers rushed forward in the darkness, rifles to shoulders as they squeezed off short three- and four-shot bursts. The ground around Svetlana was chewed up by the projectiles. The bullet that had caused the grass to jump had struck the ground just to the right of her forearm, missing Tatiana by less than an inch.

Svetlana fired with bullets spaced an even second-and-a-half apart. The first two rounds were high, both ricocheting against the mansion's marble exterior far behind her intended target of flesh and bone. The third bullet Svetlana fired caused the nearest of the soldiers to stumble slightly. Svetlana fired again. The soldier staggered and squeezed the trigger of his rifle. The weapon bucked and roared as bullets were fired at hundreds of rounds per minute. The magazine was quickly emptied. Svetlana fired once more at the soldier, and though he remained standing, the weapon dropped from his fingers to the grass at his feet.

He doesn't even know he's dead, Svetlana thought.

The second soldier rushed forward, moving past his comrade without so much as a sideways glance. He was pulling something from the pocket of his trousers. As Svetlana shifted her aim, seeking this new target in the pistol's sights, she caught a good look at the soldier's face in the moonlight. It was Stefan, the man who had been in both Colonel Mendoza's camp and in Colonel Galiano's. Stefan's left arm went upward in an arc while he continued holding the assault rifle in his right hand.

Svetlana did not take her focus off Stefan. She squeezed the trigger, but he zigged to his left, no longer rushing straight at her, and Svetlana's bullet passed harmlessly by. In her peripheral vision she caught the fleeting impression of something palm-sized and fairly round arching through the air.

"Stay down!" Tatiana screamed.

Svetlana heard the *thud!* of a solid object hitting the grass twenty feet to her right. Then the ground seemed to lift up beneath her, tossing her into the air. The roar of the grenade was deafening, and the breath was knocked from her lungs. She sensed more than actually felt herself coming back to earth, landing hard on her left hip. Her head snapped back on her shoulders when she made contact. She couldn't feel her head striking the grass. Her ears were ringing. Her eyes were open, and Svetlana could see stars overhead, twinkling in the sky. It was all she could see.

Faintly, from somewhere nearby, Svetlana heard the *pffft pffft pffft* of an Omega Force silencer hissing. The roar of the assault rifle became sporadic. The precise three-shot bursts no longer came so neatly separated. Then, suddenly, there was a last burst of machine gun fire.

Dazed, staring into space, Svetlana couldn't feel her body. Did she even have one? All she seemed able to do was blink. She blinked several times, then Tatiana's lovely, frightened face came into view.

"Are you hurt?"

Svetlana moistened her lips and was a little surprised to hear her own voice as she replied, "I don't know."

Tatiana helped Svetlana sit up. Slowly, as her breath returned, feeling also returned to Svetlana. She saw the crater in the ground, not far away, where the grenade had exploded. Had she not been lying down on the ground when the grenade exploded, the shrapnel would have cut her to ribbons.

From far off, a police siren began its irksome, three-toned wail.

"We've got to get out of here," Tatiana said. She slipped under Svetlana's arm and helped her to her feet. "Come on, you've got to help me help you!"

Tatiana pulled Svetlana to her feet, then together they hurried to the gates. The security system was designed to keep people out, not to keep people in, so Tatiana opened it easily enough. Tatiana hurried Svetlana through the gates and together they escaped to the nearest shadows. Police sirens converged from all directions.

Svetlana was unbelievably proud of Tatiana. She made a promise that, no matter what, some day she would explain this to her.

Stefan felt blood pouring through his fingers. He held more

tightly onto his chest, but the blood kept pouring out. He was a soldier, and he'd been shot before, so this was not something entirely new to him. The only other time a bullet had struck him, it was just a glancing shot that had drawn blood from his calf. That wound burned, and afterward, Stefan felt more manly for having experienced the bite of a bullet in combat. It was something he got to brag about with the other soldiers.

But this time it was different. He wasn't going to brag about it and he wasn't going to look heroic. This time he was dying, and he knew it. And what was worst of all was that it was suddenly very clear to him that nobody cared, really, whether he lived or died. Colonel Mendoza, whom Stefan had secretly betrayed, did not care. Neither did Colonel Galiano, who had promised that when they all finally returned home, the peasants would speak Stefan's name in the same breath they spoke of all the other great heroes of the struggle.

What had gone wrong? Four heavily armed, trained soldiers had entered a private residence. They were given orders to kill everyone inside. The soldiers were not expected at the mansion. The surprise attack was planned to be quick, efficient, and bloody.

But someone had shot back. Two women. The women had already been inside the mansion when Stefan and his men entered. The women were armed with silenced pistols. And it seemed to Stefan that he recognized one of the women. No, that could not be. He did not know any women who carried the weapon of an assassin and could shoot as straight and true as these two women obviously could.

Stefan began to feel cold. It was an odd sensation. The screaming wail of police sirens drew nearer.

Exhausted, feeling betrayed but still confident that his cause was just and that he would in the end be triumphant, Stefan closed his eyes for the last time.

Colonel Galiano put the van in gear and pulled away from the curb. He drove swiftly, but carefully. All around him there were sirens screaming. When he heard the first siren, he had started the engine. When the gunshots began ringing out—gunshots that had been fired from *outside*, not *inside* the mansion—he put the van in gear.

Everyone had failed him. Everyone. He had always pictured himself as the world's next *el Presidente*. He was a man of the people. He would lead the world . . . if only they would listen. Listen and learn the wisdom that he had to share.

But the people had failed him. They did not listen. And his men had failed him, too. Even Stefan. The soldiers pretended to be loyal, but if they were truly loyal, they would follow his orders and not get killed. Instead, he had sent them on a mission, and they had not returned. What else could he believe but that they had failed him?

So, what was he, the great Colonel Galiano, to do now? Colonel Mendoza was an enemy of the state, as well as an enemy of Colonel Galiano. Had the arms dealer, Sigmund Dornan, been killed?

He decided that the first thing he had to do was get his hands on Sigmund Dornan. That insufferable prick had answers, and the colonel intended on getting those answers—and he knew just how to go about with the interrogation.

Confusion welled up inside the colonel's head like a clogged cesspool, something ugly and foul. As he drove, he kept asking himself what his next move should be . . . and the worst of it was, he couldn't think of any move to make at all.

At least, not at first.

So where would a man like Sigmund Dornan hide? His home? No, he'd avoid that like the plague. But he did have a yacht at the pier, a beautiful yacht that could motor his sorry ass far away from here.

Washington D.C.

Jefferson Burke had on his desk a written report regarding a shooting, the previous night, at the Rio de Janeiro home of international arms dealer Sigmund Dornan. He had already read the Central Intelligence Agency's report, and now he was reading the alleged version of facts printed by the Associated Press in the morning's daily edition. The AP had gotten a few more facts that the CIA hadn't included, but not many more.

Pity about Anni de Chevreaux. She hadn't been a player. Just a young woman with an attractive face and gorgeous body who had figured out how to live lavishly without actually making any money of her own. That certainly shouldn't have been enough to give her a death sentence, Burke thought. She had apparently been attacked in her sleep. Her throat had been sliced open nearly to the vertebrae.

Dornan's household staff had also been summarily murdered, their bodies riddled with machine gun bullets. Neither the very old nor the very young had been spared.

"Savages," Burke said softly to the empty office. "Only savages kill civilians. Only monsters kill like that."

The soldiers had been killed by bullets apparently fired from small-caliber pistols. That sounded like the work of Svetlana and Tatiana. How had the two women, armed with mere handguns, survived a gunfight against men carrying AK-47s—a weapon that was arguably the finest assault rifle in the world?

Burke pushed the question out of his mind. It made no difference, really, how Svetlana and Tatiana survived the gunfight. What mattered now was finding the ZT-550—and gaining secure possession of it.

Rio de Janeiro, Brazil

"I'm willing to listen to any theories you have about what is going on," Tatiana said wearily. "Please, just make me understand what the hell is happening."

She was on her bed in the hotel room with her legs folded beneath her, sitting on her feet with her knees splayed outward. The young woman was completely naked, her body still moist from the hot shower she had just taken. There was a white towel over her thighs.

She and Svetlana had returned to the hotel an hour earlier, and though Tatiana kept expecting the Brazilian police to show up at their door at any moment, Svetlana was convinced that their escape from Sigmund Dornan's mansion had gone undetected.

On this, her first assignment, Tatiana had already shot and killed a man. She had willingly had sex with a man she understood was a mass murderer. She was thoroughly and completely confused regarding just about everything that mattered, and as near as she could tell, she was not one tiny bit closer to gaining custody of the poison-filled suitcases than when she'd set out on her mission.

Her personal confidence meter was hovering close to empty. It would hit bottom very soon unless something favorable happened.

"Colonel Galiano's competition with Colonel Mendoza has kicked into high gear. What happened last night was a planned assassination. No doubt about that. We just happened to get caught in the middle of it. Those soldiers hadn't figured on anyone shooting back at them. That's why we did as well against them as we did."

"So, in other words, we pretty much just got lucky?" Tatiana asked.

"Get some sleep," Svetlana said quietly to Tatiana. "You're exhausted, and so am I. Later, we'll figure out what our next move should be. Someone has the ZT-550—either Colonel Mendoza, or General Ragga. If what happened at Dornan's was an attack intended to include Mendoza, then there's going to be all-out war between Mendoza and Galiano."

"This is all getting so confusing." Tatiana sighed as she ran fingers through her long, silky hair. "These are all such bad guys. For the life of me I can't figure out who the worst one of the bunch is."

"The worst one right now is whoever has possession of the ZT-550. Until we've got our hands on that chemical weapon, nothing else matters. That means we're going to have to stick close to the men."

"I'd like to hear some ideas on how you intend to find them, particularly if it *was* Colonel Galiano who attacked the mansion last night. For all we know, he's got a hit-squad searching for us right now."

"We know it was Galiano. Those were his men we killed. What we don't know is whether he wanted to kill Mendoza along with Dornan. That's the intangible."

"Why kill the arms dealer?"

"To disrupt any sale Mendoza and Dornan might have had with a third party?" It was more of a question than a statement of fact. Svetlana stepped out of her panties and tossed them aside. "The situation keeps getting more unstable by the moment. Get some sleep. I get the feeling we're going to have to be at our absolute sharpest—and I do mean razor-sharp—very, very soon."

Rio de Janeiro, Brazil

Colonel Galiano looked at the man seated in the straight-backed chair. Though the man—international arms dealer Sigmund Dornan—was bleeding from numerous cuts all over his body, Colonel Galiano felt no sympathy for the man.

"You have a choice of living or dying," Colonel Galiano

explained quietly. He leaned closer to the chair, visually inspecting the ropes that bound Dornan's wrists and ankles. "If you tell me where the weapon is, you will live. If you continue to withhold information, I will continue to cut little pieces off you until you finally tell me everything it is that I want to know." Colonel Galiano inspected the silver blade of the knife he held. The blade was razor sharp and stained with Dornan's blood. "Be reasonable. You know you'll talk eventually. Why put yourself through such pain and suffering needlessly?"

Sigmund Dornan looked down at his thighs. Both thighs were bleeding. Colonel Galiano had stabbed each one several times already. Not terribly hard. He didn't drive the knife to the hilt into the soft flesh. Instead, he just jabbed it a half-inch deep, cutting the skin and causing hideous pain without ever actually putting Sigmund's life in jeopardy. This was what frightened Sigmund more than the pain.

"The ZT-550 . . . it's all I have left," the arms dealer said quietly, more to himself than to his tormentor, Colonel Galiano. "It'll be my last big sale. My last big score, and then I retire."

"Yes. Retire. A wise move for you to make." Colonel Galiano looked down. There were two severed fingers on the floor. He nudged them with the toe of his shoe. "Tell me where the weapon is before you have nothing but stumps for hands."

Sigmund looked at the fingers on the floor. Twenty minutes earlier they had been attached to his hands. Now they were lifeless gray organic matter on the floor.

He tried to remember a time when his life had been so golden, so blemish-free. All that now seemed so distant.

"The ZT-550 is in two stainless steel suitcases. There's a hidden compartment in the library . . . a bookshelf pulls away from the wall. I hide things behind it." He looked up into Colonel Galiano's impassive face. "On the north wall. You'll find the activator switch behind my copy of *War and Peace*."

Colonel Galiano smiled. "'War and Peace'? How appropriate. And now your reward for cooperation."

"You promised to set me free."

"Yes, I promised, and I loathe men who cannot keep their word," the colonel said as he plunged the blade deep into the bound man's chest. "Now you are free from pain . . . you pig."

Cancun, Mexico

More than a week later, Colonel Galiano sat in his hotel room, staring at the two stainless steel suitcases. Inside the suitcases were four cylindrical canisters. Each canister contained fifteen pounds of ZT-550. The sixty pounds of deadly powder was enough to kill hundreds of thousands of people, provided the chemical was dispensed into the atmosphere properly, and in an area with a compact population base.

Since taking possession of the ZT-550, the days had melded one into the other, each one almost indistinguishable from the one before it. Colonel Galiano no longer knew who his friends were, and who were his enemies. He had thought of going home, but he discarded that. He couldn't go there just yet. Not until he had someone in his corner to protect him, someone powerful enough to make the military leaders pay attention to what Colonel Galiano had to say. He needed a country like Cuba to defend him against the charges of treason that would surely be leveled against him by Colonel Mendoza.

In the darkness of his inexpensive room, Colonel Galiano smiled. He had escaped from Brazil without anyone knowing where he was headed, and he'd managed to do it while maintaining control of the ZT-550. He was now within easy boating distance from Cuba. Soon . . . very soon . . . he would have a meeting with *El Presidente,* and then the colonel would explain just how valuable the two suitcases were, and how valuable the colonel himself was.

Cuba's leader would see the brilliance of Colonel Galiano's mind. He would see the wisdom of releasing the ZT-550 on United States' soil. Colonel Galiano was convinced of it.

He just had to wait until his messages to Cuba went through the proper channels. Once he was summoned to Cuba's leaders, all of the colonel's dreams would begin to come true. Of this, he had the confidence of a True Believer.

Cancun, Mexico

Svetlana crossed the room slowly, feeling the eyes of the men on her. She was dressed in a white lacy bra with matching bikini panties. She wore pumps with five-inch stiletto heels. Her tanned flesh glowed healthily. Her makeup was delicate, highlighting her features, defining her cheekbones and the full-lipped mouth that seemed to give silent promises of heavenly pleasure.

"Here you go," Svetlana said as she handed General Ragga a crystal glass with ice cubes and scotch in it.

The general smiled and nodded, though he did not say anything. He tried to keep from staring at Svetlana breasts inside the bra, but looking elsewhere was all but impossible. With each step she took, her breasts jiggled and swayed erotically. Ten minutes earlier, while standing in the three-room hotel suite, Colonel Mendoza had casually asked Svetlana if she wouldn't mind removing her dress so that he and the general would have someone pretty to look at while they discussed the important business matters that had caused them to leave Rio de Janeiro in such a hurry. Svetlana simply smiled and removed her dress. She walked to the closet, took out a hanger, and hung her dress up. Then she returned to the small wet bar where she poured herself some champagne before fixing drinks for both Colonel Mendoza and General Ragga.

The men were sitting on high stools by the small bar. Svetlana made a point of standing so close to them that they could smell the delicate perfume she had applied earlier between her breasts and to her wrists. The perfume was called Opium, a fact both men, had they known its name, would undoubtedly find ironic and appropriate.

"The men will pick up his scent soon," Colonel Mendoza said, turning his attention away from Svetlana and toward his superior officer. "Once they do, Colonel Galiano is a dead man and the ZT-550 goes to the highest bidder as soon as possible."

"Have you heard from your men?" the general asked.

"Nothing yet. We hit Cancun eighteen hours after Galiano. That's not enough time to make the trail cold. My men will find him. Don't think they won't."

Svetlana pretended to be concentrating on the contents of the dry bar, inspecting this bottle and then that one. What she was really concentrating on was the conversation between General Ragga and Colonel Mendoza. During the days that she had been with them, they had dropped their suspicions of her and had begun to speak more openly in front of her — exactly as she had wanted.

Svetlana suspected that Colonel Mendoza had intended on leaving her behind after he discovered that Sigmund Dornan had been murdered and the ZT-550 was missing. But then, as he and General Ragga were screaming at each other in the hotel room back in Rio de Janeiro, each blaming the other for the lousy turn of events, she showed up at the hotel with Tatiana at her side. The women calmed the men down and made them realize they weren't mad at each other, they were mad at someone else. It was foolish, Svetlana had said, to be angry with a person who has done nothing wrong.

Svetlana had played Mendoza like a violin, and when it was discovered that Colonel Galiano had taken a flight from Brazil to Mexico, it wasn't too difficult for her to get invitations to come along to Mexico. Svetlana and Tatiana had become a package deal. One did not go without the other.

There was a soft knock at the door. Svetlana glanced at Colonel Mendoza. She wasn't interested in flaunting her charms in front of the three cold-eyed, battle-hardened soldiers that had traveled with them from Brazil to Mexico.

"I'll answer it," the colonel said, getting off the padded stool, leaving his drink behind on the bar.

A moment later Colonel Mendoza opened the door wide and Tatiana stepped in. Unlike the typical appearance of an eighteen-year-old she had originally adopted, she was now wearing a chic cotton dress of pale blue that came down to the middle of her slender thighs with a wide, white leather belt surrounding her waist. When she saw Svetlana standing near the dry bar wearing only her bra and panties, Tatiana's stride faltered briefly.

"This is a little more casual than I had expected," Tatiana said as she approached. "Actually, it's one hell of a lot more casual — to be truthful."

"It was my suggestion," Colonel Mendoza explained as he ushered her across the room. "Your sister doesn't seem to mind putting her loveliness on display. Gentle on the eyes, isn't she?"

"What's happening?" Tatiana asked, her tone soft. She was looking at General Ragga when she asked the question, though it could have been for anyone in the room.

"Waiting for news," General Ragga answered.

He slipped his arm around Tatiana's slender waist and pulled her closer, forcing her to stand between his spread knees as he remained seated on the tall bar stool. He had spent the past couple nights in bed with Tatiana and he still hadn't gotten his fill of her.

"General, please," Tatiana protested mildly, pushing

against his chest.

"How about a little kiss?"

"General, there's a time and place for everything, and this is not the time and certainly not the place."

"Why not?"

Tatiana forced herself to laugh. She answered, "Because we're not alone, that's why!"

"Your sister's standing in her bra and panties," General Ragga replied. His right hand slipped down from the small of Tatiana's back to the taut curve of her bottom. He squeezed her through her dress, and she squealed in protest. "Your sister's not a prude," he continued. "Not like you. Why don't you stop acting like a child and loosen up a little?"

"But General . . ."

Tatiana felt her dress being raised up in back. She wanted to push the general's hand away, but she had already seen what his temper was like when he was angry. Any resistance to his wishes could set off his fury.

"Give a little kiss," General Ragga continued. He cupped her ass in his hand, squeezing her through her panties. As he did this, he brought his mouth to hers. When he kissed Tatiana, he forced his tongue between her lips.

Tatiana felt his powerful hand slide inside the waistband of her panties. By the time the kiss ended, there was a bulge in the front of the general's trousers. When the kiss ended, he looked at Tatiana, his right hand inside her panties, his left hand at the small of her back to hold her so that she couldn't move away.

Like Tatiana, the general had changed in the past few days. The general was now a lecherous, authoritarian leader who enjoyed lording his power over her, especially in front of Colonel Mendoza.

"For a kid, you're one hell of a kisser," General Ragga said, his voice low, tense with the burgeoning lust going through his system. "How about getting down on your knees?"

Tatiana gasped at the suggestion.

Colonel Mendoza said quietly, but with great authority, "Go on, Tatiana. You don't need to be shy." He slipped his arm around Svetlana's waist and pulled her against his hip. "Your sister's not shy at all."

"That's not true," Svetlana replied. Her voice displayed tension now. "I don't mind walking around to let your friend look at me, but I didn't know my sister would be here to see the show."

For long seconds there was absolute silence as the men looked at Svetlana and Tatiana. The unspoken question that hovered in the air was: would the men accept *no* as an answer?

Colonel Mendoza broke the silence. He placed his hand atop Svetlana's head and curled his fingers slowly, entwining his fingers in her hair until it was wrapped around his fist. His dark eyes glittered menacingly.

"You're the older of you two," Colonel Mendoza said through clenched teeth. "Show her how it's supposed to be done."

Colonel Mendoza pushed down on Svetlana, forcing her to sink slowly to her knees. He did this with his right hand, and with his left he unzipped his trousers and brought his cock out.

Svetlana looked up and over at Tatiana. For a moment the two simply looked at each other. And then Svetlana, while still looking into Tatiana's eyes, leaned forward and kissed Colonel Mendoza's offering. She began licking his cock, and as she did, she closed her eyes.

"I love a powerful man," she said in a carnal whisper. She looked up into Mendoza's eyes. "You understood that about me from the beginning, didn't you?"

Tatiana knew that Svetlana had said precisely what he had

wanted to hear.

"And you're my powerful man now." She gave him a sultry smile. "Or should I say you are *our* powerful man now?"

Tatiana knelt beside Svetlana, then leaned to the side and kissed her on the cheek.

"Let me help," Tatiana said quietly. "I think he'd like us both." She looked up at Mendoza. "And I know that *I'd* like to help."

General Ragga watched Svetlana with eyes practically bulging out of his head. He stared, hardly breathing, at what was happening so nearby. He hadn't really thought that the two gorgeous sisters would go along with his lewd, hastily conceived little plans. He'd given the orders more as a bluff than anything else, something to have a few laughs about later with Colonel Mendoza when the idea went nowhere. But instead, he was watching one of the most beautiful women he'd ever met in his entire life — Svetlana Simonov — giving an intimate performance for his voyeuristic pleasure, while her sister kneeled beside her!

For more years than Tatiana had been alive, General Ragga had bullied his way through life and into a position of power. He wasn't about to be standing there doing nothing while Colonel Mendoza, an officer but one of inferior rank to himself, had a stunningly beautiful woman on her knees and giving him a blow job. General Ragga looked at Tatiana's profile. She was truly gorgeous to look at, with her blonde hair that cascaded over her shoulders, her trim figure, her pert little nose and her luscious little bosom. She was staring as though in a daze at Svetlana.

"How old did you say you were?" General Ragga asked her.

Seconds passed before Tatiana seemed to realize that she

had been given a direct question by the general. She replied quietly, "I don't think I ever really did tell you how old I am."

"Old enough," General Ragga replied as he pulled down his zipper.

"General Ragga," Colonel Mendoza said, calmly even though his cock was hard as stone and Svetlana Simonov was nibbling on it with her lips like she was a woman starving for a *real* man. "Would you like to have both ladies at the same time?"

"You don't mind?" General Ragga replied, clearly surprised that Svetlana was being offered.

"Consider her a gift from me."

Svetlana heard the words, and she wondered about just how slow and painful her execution would be if she castrated the colonel with her teeth right then and there. She hated the colonel for his attitude . . . but she also felt a pleasing twinge in her pussy at the thought of sexually sharing a man with another woman—more specifically, with Tatiana. Svetlana and Tatiana crawled closer to each other. Svetlana leaned in close, so that her shoulder was touching Tatiana. She looked up into the general's face.

I could kill you without losing a moment's sleep, she thought.

With the mission in mind, she said to him, "I want you." And then more softly, with a distinctly erotic and not-so-vaguely obscene lilt to her Russian-accented voice, she added, "In my mouth." She put a hand demurely over her eyes, as though she could hardly believe the words that had just passed between her lips. "Especially in my mouth."

She uncovered her eyes and looked up into his. And without another word, Svetlana reached out, grabbed the man's shaft, and rather rudely pulled him out of Tatiana's mouth.

"It's my turn," Svetlana boldly declared with a theatrical

flourish before opening her mouth wide and sucking General Ragga's cock in so deeply that the rigid flesh nearly entered her throat. She moaned loudly, understanding that the men wanted her to be uninhibited.

This wasn't her first mission for Omega Force, and she had no illusions regarding what her mark wanted from her. She intended to give him everything he wanted and more . . . though the latter wasn't something that he wouldn't be quite so pleased to experience.

Tatiana watched as Svetlana dragged her lips back and forth over the general's lust-swollen cock. She could hear the old man's breathing quicken rapidly, and in the short span of time that she had been with him, she could tell that his lust was quickly soaring out of control. Tatiana heard the colonel and the general whispering to themselves above her. Apparently neither man could quite believe what was happening. Tatiana didn't care. All she wanted was to excite them so completely that neither one considered her or Svetlana a threat. It would be at that moment, when they looked at her and all they saw was a beautiful young woman who could provide licentious pleasure, that she would be their personal executioner.

"I thought we were supposed to share," Tatiana said after several more seconds passed. As though she was simply dying to have the general's cock back in her mouth, she made a pouting sound. For several seconds, she and Svetlana did a mini battle for control of the general's erection. Then Tatiana whispered, "Come on, be nice and share."

Tatiana pulled the general's cock out of Svetlana's mouth. When Svetlana looked at Tatiana, she said with just the expression in her eyes, *we've got them now!*

Tatiana's silent reply was, *Let's turn them inside-out and upside-down! When we close the trap on them, they'll never know what hit them!*

From that point forward, Tatiana and Svetlana were determined to give the general more pleasure than he was capable of accepting, and to that end, they succeeded in spectacular fashion. Not two minutes after they began giving him a tag-team blow job, with Svetlana caressing the head and shaft with her lips and tongue while Tatiana tantalized the testicles beneath, the general erupted, releasing his sperm into Svetlana's mouth.

"Kiss . . . kiss your sister," General Ragga said, his fingers entwined in Svetlana's hair, his cock still filling her mouth. He was gulping in air.

Svetlana held the pungent tasting cum in her mouth. Still on her knees, she looked into Tatiana's eyes. Then, very slowly, she leaned toward Tatiana, her hand on Svetlana's shoulder. For long seconds she simply looked into Tatiana's eyes. Then, as she leaned closer, Tatiana was aware that her heart was hammering against her ribs as hard as it ever had. Their mouths touched, and it was Tatiana who first opened her mouth. She eased her tongue between Svetlana's lips, felt the early hesitation, and then the acceptance. Tatiana felt a tightening in her own pussy as unexpected pleasure surged through her system.

The evidence of satisfied passion—cum that was salty, thick, and slippery—passed between their mouths. Svetlana and Tatiana kissed deeply, tongues moving from mouth to mouth. They continued kissing long after the cum had been swallowed. Neither was in any hurry for the kiss to come to its logical conclusion.

CHAPTER THIRTEEN

This is more than I had bargained for, thought Svetlana as she looked into Tatiana's eyes and saw the uncertainty there. *She's so young and inexperienced,* she thought next. But then another thought came into her consciousness, and when it did, a shiver went up her spine. *Young . . . and beautiful.*

How long had it been since she had truly enjoyed been with another woman? It was a tempting question, especially since she really didn't have an answer that came readily to mind. Whoever the last woman was obviously hadn't left much of a memory. But an even more tempting and tantalizing question immediately made an entrance into her consciousness. How long had it been since she had sexually been with another young woman as lovely, innocent-looking, and tempting as Tatiana?

The answer to that question came to her in an instant. Never. Tatiana was the most beguiling mix of sensual allure and charming, milky-skinned, blue-eyed innocence she'd ever come across. And the combination of physical and emotional innocence made Svetlana's clit both tighten and tingle and fresh cream ooze to the lips of her cunt.

It had been a long time since a female had aroused Svetlana's libido to such an extent.

Svetlana tried to tell herself that Tatiana wasn't one of the perks that came along with being an Omega Force agent, but this effort at self-deception was woefully inadequate for the feelings that were quite suddenly going through her system, and firing up a libido that she had thought she had trained sufficiently to always be professionally aloof regarding such matters.

"Can I kiss you again?"

It took a moment for Svetlana to realize that she herself had spoken the question.

Several seconds passed before Tatiana closed her eyes, then almost imperceptibly nodded her head.

She's so very lovely, Svetlana thought. *So very, very lovely. There's an innocence to her that makes me want to protect her.* She closed her eyes for just a moment as another thought came to her—one that was as real as the first. *And seduce her. I want to see her face between my thighs. I want to feel her mouth against my pussy. I want to feel her tongue pushing between the lips of my cunt, and then caressing my clit.*

"Are you sure?" Once again Svetlana was a little surprised to discover that she herself had spoken the words. When Tatiana gave the briefest of nods, Svetlana whispered, "Fuck, I could come right now without even kissing you."

"Then you should kiss me now . . . shouldn't you?" There was a faintly tremulous quality to her words that Svetlana found extraordinarily erotic.

On her knees on the floor with other people so nearby, Svetlana was suddenly able to completely block everyone other than Tatiana out of her consciousness. She looked down at the young woman's pink-tipped breasts and was pleased to see that her nipples were distinctly erect—no doubt with passion.

We're on a mission, and there are certain things that she's got to do and I've got to do, Svetlana thought, trying to rationalize the erotic feelings that were now going through her with lightning speed. *But that doesn't make the fact that I want to taste her pussy any less real.*

She placed her palms lightly against Tatiana's cheeks, and for a moment simply looked into the young woman's eyes. She heard a masculine sigh, and was reminded that she and

Tatiana were not alone, and though she tried to tell herself that she was only playing a role like an actress would, the fact that she was ravenous to taste Tatiana's kisses was very real in her heart and soul — and it had nothing to do with being an actress playing a role, or being an agent for Omega Force.

She moved forward, and when her lips were an inch from Tatiana's, she whispered, "You make me wet. You have from the very first moment I saw you." The breath caught in her throat. "That's never happened before. I don't always tell the truth, but this time I am."

"If you don't kiss me right now," Tatiana replied, in a voice so soft only Svetlana could hear, "I'll either kill you or eat your pussy until you think you're going to die." She closed her eyes. "But one way or another, I think one of us is going to think she's going to die." She inhaled deeply. "But only the little death," she said, using the euphemism for an orgasm.

"If we're lucky, we'll both die . . . just a little."

The kiss started slowly, hesitantly, Svetlana not entirely sure how far or forcefully she could go with Tatiana. Since she was the superior officer on the mission, she could literally command Tatiana to do whatever she wanted. It was tempting for Svetlana to pull rank . . . but she wouldn't . . . though if she did . . . .

Colonel Ragga's voice interrupted Svetlana's concentration when he said, "No! I want more than that! Let's see some tongue action!"

You insufferable bastard, Svetlana thought bitterly. There were times when she despised men. *You ruin everything you have influence over.*

She ended the kiss with Tatiana, then leaned back and looked into the young woman's eyes. She saw an understanding in those blue depths, and an awareness that what they were doing to each other wasn't just about giving each other pleasure, it was also about satisfying the voyeuristic desires of the men they both despised. Svetlana wished it was otherwise, but she couldn't say that to Tatiana.

Svetlana put her arms slowly around Tatiana's naked body, and pulled her into a soft, warm hug. For thirty seconds they were naked and breast to breast, then Svetlana whispered into Tatiana's ear, "There going to come the time when we're going to kiss without an audience."

They separated for a moment and looked into each other's eyes. After several seconds, Tatiana smiled — a bit sheepishly, Svetlana thought — and said, "Sister, make me come. Give me the best orgasm of my life, and do it with your tongue." She spoke loudly enough so that the men could hear her taboo desires.

She's got it! Svetlana thought. *She's in character, and she knows exactly what the mark wants to hear.*

In an exaggerated move, Svetlana stuck her tongue out between her lips, and Tatiana leaned forward and began to suck lightly on her tongue, almost sipping it, like she was taking small sips of a very expensive champagne. The sensation of Tatiana's lips surrounding her tongue was nearly sensual enough to make Svetlana come instantly.

"Holy fuck," General Ragga said softly. "Sisters. Real fucking sisters kissing like that."

Svetlana thought, *No, you stupid fuck. We're pretend sisters, just like you're a pretend stud. You're just too stupid to understand the difference.*

The thought almost made Svetlana smile, but her lips were busy at that moment making delightful and delicious contact with Tatiana's. The fact that she was pretending to be kissing her own sister added spice to the kiss, though Svetlana tried very hard to pretend this wasn't so. There were taboo passions that she wouldn't cross . . . but the fact of the matter was, she wasn't Tatiana's sister, and in point of fact, hadn't even met her until very recently. But to pretend she was kissing her own little sister . . . .

Pleasure is fleeting, she thought. *Better to accept it while you can.*

Svetlana felt only a little guilty about her own self-justification.

As Tatiana's tongue slipped delicately, almost hesitantly between Svetlana's lips, another groan came from the audience, though this time Sven wasn't sure whether it was General Ragga or Colonel Mendoza who had reacted to the lesbian performance she and Tatiana were providing under only a little coercion.

Blindly, since she was still kissing Tatiana, Svetlana reached her left hand out slowly, tentatively, her fingers splayed, every nerve in her body vibrantly alive. First, she touched the girl's thigh. It was naked, and the skin was soft as velvet. When her fingertips came in contact with Tatiana's thigh, it was as though an electrical charge had gone through Svetlana.

I'm not really like this, Svetlana thought. *I just don't react this way to kissing a woman, especially not on assignment.*

But Tatiana wasn't just a woman. She was a *young* woman, and she was both innocent and cunning, naïve and wise . . . and beautiful. Blonde and petite and her breasts looked as delicious as anything Svetlana had ever seen, with the exception of Burke's cock and her grandmother's Thanksgiving turkey.

Svetlana slipped her hand slowly up Tatiana's thigh, touching her only with the pads of her fingertips. The contact of flesh to flesh made Svetlana's juices flow freely, and she felt her pussy become more moist and ready for penetration — even though no man was involved in turning her on so much.

"You can touch me," Tatiana said, her lips nuzzling Svetlana's as she spoke. "Your touch is divine. You can touch me wherever you want . . . whenever you want."

A moment later Svetlana's fingertips were gently caressing the lips of Tatiana's pussy, and she could feel the dampness there, and knew exactly what it meant. A woman always knew when another woman is faking it — or if she was really excited.

She's as turned on as I am. The revelation caused juice to lubricate her own entrance even more. She was ready for a cock, but that didn't seem to be on the menu just now. *I'll bet she eats pussy divinely.* That thought brought another surge of fluid to the lips of her cunt. Svetlana found virtually every aspect about the situation to be a pussy-wetting awareness.

Svetlana was about as ready to have her pussy get pleasured by another woman as she ever had been in her life — and she knew it. Tatiana had brought her to the brink of ecstasy in an astonishingly short period of time. She had done it with only a few kisses and some blue-eyed glances that said without words that she would do everything she could to please.

With just the tip of her middle finger, Svetlana separated the lips of Tatiana's sex. When she did, Tatiana moaned directly into her mouth as they kissed, letting her know that she approved of what was being done. With very little hesitation, Svetlana slid her finger upward over the delicate folds, found the young woman's distinctly erect clit, and began caressing it with a firm, circular motion.

"Oh, God," Tatiana gasped, her lips still touching Svetlana's. "You're magical."

Svetlana smiled, ran her tongue around the circumference of Tatiana's mouth, then said loud enough so that the men could hear, "Not magic, just very, very . . . *inspired.*"

Svetlana kissed Tatiana's neck, and the soft purr of approval she received was nearly a narcotic to her senses. To feel the girl responding to what Svetlana was doing to her was everything and more that Svetlana could want.

"Deeper," Tatiana said, her tone somewhere between being conversational and a whisper.

She knows how to play this game, Svetlana thought, then pushed her finger into Tatiana's pussy until her palm was pressed against the agent's sex lips.

"Sisters," General Ragga said with awe in his voice.

Shut up, you bastard, Svetlana thought, hating the fact that the odious man could so easily destroy the fantasy that Svetlana was trying very hard to create as she kissed her way slowly down from Tatiana's neck toward her small, perfectly formed, pink-tipped breasts. *I can give her more pleasure than you ever could.*

Svetlana kissed Tatiana's abdomen, taking her time, kissing slowly and a bit loudly. She was headed for Tatiana's belly button, and as she made her way there, she could sense that she was being watched closely. The men in the room were breathless with anticipation, wondering whether or not Svetlana would go down on her own little sister.

"Do it," General Ragga said when Svetlana was kissing Tatiana's abdomen, inches above her pussy. "And tilt your head back a little. And keep your hair out of the way. I want to see it when your mouth presses against your own sister's cunt."

Burke was so right about putting Tatiana on this mission and making her cover story being my younger sister. I'm about to put a hook in the men they'll never get rid of. All I have to do is pretend that Tatiana's my little sister and they'll be under my spell.

Svetlana flicked her tongue into Tatiana's navel, and was pleased when she heard the soft, somewhat high-pitched cry of erotic delight that immediately followed. She then stuck her tongue deeply into Tatiana's navel, and the shocked gasp of erotic pleasure confirmed that the young woman was in a state of deep eroticism.

"Come for me," Svetlana said softly, but loud enough so that the men in the room could hear what she said. Though she found herself inexorably drawn deeper and deeper into the eroticism of the scenario, she was professional enough to know that she was being judged by people who could do her fatal harm if they thought she was someone other than who she was pretending to be. "I want to taste your pussy when you come on my mouth."

Svetlana captured the small, throbbing nub of Tatiana's clitoris between her lips and started to suck on it softly, very tenderly, and as she did so, she worked her tongue from side to side, adding gentle oral friction to her caresses.

"Un . . ." Tatiana said, but then the words died away in her throat. Finally, she said, "Un-fucking-believable."

Svetlana sucked somewhat harder on Tatiana's clit for several more seconds. Then she said, "Not while you're with me. When you are with me, ecstasy is what you can expect, not what you'll be surprised by."

"Oh," Tatiana purred as the warm, rasping tongue slid over her passion-aroused clit. "That's it. That's it. Right there."

Come for me. Svetlana was shockingly aware that she'd never thought that before while giving cunnilingus to another woman. *I want you feel you shiver when you come on my mouth.*

"Oh, God! That's so good!" Tatiana said, her body quivering.

She's going to come soon, Svetlana thought, her sexual self-confidence about giving pleasure to other women skyrocketing by the second.

Svetlana tried to pretend that her actions were entirely assignment-oriented, but she knew in her heart that this wasn't true. She wasn't licking Tatiana's pussy with an almost fanatical desperation because she had an audience of enemies she wanted to impress, she was doing it because she wanted to give Tatiana more pleasure than she could withstand. Once Tatiana reached her upper level of ecstasy, she'd have to climax—and when she did, Svetlana wanted to be there, tonguing her clit when the release of ultimate sensation ripped through her body like a hurricane.

Come for me, Svetlana thought as she sucked on Tatiana's clit. *And scream when you do.*

As though following orders, Tatiana instant arched her back, mashing here pussy against Svetlana's mouth, and cried out, "Oh, God! Oh, fuck! I'm going to come."

She wasn't lying. A moment after putting words to sensation going through her, she climaxed. It wasn't a gentle, mildly satisfying orgasm. It was a rip-the-spine-out-of-your-back variety.

Svetlana's mouth was still against Tatiana's pussy when she smiled, knowing that she had inspired a climax to be remembered.

Someday, I'll make her give me one of those, Svetlana thought with selfish greed. *And as soon as she does, I'll give her another one so that she'll owe me.*

Suddenly the hotel door burst open, and three young soldiers in civilian clothing burst into the room.

The eldest of the three deadly young men said rapidly, "General! Colonel! We've found Colonel Galiano! He's at the pier on his way to Cuba right now!"

"You're not leaving us behind!" Svetlana declared, standing on the pier as Colonel Mendoza and General Ragga, along with their three unsmiling soldiers, readied the boat.

"Svetlana, you don't know what's going on here," Colonel Mendoza said, putting his hands on her shoulders. "We've had a lot of fun recently, but what I'm about to do could be very dangerous, and I can't have you along. I don't want to put you or your sister in jeopardy."

Tatiana stepped forward. "Being with you and General Ragga is the most excitement I've ever known. I want to go with you, just like Svetlana does."

Colonel Mendoza looked at the beautiful ladies, with their pale flesh, their naked bodies, their lovely eyes and honey blonde hair. All they had taken with them when they all hurried out of the hotel was two suitcases each, but that wasn't surprising, considering their feverish departure from Rio de Janeiro earlier.

Colonel Mendoza looked at General Ragga and shrugged his shoulders.

"I don't want to hear a word of complaint from either of you," Colonel Mendoza said, wagging a threatening finger at the women. "When I tell you something, it's an order, not a suggestion. When you're with me you're under my command . . . and people under my command follow my orders — or suffer greatly. Agreed?"

Behind them, one of the soldiers fired up the big diesel marine engine. Blue smoke coughed out before the engine began chugging properly.

Svetlana kissed the colonel on the cheek and pulled her suitcases onto the boat.

Colonel Galiano was sweating. It was a hot evening, and even though the boat he had rented was moving at a nice pace, he just kept perspiring.

On the deck at his feet were the two stainless steel suitcases containing the ZT-550. He was certain that when he finally reached Cuba, he would be rewarded for his heroism. Back in his home country, there would be parades in his honor. The civil wars would end and finally there would be peace in his country, as there was peace in Cuba. Yes, Cuba was the answer for everything that he could hope for.

Vague images of himself as an older man drifted through the colonel's brain. He imagined what he would look like with a beard, one like *el Presidente* had grown. Yes, that would be just the right touch to give him the kind of political immortality that previous presidents of the island nation had enjoyed.

He smiled. It was just a matter of time before he experienced all that he had dreamed of for so long. He told himself that he only had to be patient. Just for a little while longer, he had to be patient.

The colonel checked his compass heading and smiled, resisting the urge to give the old diesel engine more fuel.

Patience, Colonel Galiano told himself. *Cuba's less than a hundred miles away by now. You'll get there soon enough. Soon enough. Push the engine and it'll blow a piston.*

He looked in all directions. Nothing but endless night. Clouds overhead obscured what little moonlight and starlight tried to illuminate the Gulf of Mexico.

The colonel was tired, but he didn't dare sleep. When he was in Cuba, then he could sleep. He would curl up with young virgins that the Cuban government would provide for him, and he'd sleep the sleep of the blessed.

He decided it wouldn't hurt to close his eyes for just a moment.

Soon enough he would be a hero. Soon enough Cuban journalists would be asking him questions and hanging upon his every word.

Soon enough.

"What are we going to do when we find him?" General Ragga asked.

He was sitting in the small cabin below deck. The throb of the diesel engines was continuous, and the sound was beginning to get on his nerves. To make matters worse, he wasn't at all interested in getting too close to Cuba. While some of his countrymen considered the Cuban leaders as saviors, the general wasn't one of them. He knew how impoverished the Cuban soldiers were, and he didn't like the thought of being impoverished. More significantly, he knew what the penalty was for disobeying even the most inconsequential order given by *el Presidente.* The *person* holding the title wasn't all that important. What was *really* important was the title. With that, you could have or do anything. Without it, a person's options in life suddenly became decidedly rather different.

"The man at the pier said he was alone," Colonel Mendoza answered. "That crazy fool thinks he can make it to Cuba."

"I knew I should have had that bastard killed years ago," General Ragga said. He made a growling sound in his throat, angry with himself. "You've got to kill the sick ones while they are weak, not wait until they're strong. That only makes matters worse."

He looked down to see Svetlana's hand moving up and down on his cock. She was curled up on the deck of the boat, completely naked, occasionally giving him a leisurely delivered blow job. The general couldn't remember the last time he'd been aroused so many times in a day.

Between Svetlana and Tatiana, General Ragga couldn't seem to get enough sex. He hadn't been this insatiable in the last thirty years. He had also stopped being careful of what he said in front of Svetlana and Tatiana. It was abundantly clear to him that the women had a fetish for powerful older men, and they liked exciting new adventures. It made the rest of his life so much easier to deal with.

Svetlana looked up at the major general and said, "Let me in on what's going on. Maybe Tatiana and I can help."

Colonel Mendoza, who was getting a casual blow job from Tatiana, said, "It's a bad business, but nothing for you to worry about. A man stole something, and we've got to get it back from him."

Tatiana raised up onto her knees, releasing Colonel Mendoza from her oral embrace. She said, "You're talking about Colonel Galiano, right? Well, he's got the hots for me. Maybe that'll help you somehow."

Colonel Mendoza looked down. He caught a long, silky tendril of Tatiana's hair and twirled it around his forefinger. His cock was hard as rock once again, his erection sticking out through the fly of his trousers.

"You know, you just might be able to distract him, at that," the colonel said after a full thirty seconds of thoughtful silence. "It might be dangerous, though. He's an unstable man. Very savage."

General Ragga smiled. Perhaps he had around him men more capable than he had thought.

General Ragga was beginning to get nervous. No, that wasn't accurate. He wasn't *beginning* to get nervous, he *was* nervous. Very nervous. To say the word *scared* wouldn't have been an overstatement by any credible standard of judgment. The sun would be up soon, he had been on the water for hours, and still there wasn't any sign of Colonel Galiano's boat. Peering through the ten-power binoculars, the general scanned the horizon, searching for any sign of another boat. He hadn't moved in twenty minutes, and he could feel sweat trickling down his spine, making his shirt stick to his body.

"It's going to be a hot one today," Colonel Mendoza said as he approached.

The general did not take the field glasses from his eyes as he continued to scan eastward into the Gulf of Mexico.

"It's going to be *too* hot if we can't catch Colonel Galiano." General Ragga studied his partner in crime. "You don't suppose that crazy bastard might find an ally in Cuba, do you?"

"No," Colonel Mendoza replied. He handed the general the binoculars. Then, after a beat, he said with obvious unease, "I hope not."

General Ragga said in a raspy, violence-laden voice, "I've been spending too much time between a pair of silky thighs and not enough time thinking! I've underestimated the threat that Colonel Galiano poses to all of us with his stinking grandiose schemes. These damned women are going to be the death of me yet!"

Tatiana walked toward the bow of the boat. Her slender, petite body was completely naked, her breasts bobbing tautly with her steps.

"Oh, gentlemen," Tatiana said, a smile on her lips, a slightly sarcastic tone to her voice. "I think you're missing something."

"Shut up!" General Ragga said venomously.

Tatiana stepped closer, obviously ignoring the three soldiers who were standing with her. She put her hand on General Ragga's chest and smiled up into his face, ignoring his bad mood.

"Still can't find your man, can you?"

"Think that's funny? How about I throw your ass overboard and see how funny that is?"

"You've been so locked in on what you're looking for that you've got blinders on," Tatiana explained. "Look over there." She pointed in a southwesterly direction. "See? You can just barely see the bow."

"What the — ?"

General Ragga and Colonel Mendoza both turned in the direction that the teenager had pointed. The general held the binoculars to his eyes.

"Son of a bitch," General Ragga whispered, turning the focus adjustment on the binoculars to get a better view. "I'll be a son of a bitch . . ."

Tatiana said, "We passed him in the darkness. Now he's behind us, and from the looks of things, he's off course. Svetlana spotted him a moment ago and told me to tell you. It would seem us ladies are more than just window dressing in your lives, gentlemen. And we're more than just your personal sex slaves. We're soldiers . . . and we do the job better than your own men!"

General Ragga tried to hold the binoculars steady. There, perhaps two miles in the distance and just barely visible, was a boat. It looked old, and though he couldn't be sure it was the one that the renegade Colonel Galiano had rented, the odds were favorable that it was one and the same.

"Tatiana," the general said, holding the binoculars to his eyes, "you and your sister are going to get treated like princesses just as soon as we sell the ZT-550. That's a promise from me to you. You'll be treated like royalty."

"What's ZT-550?" Tatiana replied.

The general was pleased with her complete lack of understanding. He liked his women stupid, and was both pleased and confident that the one he was with was clearly stupid.

Colonel Galiano felt the gentle rocking of the boat, heard the splash of waves against the hull, and the constant, steady thrum of the engine turning the propeller. It felt so restful, so peaceful, to be sleeping at sea . . .

His eyes flew open, and he sat bolt upright. He had fallen asleep!

In an instant he was fully awake. He was still at the wheel of the rented boat. How long had he slept? A thousand unanswered questions ricocheted through his skull.

He looked at the compass and a string of obscenities were ripped from his throat. He was moving in a southeasterly direction, which meant that he was going too far south. His heading for Cuba had been straight as an arrow due east.

He checked the rest of the gauges. There was still plenty of fuel in the twin tanks, he saw reassuringly. He turned the wheel, changing course, watching the dial on the large compass turn slowly. Seconds ticked by as the colonel stared at the slowly spinning compass. When the compass was steady again, the arrow pointed north by northeast. Colonel Galiano at last breathed easily. He had made a mistake, but it wasn't a fatal one. Too many hours without sleep had taken its toll on his body, and though he had gone off course, the adjustment necessary to correct the problem was minor. He had lost time, but nothing more than that.

He looked into the eastern horizon and saw the pink hue of approaching sunrise. A new day was dawning in more ways than one, the colonel thought. Squinting in the darkness, he wondered just how far he was from Cuba. Would they send a boat out to greet him? It was a pleasant notion, though in his heart he knew such a thing wouldn't happen. *El Presidente* didn't yet know that a comrade hero was about to step upon the shores of Cuba with the most devastating weapon ever to be unleashed upon the United States.

In the distance he saw movement on the water. The colonel squinted, leaning over the wheel of the ancient boat that had cost him all the money he had. It was a boat, headed straight toward him.

A smile curled Colonel Galiano's lips. Though the approaching boat was still a solid mile away, the boat appeared old. That was a good sign. If General Ragga or Colonel Mendoza had followed him, they would be using a new speedboat. They never went anywhere unless they were blessed with creature comforts only the wealthy could afford.

I must be getting close to Cuba, the colonel thought. *It's some old fisherman coming out to complain that I'm fishing in his waters, stealing his catch.*

The colonel cursed himself for not having binoculars. As the boat drew nearer, coming from the northeast, Galiano could see someone was standing at the bow. Even from a distance he could tell that whoever stood at the bow was small and slender, not tall and broad-shouldered, like the soldiers that Colonel Mendoza surrounded himself with. He decided that the old fisherman probably had his young grandson with him.

Another smile touched the colonel's lips. Soon he would be surrounded by school children. He would thrill them with tales of his daring his exploits, telling the adventure of how he had single-handedly fought the United States, and delivered a crippling blow. In his mind's eye he could picture a sea of young faces with rapt expressions listening breathlessly to his exploits. Those young people would either want to be like him, or they would want to have sex with him because he was a hero to the country that could never be replaced.

The little boy on the bow of the approaching boat wasn't a little boy, though. In fact, it was a slender girl with long blonde hair, pale skin, and a way of walking that was distinctly erotic without being glaringly obvious about it.

Tatiana! It had to be Tatiana!

The boat continued approaching, and as it did, whatever doubts Colonel Galiano had vanished. His teenage lover had returned to him ... but how did she know where he was? How had she gotten this far from Rio de Janeiro?

Then, with fifty yards separating the boats, he saw her waving her arm frantically over her head. The girl began jumping up and down on the bow joyously. Across the surface of the water, the colonel could hear Tatiana as she shouted, "Svetlana! It's him! We've found him! I told you we would!"

And then, when she turned away from the wheel of the old boat and back toward the bow to face Colonel Galiano, Tatiana did something that shocked him.

She pulled her dress over her head and tossed the garment in the air. It was a seemingly spontaneous, light-hearted gesture, and it caused the colonel's jaw to drop open. He saw her small breasts bouncing, and there wasn't so much as a hint of pubic hair at the juncture of her thighs. Beneath the dress that here been nothing but Tatiana Simonov, and now the teenager was showing everything she had to offer him.

"Permission to come aboard, sir?" Tatiana called out, her smile beaming as the boats drew within yards of each other.

It was against his better judgment, but Colonel Galiano was helpless against Tatiana's naked allure. Since taking custody of the stainless-steel suitcases, he had hardly slept and had been on the run, almost literally, from morning to night for days on end. He was exhausted to the bone. Now, seeing his teenage lover so joyously greeting him, he cut the throttle and slowed the old boat.

"How did you find me?" he asked when the two boats were side by side.

Svetlana was at the wheel, wearing a light sundress. In the first rays of early morning, she looked gorgeous, and though she wasn't a youngster — which meant that she was too old to truly appeal to the colonel — he wondered what it would feel like to have her thrashing beneath him as he unleashed his sadism upon her.

It was General Ragga who answered, coming onto the deck from below. He said, "We bribed the men at the marina more than you did, that's how we knew where you were headed."

Three soldiers hurried out from below deck, each one carrying a big revolver. They stood shoulder to shoulder, holding their revolvers aimed at the colonel.

"You have something that belongs to me, Colonel," Colonel Mendoza said as he stepped out from behind a mound of folded, mildewed canvas. "And you've caused me a great deal of trouble."

Galiano's shoulders slumped as defeat washed over him. Then, summoning strength from within, he squared his shoulders, spit toward Colonel Mendoza, and made a dive to his left.

The roar of the revolvers was simultaneous. Heavy-caliber bullets slammed the colonel's body down hard into the deck. The first volley ripped through his side; the second punched into his back when he was face-down. The three soldiers each fired six shots, emptying their weapons into the corpse.

"Find the suitcases!" General Ragga commanded, barking orders to the three soldiers.

As General Ragga and Colonel Mendoza knelt on the deck, leaning over the railing to hold the old wooden boat close, the three soldiers leaped from one boat to the other. The soldiers quickly found the stainless-steel suitcases.

"I'm rich!" the general shouted.

"I don't think so."

It was the sound of Svetlana's voice coming from behind that made the general freeze in place. He turned slowly to find himself facing Svetlana and Tatiana. They were an unlikely pair, it seemed, to be threatening him, especially since Tatiana was completely naked. But at the feet of the women were the two suitcases they were never without — the ones that the general himself had inspected to make sure they carried nothing but clothes.

Except Svetlana and Tatiana were holding small automatic pistols, and those pistols were held with steady hands that indicated experience and training.

The general went for his gun. He was too close to his dream of wealth for him not to go for his gun.

And that was what started the final carnage.

Tatiana's Walther jumped in her fist, screaming angrily, and spontaneously a small, red dot formed on the general's shirt.

Svetlana's reaction was immediate. She spun away from the onrushing Colonel Mendoza, toward the three soldiers trying to leap back aboard their commanding officer's boat. But they had emptied their weapons assassinating Colonel Galiano, and the Mauser Svetlana held securely in both hands fired straight and true. She had just finished off the third soldier, putting a neat, round hole in the side of his skull just above his ear, when she turned back toward Mendoza.

By this time Tatiana had already turned him into a dead man, though the colonel didn't quite know it yet.

Colonel Mendoza had taken two rounds in the stomach. He looked at Tatiana and smiled menacingly, whispering, "You little slut. Now you're going to get it!"

Tatiana raised her aim. When she squeezed the trigger again, the colonel's smile changed abruptly when his two front teeth were shattered by a bullet.

It ended nearly as quickly as it had started. Tatiana looked around, almost in a daze. She was naked, but hardly aware of this fact. In the water were two soldiers. They were sinking slowly. On the deck were the corpses of Colonel Mendoza, and Colonel Ragga. On the nearby boat was the bloodied corpse of the bullet-riddled Colonel Galiano.

"Get the suitcases," Svetlana said, her voice stern, level, commanding.

"What's wrong?" Tatiana asked.

"Take a look." Svetlana pointed eastward.

Far off in the distance, even with the naked eye, Tatiana could see a boat approaching. It was a big white boat, clearly new, and moving swiftly over the water. She couldn't see what flag the vessel flew, but Tatiana suspected when the boat was closer she'd see the blue, white, and red flag of Cuba.

Several minutes later, the corpses had all been weighted down and were sinking to the bottom of the Gulf of Mexico. The boat that Colonel Galiano had rented was wood, and it was soon engulfed in flames.

Svetlana slipped the rope through the handles of the suitcases to keep them together, then checked to see that the knot securing the suitcases to the toolbox wouldn't slip. She pushed the toolbox over the edge of the deck and it dropped into the water. It sank quickly, pulling the two suitcases with it on its hurried path to the bottom of the ocean.

Picking up her suitcase, the one that so artfully and secretly had held her Mauser from even the most careful inspection, Svetlana tossed it overboard, then flipped her weapon into the water, too. Tatiana did the same with her weapon and suitcase.

The speedboat was close enough now for Tatiana to see men standing on the deck. "Cuban sailors," she said, looking around for the dress she'd earlier discarded.

Svetlana's reaction, though equally as swift, was just the opposite. She pulled off her dress and tossed it overboard so that she, too, was completely naked. She smiled at Tatiana.

"Mission accomplished, my friend," she said. "The ZT-550 will rot on the bottom of the ocean and eventually dissipate into harmless nothingness, the bad guys are all dead, and unless I'm mistaken, very soon you and I are going to be giving Oscar-winning performances as two helpless women who were attacked at sea by pirates." Svetlana gave her shoulders a shake, sending her big breasts swaying. "Wanna bet those sailors coming to rescue us are going to believe we're victims?"

Tatiana smiled and replied, "You think of everything, don't you?"

The End

YOU MAY ALSO ENJOY THE FOLLOWING FROM eXTASY BOOKS INC:

Deadly Secrets
Robin Gideon

Excerpt

The mansion in the cove was surrounded by an eight-foot-high white marble wall. The original owner had been a member of the New York Mafia, and he'd been more than merely paranoid for his safety, since he had ordered the murders of enough of his former associates, enemies, and friends, to have an on-going "contract" on his head.

As it turned out, the mobster had been safe and protected within the marble walls of his Florida Keys retreat. But his taste for Chinese cuisine was his undoing. He'd been hunched over a heaping plate of sub gum chow mien in a tiny Chinese restaurant when a lone gunman put a .45 automatic to the back of the mob kingpin's head and pulled the trigger.

The current owner of the residence—which included a main house with five bathrooms, five bedrooms, a ballroom large enough to accommodate a party of one hundred comfortably, and three separate fireplaces that had been converted to gas within the past decade—enjoyed the privacy the marble wall gave him more than the protection.

He should have been more concerned with his protection.

Four men and one slender woman, all wearing camou-flaged uniforms, slipped quietly over the marble wall. Each soldier was equipped with a Colt Police Positive .38 Special, fitted with a silencer and loaded with hollow-point bullets that had been made into "dum-dums" by having an "X" filed into each one. Upon impact the bullets didn't merely mushroom, they splintered into small segments. The woman did not carry a pistol. Instead, she had in her back pocket a black-handled, stiletto-bladed switchblade. It was her weapon of choice. She preferred her killing to be done up close and with a personal touch.

The secluded mansion's owner was an English gentleman named Sir Malcomb Sitwell. His family — a wife and two sons — owned three cats but no dogs. The cats, upon discovering the intruders, quietly crept to safe shadows, concerned only with their own welfare as the Sitwells slept.

The maid, an elderly immigrant from Germany who often had trouble sleeping throughout the night, had taken two sleeping pills at midnight, afraid that her chronic insomnia would afflict her. She was dreaming of her childhood home in Munich when Jacques entered her bedroom. The room was far removed from the other bedrooms, separated not because of her social status compared to the Sitwells, but because of the volume at which she snored.

Jacques paused a moment to look at the old woman. He waited a second. No more than that. He aimed his Police Positive at her forehead and squeezed the trigger. The long silencer reduced the pistol's roar to a hiss. The hollow-point dum-dum, upon striking the maid's skull, fragmented into four separate pieces of lead and copper. The old woman's head literally exploded.

In other rooms in the mansion, victims were dispatched in similar fashion. Neither of Sir Malcomb's sons heard a thing as they were executed while sleeping.

Sir Malcomb had retired while in his late forties from the

British military. He had bravely served his twenty years, and when he met a wealthy American widow, he moved from London to Florida without remorse. Peace, love, and family contentment had dulled what had for many years been battle-honed senses.

Jacques, Arturo, Deiter, and Petyr were all in the bedroom when Sir Malcomb was shaken awake, a large gloved hand over his mouth to prevent him from making even a sound. Jacques looked into Sir Malcomb's eyes and put a gloved finger to his own lips, indicating silence. Then Sir Malcomb was assisted out of the bed while his wife slept peacefully.

In the library, Juanita extracted from a canvas pouch a bottle of vodka. It was one hundred proof. She opened the bottle, breaking the seal, and pointed toward the overstuffed chair near the fireplace.

"What's the meaning of this?" Sir Malcomb asked, finally finding his voice.

The uniformed soldiers said nothing. Juanita extended the vodka bottle.

"Take this. Drink."

"No."

"Drink it," Juanita said quietly. "If you don't, we'll kill your wife."

The defiance drained quickly out of Sir Malcomb. His eyes darted left and right as he assessed the situation, calculating his chances of fighting back successfully.

"What are you worried about?" Juanita asked. "If we wanted you dead, your brains would be on the floor. Now take the bottle and drink. Finish it all and nothing will happen to you. I promise."

Malcomb took the bottle and brought it to his lips. It took him almost five minutes to drink the entire pint of liquor.

Deiter stepped into the library. He nodded his head, saying nothing. When he did, the faintest smile curled Juanita's lips.

"Very good," she said. She placed the bottle on the carpeted floor beside Malcomb. "Just sit there now. Everything will be just fine in a matter of minutes."

Juanita watched as the alcohol began clouding Malcomb's brain. She saw him blinking his eyes as he tried to clear his vision. It was a pleasure to watch the capitalist trying to intellectualize his way past the alcohol that was fogging and diluting his reasoning. Three times Juanita walked past him, moving just a little closer each time. He stopped watching her carefully.

Juanita brought out a second bottle. She opened the vodka, breaking the seal. This time she did not hand the bottle to Sir Malcomb. Rather, she put it to his lips and forced his head back. He knew what was expected, and gulped the clear, fiery liquid as best he could. Vodka dribbled over his chin and down his neck, only to get soaked up in his fine silk pajamas.

"That should do it," Juanita said when the last of the second bottle of vodka had, quite literally, been poured down Sir Malcomb's throat.

She waited until she was on the verge of losing consciousness before she took the .38 Special from Deiter. She unscrewed the silencer and then placed the weapon in Sir Malcomb's relaxed hand. He said something, or at least tried to say something. Saliva trickled from the corner of his mouth.

Juanita turned the weapon inside Malcomb's hand so that the muzzle touched his temple. He started to protest, fighting against the young Mexican woman with the fathomless black eyes.

The Colt Police Positive roared, the deafening noise of the .38 Special being fired echoing off the walls. The force of the fragmenting round bursting through hard skull and soft brain tissue tossed Sir Malcomb out of the chair. The left side of his head had disintegrated.

ABOUT THE AUTHOR

Robin Gideon is the author of over 50 novels and novellas in paperback form and for e-publishers. She is currently writing erotic action-adventure stories starring the secret agent Svetlana Simonov exclusively for eXtasy Books. She was the featured author on the nationally syndicated TV series CBS Sunday Morning. She loves hearing from her readers, and can be reached at: robin.gideon@ymail.com.

www.ingramcontent.com/pod-product-compliance
Lightning Source LLC
Chambersburg PA
CBHW070816120626
46556CB00002B/525